The Collected Stories of
Pinchas Goldhar

The Collected Stories of
# Pinchas Goldhar

## A Pioneer Yiddish Writer in Australia

HYBRID
PUBLISHERS

Published by Hybrid Publishers

Melbourne Victoria Australia

© Joshua Goldhar 2016

First published 2016

National Library of Australia Cataloguing-in-Publication entry

Creator: Goldhar, Pinchas, 1901–1947, author.

Title: The collected stories of Pinchas Goldhar: a pioneer Yiddish
writer in Australia / Pinchas Goldhar.

ISBN: 9781925272246 (paperback)

Subjects: Short stories, Yiddish – Translations into English.

Dewey Number: 839.3

Cover design by Art on Order

*The illustrations on pp. 196, 253 and 285 by Noel Counihan
are reproduced with the kind permission of Michael Counihan.*

# CONTENTS

# PREFACE

Any study of Australian Jewish literature must include the works of Pinchas Goldhar. Having arrived in Melbourne from Lodz in 1928 as a twenty-seven-year-old with a background in journalism and an affinity for poetry, Goldhar brought an Eastern European Jewish learning and sensibility to his encounter with, and observations of, Jewish existence in the urban and rural Australia of his time. He was the first to bear witness to the lives and concerns of its Eastern European Jewish migrants, pre-empting his contemporaries Judah Waten and Herz Bergner. Through his short stories and journalism, he introduced into the nation's literature – both Jewish and Australian – an expanded canvas and incisive description of Jewish immigrant life.

As H. Brezniak wrote: 'He was the first to publish a Yiddish literary book, the first editor of a Yiddish paper, the first Yiddish writer to be included in Australian anthologies, the first to translate Australian writers into Yiddish and certainly was one of the founders of a literature written by "New Australians" before the term New Australian even existed.'

Paradoxically, notwithstanding his seminal importance, Goldhar's works have had limited publication and distribution until now. Although over the years a number of his stories have been translated from Yiddish and published in scattered Australian literary publications, no comprehensive collection of them has thus far appeared in English. This volume, which incorporates for the first time all of his stories known to us through his Yiddish anthologies, *Dertzeilungen fun Oystralie* (*Stories from Australia*, 1939) and the posthumous *Gezamlte Shriftn* (*Collected Writings*, 1949), aims to rectify this anomaly and bring his creative works to a broader readership.

If reasons are sought for why these writings should be brought to light at this time, some seventy years after Goldhar's passing, it should suffice to highlight two salient and closely entwined motivations.

As narratives, his stories are in line with the best tradition of twentieth-century Yiddish literature in their blending of individual, existential, collective communal and national dramas set against a contemporary backdrop of major developments affecting Jewish populations in Europe and Australia alike. Eastern European Jewry from the late 1920s and well into the 30s was finding its safety and continuing existence coming increasingly under threat. At the same time, since white settlement in 1788, Australia had already shown itself to be a congenial home for earlier Jewish arrivals, and was evolving into a destination to which successively greater numbers turned in search of a more secure haven.

That same tide brought with it the young Goldhar who, as much as he was a storyteller, was also to become the literary voice of his generation, as well as a leading cultural and social commentator through a succession of Yiddish-based journalistic initiatives, essays, editorials, reviews and communal polemics in an era which has thus far been much under-investigated and under-recorded in Australian Jewish historiography. Goldhar was deeply imbued with *Yiddishkeit* which he sought – as if in pursuit of a personal mission – to foster, enhance and consolidate it in Australia.

His stories are poignant and touching, featuring mainly Polish-Jewish protagonists who wrestle with the strange ways of their new home, but resonating for any migrants or refugees who have come to Australia. Often told with bitter irony, the stories express the loneliness and isolation of the immigrant, for whom cultural differences seem in-surmountable, the longing for familiar Jewish life, and his sense of uprootedness and disappointment in his adopted homeland.

His protagonists are those who he knew best and for whom he wrote: uprooted and transplanted fellow immi-grants in an alien, isolated and sparsely populated country, far from the familial, communal, cultural and religious intimacy and immersion of *di alte heym* (the old country). The stories depict a monocultural Australia, in thrall to the most conservative aspects of British traditions and values, where even Jews who had emigrated in earlier years emu-lated English manners, customs and dress.

Had Goldhar lived beyond his forty-five years he might

have been pleased to see his fears were unfounded. With the influx of post-Word-War-II Jews in the late 1940s and 50s, there sprang up a new vitality in Jewish life, which saw the growth of strong Jewish cultural life in the following decades. This new collection will ensure that this wonderful writer is not forgotten.

—Serge Liberman

## Publisher's Note

Thank you to Freydi Mrocki and Andrew Firestone for assistance with Yiddish vocabulary, and to Philip Rosenbaum (Pinchas Goldhar's grandson) for input and suggestions.

# INTRODUCTION

## The convergence of cultural worlds –
## Pinchas Goldhar: A Yiddish writer in Australia

### Pam Maclean

PINCHAS GOLDHAR was born in Lodz, Poland, in 1901. From his schooldays onwards he was involved in literary activities, contributing poems and songs to experimental Yiddish journals in tandem with a group of other young expressionist Yiddish poets and writers heading towards renown. After he left school, Goldhar studied journalism in Warsaw and at the conclusion of his studies returned to Lodz to write for a daily newspaper while also undertaking some private teaching.

In May 1928, Goldhar left the increasingly troubled, anti-Semitic atmosphere of Poland to join his father, who had previously emigrated to Australia. For Goldhar, life in Australia was both intellectually and financially difficult, for after having lived in the centre of an active Jewish cultural life, he now found himself embedded in the unsympathetic

Original cover illustration of *Dertzeilungen fun Oystralie*
by Noel Counihan

environment of – with some exceptions – a predominantly Anglophile Melbourne Jewish community. Economically too, he struggled, working first as a house painter before he found more secure employment in his father's dyeing factory. His involvement in the factory resulted in ICI (Imperial Chemical Industries) awarding him a scholarship to study in Germany where, in 1932, he witnessed Hitler delivering a speech. Goldhar's period in Germany heightened his awareness of the pernicious nature of European anti-Semitism. During this trip to Europe, Goldhar visited Poland for the last time.

Three years after arriving in Australia, Goldhar resumed his literary and cultural activities as editor of the short-lived newspaper *Di Oystralier Leben* (*Australian Life* 1931–33), the first Yiddish newspaper published in Australia. No longer a poet and lyricist, Goldhar emerged as a consummate prose writer. His early writing not only explored the fragility of Jewish life in Australia, but, drawing on his European experiences, Goldhar also exposed the precarious situation confronting Jews in Europe. After the closure of *Di Oystralier Leben*, Goldhar continued contributing stories and other social and cultural observations to the Melbourne-Yiddish press. Now his stories focused on his growing disillusionment with the Australian Jewish community and culminated in the publication of *Dertzeilungen fun Oystralie* (*Stories from Australia*, 1939), with illustrations by Noel Counihan.

As news of the tragic fate of Jews in the wake of the Holocaust percolated into Australia and refugees started to arrive in Melbourne, Goldhar's despair intensified. The posthumously published *Gezamlte Shriftn* (*Collected Writings*, 1949), included further unpublished material in addition to the previously published essays and stories.

While Goldhar's contribution to Australian-Yiddish writing and Jewish cultural life is indisputable, his contacts extended far beyond the Jewish community of the 1930s and 40s to progressive and innovative Melbourne cultural figures of the period. Often fascinating interconnections between the two worlds that Goldhar shared provided him with fresh insights into the experiences of the group of two thousand Eastern European Jewish immigrants who came to Australia in the years 1926–28. This group found itself having to undergo a twofold cultural adjustment: the adjustment of establishing itself in a totally alien land in which immigrants of non-British origin were viewed with suspicion, and the adjustment of the Anglo-Jewish assumptions underlying the operation of the local Melbourne Jewish community. In addition to being faced with the problems common to his generation of immigrants, Goldhar was attempting to write under what proved to be extremely adverse circumstances. Pursuing a literary career in the 1930s was itself problematic for many Australian writers, but for someone like Goldhar, whose literary language was Yiddish, for which there was only a limited audience and few avenues of publication, the obstacles were almost insurmountable.

By sharing comparable concerns and difficulties with Australian writers and activists with whom he mingled or entered into correspondence, e.g. Vance and Nettie Palmer, Alan Marshall and Brian Fitzpatrick, with whose works he became familiar, his literary activities extended beyond the narrow confines of the Yiddish-speaking community. Such contact helped him to transcend the isolation that could well have prevented him from writing at all. As well as a sense of marginalisation, he shared with them an interest in the construction of minority national literatures and the conviction that culture should be outward-looking and international in orientation. In common, too, with the writers and artists with whom he had contact, Goldhar was sympathetically inclined towards socialist political aspirations.

Conversely, through his knowledge of European litera-ture and his ability to place Australian literature within a broader context, Goldhar was able to offer something in return. It seems that for Australian cultural figures of the 1930s and 40s, located across a remarkably broad spectrum of interest and activity, contact with European immigrant writers such as Goldhar contributed an important element in their attempts to break down their own feelings of isolation and entrapment in what they regarded as a me-diocre culture, dominated by conservative, parochial and often second-rate derivative British values. By tracing the interconnections between Goldhar and other Yiddishists in his circle with some of these figures, a fascinating picture of cultural and intellectual cross-fertilisation between the Jewish and Australian communities emerges.

To characterise Pinchas Goldhar simply as a Yiddish

writer in Australia does not adequately throw into relief the issues raised by his writing, both in the sense of practice and theme. More properly, he might be referred to as a multicultural writer before multiculturalism: as a writer whose work explicitly explored the issues of cultural disjunction in Australia before there was any general acceptance for or means of conceptualising such an approach. Looking back at interwar and wartime Australian society, one of its most striking features was its explicit and increasing concern to reinforce social and cultural orthodoxy. The official stance of the day, as reflected by the Joseph Lyons and Robert Menzies governments of that time, was a homogeneous Australian artistic culture, as a bulwark against the challenges posed by European modernism.

Running parallel to such attempts at artistic control was the tightening of restrictions on non-British immigration. Once again, homogeneity was the crucial social value. Such policies were designed to limit non-British immigration and were based on a growing xenophobia, reinforced by popularly accepted racial theory proclaiming the inferiority of non-British 'races'. The society in which Goldhar found himself was therefore one that was generally intolerant of the potential heterodoxies posed by the cultures of what today would be called 'marginal' groups. Hence Goldhar did not enjoy the luxury of writing and publishing in a society that at least pays lip service to the benefits of cultural pluralism.

Even the Melbourne Jewish community, which provided the cultural framework and eventually much support for his work, was itself divided on class, national and linguistic lines and was by no means united in regarding his Yiddishist cultural orientation as reflecting its own social values.

Although, on the issue of language, Goldhar was a dedicated Yiddishist, arguing, along with Herz Bergner and others, that it was not merely a linguistic prerequisite for the perpetuation of a Jewish literature, but the *sine qua non* for the preservation of a Jewish national identity, to assume from this that he sought to cut himself off from the Australian environment would be wrong. Certainly, these writers – in the main affiliated with the Kadimah Jewish Cultural Centre and National Library in Melbourne – actively promoted the cause of Jewish cultural nationalism, but as already intimated earlier, this did not preclude contact with non-Jewish Australians and their writings, about which more will be written below.

For all that, despite evidence that Goldhar was able to obtain support for his writing both from within a section of the Jewish community and from some Australian writers, it is clear from the subject matter of his *Stories from Australia* that no matter how energetically Goldhar pursued his Yiddishist activities, this did little to allay his sense of being isolated from the real centres of Jewish culture. He remained painfully aware that the reality of Jewish life in Australia fell far short of his own ideals.

His *Stories,* as mentioned earlier, focus on the nature of Jewish life in Australia. Herz Bergner finds Goldhar's Australian settings somewhat curious. He argues that Goldhar's use of Australian themes contrasts with the work of other migrant Yiddish writers living elsewhere in cities such as New York. These writers were content to evoke memories of their *shtetl* childhoods 'in the old country' and therefore did not need to develop a style of writing that moved beyond an established literary tradition. It was easier, according to Bergner, for those who wrote in the context of an American immigrant society that was accepting of Jews and possessed a large active Jewish community, to retain a sense of continuity and connection with their earlier lives. This was not possible for Pinchas Goldhar whose writing was dominated by the themes of loneliness and rootlessness. His ironically realised narratives construct a pessimistic universe peopled by Jews unable to maintain a coherent identity within the constraints of Australian society. Therefore, while Goldhar does follow in the tradition of well-known Yiddish writers like Sholem Aleichem, it was their realist techniques rather than their positive visions of Jewish life that found resonance.

Bergner's interpretation stands in stark contrast to the assessment of a contemporary review by émigré Russian lawyer and commentator, Aaron Patkin, who wrote:

> He has taken with him on his long voyage to Australia, the dreams of his childhood and youth, the Jewish soul burning with the sparkling spirit of generations and this helped him to reveal such features in the characters of his heroes that made many of them so human and so convincing. The 'Australian' stories of Goldhar are therefore more Polish-Jewish than Australian-Jewish stories; their

realism breathes not with the Australian atmosphere, but with the air of the old home.

Goldhar's characters may indeed have been Polish-Jewish, but their transposition into the Australian environment creates a social dynamic peculiar to the Australian situation, and Goldhar explicitly acknowledges the particular circumstances of this situation.

Multicultural scholar Sneja Gunew's comment on the position of the migrant writer in Australia in general succinctly captures the particular situation of Goldhar. For migrant writers, the purpose of literature is to 'transmute their human subjects' own physical implausibility into metaphysical terms' and this gains special poignancy as such writers try to come to grips with their own physical displacement. For them, as for Goldhar, experience is dominated by a continual 'sense of discrepancy'.

While the narratives in Goldhar's book *Stories from Australia* focus on the narrowly circumscribed situation of Jews in Australia in the 1930s, exploring its characters' reactions almost as if they were subjects under examination in a social laboratory, later published stories and essays deal with the beginnings of the impact of the arrival of survivors of the Holocaust on the Australian Jewish community. Inevitably, as Bergner indicates, Goldhar's horizons were broadened and his attention turned to the tragedy of the Jewish community in Poland.

As if trying to recapture a lost world, he wrote autobiographical stories recounting in a softer vein incidents from his childhood in Poland. These stories, unpublished in his

lifetime, appeared in his *Collected Writing*, as do fragments
of a series of bitter stories dealing with the devastation of
the Polish Jewish communities by the Nazis. At the time of
his death he had also sketched out a plan for a novel set in
Australia, the theme of which was to be the reconciliation
between the Jewish and Gentile communities.

Reference has already been made to his explicitly
Australian settings and themes and to his Australian literary connections. Indeed, Goldhar was an avid reader of
contemporary Australian writing and was well respected
within Melbourne Leftist literary circles as someone
sympathetic towards attempts to assert the existence of an
independent Australian literary tradition. One of his last,
and unfortunately unfinished, projects was the compilation
in Yiddish translation of an anthology of Australian stories,
including writers such as Henry Lawson, Dowell O'Reilly,
Vance Palmer, Katherine Susannah Prichard, Frank Dalby
Davison, Gavin Casey and Louis Esson. His aim was to
familiarise an international Yiddish-speaking audience with
a literature that he felt embodied values that would be spir-
itually enriching for a community whose faith in humanity
may well have been shattered by the experiences of war.
This project was not, however, undertaken completely in
vain, for his *Collected Writing* does in fact contain stories
of each of these writers, preceded by a twenty-two-page
essay titled 'Australian literature', in which can be found a
number of acute observations relating to the nature of an
Australian literature, comparisons between Australian and
Yiddish literary developments and comments concerning

the formation of national literary cultures in general.

Goldhar's connections with Melbourne literary circles bore fruit in another way. The stories, 'The Funeral' and 'Café in Carlton' were translated into English and published in his lifetime, enabling an Australian audience to gain an early and remarkably sophisticated insight into the world of the immigrant before the impact of the post-war mass migration of refugees had been felt.

Evidence of the high esteem in which he was held among Australian intellectuals is revealed by reactions to the news of his premature death in 1947 and obituaries written about him by eminent writers and editors of his time, such as Nettie Palmer and Stephen Murray-Smith, and the translation and publication of his essay 'Australian Literature'. Nettie Palmer praised him as 'a true internationalist, alive to the conditions special to our own terrible century', elaborating that because of his position as a cultural outsider, a migrant writer like Goldhar could bring to the analysis of the Australian situation a pair of fresh eyes whose focus was directed outwardly, not restricted within the narrow preoccupations of Australian society – and within Australia there existed people who were receptive to the notion that dominant visions would be challenged.

Pinchas Goldhar thus straddled many cultural worlds. He did this quite consciously and in so doing viewed culture and cultural interaction from a perspective that was both remarkably tolerant of diversity and dynamic in conception, especially given the general climate of opinion that predominated during the period in which he was writing. The effect of his writing was to juxtapose Australian and Jewish themes in a way that anticipated the concerns of later explicitly multicultural writers; the contemporary framework of Goldhar's interests, however, was that of internationalism: an orientation which brought him and other Jewish writers and artists into contact with a small but diverse group of Australians who shared a similar orientation.

For instance, an internationalist perspective informs Goldhar's essay on Australian literature. As he writes:

> One can have great faith that such a literature will in time achieve an important position among the literatures of the world. But even in the present position it merits special consideration, because of its unique place in the literatures of the new continents. It is a significant product of an age-old culture transplanted to foreign soil, and from it we can learn much about the processes which have shaped the citizen of the New World. These have a more than academic interest for the Jewish people in these countries. They deeply affect our present existence and indeed the very future of Jewry.

The problem of how to maintain the cultural integrity and vitality of transplanted communities to which Goldhar here alludes, lies at the heart of discussion surrounding multiculturalism. Ironically, Goldhar identified many cultural characteristics that today might be thought to be part of a dominant, nationalistic Australian culture intolerant of minority groups – as those that could provide models for new literatures and by extension for Jewish cultural development. From the point of view of the global perspective adopted by Goldhar, Australian literary culture appeared as a subordinate literature, still in its embryonic phase.

According to Goldhar, the two central characteristics of Australian literature were 'the pioneering tradition and democratic impulse': the former resulting in a literature in which authors self-consciously portray the strangeness and hostility of Australia's natural environment, the latter resulting in a literature derived from the folk idiom of the ordinary people. These elements represented a means whereby for Goldhar, Australian literature (and in a broader sense culture) could free itself from the dead hand of English tradition and maintain its vitality. The positive lesson for Jews lay in the possibility that an adaptive people could still survive in the face of an unsympathetic environment, and that if their culture was firmly embedded in popular practice, it too would survive.

Goldhar was strongly influenced by Vance Palmer, the enthusiastic proponent of Australian literary nationalism and the 'bush tradition', sensitive to the plight of refugees, and opponent of fascism and censorship. Goldhar's view of the 'democratic' – what today might be called the 'pluralistic' or 'rebellious' tendency in Australian literature, and by extension, of its writers – appears now, with hindsight, to be rather idealised. For it glosses over the still parochial and limited cultural position adopted by even some of the most 'advanced' critics of the period. These folkloric and communalist strands in Palmer's thought, used in an attempt to legitimise notions of a distinctly Australian culture, are reminiscent of similar ideas employed by the Yiddishists, even if the circumstances of their development were rather different.

During the 1930s and 40s a broad cross-section of Australian writers, artists and political 'activists' (both of the Left and progressive Right) had been acutely conscious of Australia's position as a political and cultural backwater, the corollary being that if Australian accomplishments were to receive due recognition, Australian culture must establish itself in an international framework (a line of argument also pursued by Goldhar), thereby freeing itself from constant references to and comparisons with British cultural models. By demonstrating Australia's cultural worth on the international stage, claims for Australian cultural independence from Britain could be legitimated. Internationalist values, therefore, stood in a dialectical relationship to nationalism, tempering its tendencies towards nationalistic chauvinism and positively promoting the desirability of contact with ideas and people who were not necessarily in the Anglo-British mould.

For Goldhar, the implicit contradictions posed by simultaneous support for a nationalist and an internationalist position was expressed in different terms: the conflict between Yiddishism and Zionism. Whereas for Australians an effect of the war was paradoxically to enhance the opportunities for international contact through increased European migration, for Goldhar it represented the destruction of the cultural base upon which his internationalist, Yiddishist, humanistic orientation was built. At the same time, the narrowly nationalist claims of Zionism were strengthened. Writing after the end of World War II on 'Jewish anti-Semitism', Goldhar was scathing in his attacks on assimilated Jews who sought to hide their Jewishness from the Gentile world. He argued that such Jews in fact internalised the prejudices of anti-Semites by trying in vain to conform to a set of values set by the external world. Goldhar was also critical of Zionism. He believed that Australian Jews viewed Israel not as an end in itself 'but as a legitimisation of nationality which would assist their own assimilationist status'. He viewed Zionism as 'lacking in spirit' and as embracing a blind nationalism, which was antithetical towards Yiddishist folk culture. Goldhar argued that it was by restoring this now almost lost folk culture that Jews would rediscover a sense of nationality and self-worth and be able to counter the effects of anti-Semitism.

There was one other major social grouping whose internationalist orientation contributed to involvement with Jews: the Left, and especially writers and artists associated with the Left (who were mainly, but not exclusively, members of the Communist Party). It was with this group that Goldhar was most closely associated, its social milieu of writers, artists graphically described by Richard Haese in his *Rebels and Precursors: The Revolutionary Years of Australian Art* (1981), which included writers Vance and Nettie Palmer, Frank Dalby Davison, Judah Waten, Brian Fitzpatrick; the social realist artists, Noel Counihan,

Vic O'Connor and Yosl Bergner; and William Dolphin, a violin-maker and patron of contemporary artists. From the recent Jewish arrivals from Poland and Germany who settled around Carlton and Princes Hill and brought with them an appreciation of art and a cultural breadth rare anywhere in Australia, these artists, as personally noted by Vic O'Connor about himself and cited by Haese, gained a respect and understanding that he hardly ever received elsewhere, and were accofrded 'the warm sense of community and the values of a wider world of European humanism, which they brought with them as cultural baggage'.

By looking at Pinchas Goldhar it becomes apparent how difficult a task it is to disentangle the history of an immigrant community, or even a sub-group of such a community, from its more general environment. The interconnections between host and immigrant society are intricately realised, both conceptually and in actual social relationships. Goldhar's position as an observer of Jewish and Australian society and as a participant in their overlapping cultural and political movements placed him in a fascinating situation whose analysis throws new light on some lesser-known features of Australian social and cultural life in the 1930s and 40s.

—Pam Maclean
Honorary Fellow
School of Humanities and Social Sciences
Faculty of Arts and Education
Deakin University AUSTRALIA

This essay by Pam Maclean is an abridged and revised version of the original, which appeared in Rubinstein, William D. (Ed.): *Jews in the Sixth Continent*, Sydney, Allen and Unwin, 1987, pp. 127–50.

# CAIN

DOCTOR HERMANN LOWENSTEIN took his own life by hanging himself in a concentration camp near Dresden. He had been famous throughout the medical world for his scientific experiments and discoveries, and his death was met with a profound sense of regret amongst his contemporaries. He wrote a farewell letter to his family that the Nazis mistakenly overlooked. For a long time this letter travelled a difficult, hazardous and secret road and, when it finally reached Mrs Lowenstein, it was so torn and wrinkled that it was almost impossible to decipher – evidence of how difficult its path had been. This is what Dr Lowenstein wrote in his letter:

> My loved ones, my dear Klara and children! This letter is not being written to you by a person who has killed himself but by a murderer, someone who has spilt his brother's blood. I don't want this letter to arouse your sympathy or be used in defence of my actions. I have sentenced myself to death but I still feel that it is an insufficient punishment

for my crime. I am writing to let you know the terrible truth. I don't want you to grieve over my death, I don't want you to carry loving feelings for me. I want this confession to make you curse my name and to excise any fond emotions that you feel towards me. I have sentenced myself to death and that is why I am writing this letter to you. I will tell you in detail everything that happened when the Nazis took me away from you. Fate dealt a fearful and bloody hand to me and I am about to end it with the rope that I will soon tighten around my neck. I place the entire truth before you. View it with clear eyes and judge me without mercy. The full severity of judgment will be the one comfort for this bloodied conscience of Cain by which I am plagued.

This is what happened:

From the moment that the Nazis broke into our house in the middle of the night and dragged me from my bed, my life has been suspended in a web of uncertainty. Suddenly, I began a new life. I became a new man. Dr Hermann Lowenstein ceased to exist. His books, his laboratories, his high moral principles and ideals disappeared without trace as if they had been sucked into a vacuum. A new being was created in my body – not a person, but a creation of fear that trembled at the sound of every scream, cowered before every stare, became a slave to every superior. My entire persona was ruled by only one thought – to live, to live, to live!

What happened to me? I myself don't know. It was as if I was under a spell. The Nazis bewitched me with their gigantic faces and their steely cold eyes. I was a slave to their brawny bodies, to their brown shirts and to their jackbooted legs. I did not know what I was doing. I followed them like some sleepwalker with no memory, no will; my entire body was covered by a thick layer of sweat.

I was taken to the 'Brown House'. My mind only remembers a dark shadowy world filled with fearful screams of pain, hard piercing eyes, raw murderous voices and wild laughter. Someone screamed something into my face. The screams fell on me like heavy, painful blows. Another kicked me in the heart with his boots. I yelled out. I heard hard, irritated laughter. I felt one slap, then another. Burning snakes were circling my body; they were rubber thongs beating me. I jumped around like a maniac, begged, pleaded squirmed, desperately wringing my hands. The rubber thongs lashed my body harder and faster. I fell on my knees, I kissed someone's hard sweaty fist, my hands stroked slippery boots that kicked me in the face. Suddenly I was enveloped in blackness. Everything became confused and I fainted.

When I awoke, I found myself in a deep cellar. Day already shone through the tiny barred window right under the ceiling. The smell of dampness filled the air in the cellar along with the putrid smell of filth and sweat. Men with swollen, bloodied faces and torn clothing were sitting, lining the walls. Some of them were groaning with pain, others huddled together in the corners, secretively muttering amongst themselves. I forgot my own troubles for a moment as I stared engrossed at this picture of pain and suffering. I caught sight of an older Jew who sat in the darkest and furthest corner of the dungeon. I could tell from his black felt hat, his black clothes and his distinctively hunched shoulders that he was from the East. His face was bloodied and some of his scrawny greying beard had been ripped out with his flesh. He sat stiff and immobile, his eyes lowered to the ground, his hands pushed deep into the pockets of his long overcoat. He was surrounded by an aura of foreignness and strangeness. I don't know why, but he awoke a secret fear within me and I could not take my eyes off him for even one moment. I had such mixed feelings when I looked at him, I felt both fear and sympathy, and my heart was filled with a heavy premonition that his fate and mine were somehow to be entwined. I had a similar feeling the first time I ever saw you. But then it was a premonition of elation, but this time the premonition was filled with fear and death.

How true this premonition turned out to be.

We heard the sound of heavy footsteps and loud rasping voices behind the cell door. Everyone in the cell trembled and the room was frozen in an unearthly silence. The door opened. A few Nazis entered. Their faces looked freshly shaven and their uniforms were spotlessly clean and perfectly pressed. Their voices sounded confident and powerful, and their movements were fast and aggressive. Everyone in the cell rose involuntarily, standing, trembling, in fearful anticipation. One of the Nazis with a pot-belly, a red flushed face and watery eyes looked sternly around the cell. We followed his gaze, which stopped abruptly in the corner where the Jew from the East was sitting. He did not move a muscle. He sat stiffly, motionless, his eyes half-closed, as if he was in a hypnotic sleep.

'Get up, you filthy Jew!' he screamed with murderous hatred.

The Jew did not move.

'You filthy Jew!' the Nazi screamed again as he kicked a boot right into the Jew's face.

The Jew suddenly trembled and his eyes looked up to stare at the Nazi. I was distressed by the stare. The Jew could not have been in his right mind. His eyes were blazing with a mad flame.

'Pull him out!' a tall, thin Nazi with deep-sunken dark eyes ordered curtly. He seemed to hold a higher rank. He wore coloured stripes on the sleeve of his brown shirt, while from his thick leather belt hung a lethal knife, short and sharp, and a revolver. His tone was stilted a s if he was spitting the words out of his mouth, and while he spoke he rhythmically hit a rubber thong against his leather boot.

The fat one threw himself at the Jew. First he tore off his coat and then began pulling off the rest of his clothes. With a sadistic smile he suddenly turned around to the other Nazi and said: 'This filthy Jew stinks!'

The Nazi with the deeply-sunken eyes made a sign with his hand and moved away from the Jew. The first Nazi looked around the cell as if he were seeking something. His icy stare surveyed each and every one of us. We all realised what he was searching for and began moving further back to the wall, trying to escape his steely piercing gaze. My heart began hammering wildly as if I was already guilty of some crime. I sensed the inevitability of the moment that was coming and when the Nazi's gaze fell on me, I felt like a thief caught by the arm.

'Jew?' he asked.

I silently nodded.

'Why don't you answer, swine?' he said angrily to me. 'You have to undress him, understand!' he commanded harshly.

I approached the Jew and with trembling

hands began to undress him. The thought kept raging through my head: it's coming, it's coming …

Soon the victim stood naked. In the cold dampness of the cell his clear, almost feminine skin was covered in gooseflesh. My skin also turned to goose bumps and I could feel each bump of flesh as if it were a sharp needle. A mist descended over my eyes and my throat tightened as if someone was strangling me. The tall Nazi approached me and placed the rubber thong in my hand.

'Beat him!' he ordered.

I lifted up my arm and the thong fell with a bang on the Jew's flesh. A bright red stripe leapt out of his skin. He released a terrified maddening cry.

'Beat him!' the Nazi screamed out even louder.

And I, I beat him. I didn't know what was happening to me. My head was burning and I could not catch my breath. It was as if I was bewitched and my hand was automatically beating the Jew with the rubber thong. He collapsed to the ground. He was no longer screaming, he just yelped like some animal. All I saw before me was a red piece of flesh throwing itself about, convulsing, squirting my face with blood.

'Beat, beat, you bloody Jew!'

Wild, murderous screams fell all around me.

My hand moved down harder and faster as the thong whistled through the air.

'Beat the German, beat the German!' was the message my poor brain was trying to send to me. But the thong kept falling on the Jew. My hand would not obey my mind and I continued to beat the Jew's naked body.

This wild maniacal game finally came to an end. The Nazis left the cell. It was deathly silent. Only the groaning of the beaten man kept ringing in my ears. I lay in a corner, my face sunk into my hands. My eyes were burning but I could not squeeze out the painful cries that were choking me. Hours passed until I heard a voice, many hours filled with horror, disgust and shame as I lay unable to move.

It was already deep in the night. The cell was completely dark. I sat up and heard a soft groan next to me. It was the voice of the man I had beaten. Although I could not see I knew it was him. I stretched out my hand to touch his face, which was covered in dried blood. I began to stroke the tangled damp hair of his head, his bloodied face, his torn beard and called quietly: 'Brother, brother!'

'*Oy vay is mir, nebech*!' he said in Yiddish, and suddenly I felt his burning, parched lips. He, oh dear God, he was kissing my hand! I wanted to pull my hand away but he stubbornly clutched it, lovingly kissing my accursed, bloodied hand.

The Jew died. His soul left him as he lay in my arms, it left his body with a quiet patient Yiddish groan. I closed his eyes.

There will be no one to close my eyes and you, my children, should not say *Kaddish* for me. I am leaving this world with Cain's mark on my brow and my own curse on my head. Forget me, wipe me from your memory without mercy, may my memory be obliterated without trace. My soul will have to wander aimlessly over the world until the last days, when I will finally receive my bitter punishment.

Mrs Lowenstein read this letter to her children. Their eyes burned with a dry glaze, their hearts weighed down as if filled with stones.

They could not cry…

—Translated by Tania Bruce and
edited by Pam Maclean
*Oystralier Leben*, 4 October 1933

# CAFÉ IN CARLTON

ON THE DOOR of Mandel's kosher restaurant in Rathdowne Street, there is a chalk drawing of a swastika, and in big childish writing is scribbled:

*Jew boy Jew*
*Call him five to two.*

The swastika and the scrawl have been almost wiped away, yet whenever Mr Mandel looks at the door they hit him in the eye, but he pretends not to see them. Ever since he opened the restaurant he has been pestered by small boys who keep scrawling these insults on the wall, on the door or on the window. He rubs them out, scrubbing and washing until no trace is left, but all to no avail. As soon as he turns his back the boys are at it again. He lies in wait to catch them red-handed, but as soon as they see him they scatter noisily, poking out their tongues at him. Only George doesn't run away. He is a thin, bare-footed urchin with straw-coloured hair that stands out from his head like the peak of a cap. As he backs slowly away he screws up his green eyes, that peer at Mandel through stiff white lashes like the hair on a gooseberry. Mandel longs to twist his ear but George's insolent hairy gaze gets the better of him. He points his finger as he reproves him.

'You bad boy!'

'Bat boy, bat boy,' mimics George, wrinkling his freckled nose as he moves away with the slow confident gait of a grown-up man.

Mandel has given up chasing the boys for he can see that it doesn't get him anywhere. He has only been making a fool of himself while the children have been leading him by the nose. He has stopped taking any notice of the insulting scrawls; what he doesn't look at he won't see.

But although he kept turning his face away he still couldn't help seeing the defaced door. As if on purpose, the childish jingle and the crooked cross, although partly wiped away, have continued to hit him in the eye. He knew by heart every stroke and twist of the clumsy childish scribble and it was because he was so well acquainted with it that he couldn't resist looking at it every time he went near the door. In spite of its childishness, it radiated an unholy force, that fascinated him. Against his will he found himself staring at it and mumbling the words, *Jew boy Jew, Jew boy Jew.*

'Just childish pranks – not worth worrying about,' he thought, waving it away with his hand. But his low womanish round shoulders, which moved with such easy grace when he served his customers, stiffened and flattened like pieces of board at the sight of the scribble. Stealthily, he brushed the door with his hand, but drew it back quickly, thinking that George's green eyes were watching him from

Illustration by Noel Counihan that appeared with the original
translation by Judah Waten in *Southern Stories*

some hiding place. Involuntarily, Mandel turned around, but the street was quiet and empty as usual. The dilapidated single-storeyed houses were huddled together like a team of horses that had gone to sleep standing up, their heads resting on each other. The sloping rusty roofs cut the skyline in every direction. From the hotel on the corner, with its big windows and bright blue tiles half-way up the walls, came a constant low humming as if from a beehive. A drunkard staggered out from its open doors, his clothes crumpled as though he had slept in them. He gazed up and down the street with dull glassy eyes and stamped his feet, walking in a circle like a dog that has found a spot to lie down. He could hardly stand up, and it seemed that when at last he did lie down, all the tired and neglected houses would lie down with him.

In a deckchair on a veranda across the road, old Henderson dreamed with half-open eyes. As he smiled in his dream his cheeks puffed out, pink with age. A gentle breeze blew though his fluffy white hair and revealed his rosy scalp. He was a gentle old man who would not hurt a fly and lived on an old-age pension, which he collected at the post office every fortnight. On that day he would wear a black bowler hat, green with age, and a frayed shiny suit cut in the old-fashioned way with a shaped waist. Except to collect his pension, he never went anywhere. As soon as the sun rose each morning, he appeared on the veranda, wearing deep felt slippers and carrying a deckchair in one hand and a green cushion as flat as a pancake in the other. He would shake his head as he slowly scanned the empty street and smiled as though he were saying good morning to himself. That smile never left his face.

But now it seemed to Mandel that the old man was watching him with his sleepy eyes and laughing at him for worrying about his scribbled door and the childish Jew verse. Even the windows of the sleepy houses seemed to mock him from beneath their lowered veranda roofs. A mass of smoky white clouds straggled lazily across a sky that was flat and wan. The reflections in the window panes stood out moist and milky-blue like the whites of horses' eyes. They watched him with cold unfriendly stares. From a side street appeared two Jews who walked easily and unconcernedly. Totally absorbed in conversation, they waved their hands and shook their heads. Their gestures disturbed Mandel; in the quiet street they looked jerky and senseless like puppets. He watched them as they passed and felt bitterness and self-pity.

'Oy, Yidn, Yidn,' he sighed again as he shuffled back into the restaurant as if to hide from menace.

Those years he had spent in Berlin's Grenadierstrasse were still in his bones. He had kept a kosher restaurant there with a small hotel. On the window had been painted in gold the star of David with 'Kosher' in its centre and 'Hotel Metropole' inscribed in Gothic lettering in a half-circle around the star. But if anyone asked on the Grenadierstrasse for the Hotel Metropole, he was met with a shrug of the shoulders. Only after a while would even a German discover what he meant and answer, 'Ach so, that chassidic chapel. Certainly! Certainly!' For that was what Mandel's restaurant was called, because it was the Polish *chassidim* who stayed there when they came to the Berlin specialists for treatment. Day and night there was an uproar in the restaurant as at a fair. Polish Jews bustled in and out and called to each other in loud voices. They were dressed half in the traditional *chassidic* way and half in the German fashion, and they wore on their heads brand new black velour hats, which sat stiffly and awkwardly as if they were made of tin. They had brushed their beards under their chins so that they would not be so obvious. Sometimes they sat for hours at the tables and told stories of the wonders of the Berlin professors, or discussed politics while they puffed pompously at fat German cigars with gold bands. And if there were ten men together, without any self-consciousness, they stood between the tables and intoned the afternoon prayers.

From the kitchen could be heard the loud masculine voice of the wealthy Frau Presament from Kalisz. She had no children, and so year after year she travelled to Berlin to be treated by the most distinguished professors. Special delicacies had to be prepared for her at Mandel's – chicken soup made from capon, dumplings fried in the purest French oil and a compote of peaches.

Expensively dressed in a black lace dress like the guest of honour at a wedding and wearing an elaborate wig, which piously covered her head to the eyebrows, she looked after the cooking herself. She moved about in the kitchen and poked her fat wrinkled neck in and out like a hen picking at grain as she tasted from each saucepan. She fastidiously screwed up her strained face and, in her sing-song Kalisz dialect, boomed, 'Some bay leaf! The soup begs some bay leaf!'

Although Mandel was a Polish Jew, he had such respect for German manners that he looked down upon his guests. He couldn't stand their 'Eastern' ways. Behind the semi-circular counter piled high with dishes of calf's foot jelly covered with yellow wrinkled skin, plates of *gefilte* fish surrounded by slippery carrot rings, bowls of giblets and chicken livers, jars of pickled white-bellied herrings, loaves of spiced bread and egg rolls under glass covers, he was almost hidden. Only his silk skullcap with its knife-edged crease like newly-pressed trousers rose above the heaped-up jars and dishes. He stroked his pointed golden beard as he watched his noisy, flustered guests, and he shook his head angrily at the greatly revered *chassid,* the pious Reb Reckmiel from Radzin, who strode up and down the crowded restaurant.

He was a tall, thin man with a scholarly deeply lined forehead, his thick tangled sacred fringes with the prescribed thread of blue wool swaying with every stride. His devout eyes closed in pious meditation and hid the fear of a very sick man. He suffered from a serious heart condition and on several occasions had collapsed at the court of his revered rabbi and had barely been revived. There had been a great commotion among the *chassidim* and even the rabbi, who was not easily excited, had been gravely perturbed and had declared that his favourite Reckmiel must be put on his feet again. This was a command and, although Reckmiel made a bare living as a timber merchant, a few rich *chassidim* took him at their own expense to Berlin, where they were themselves travelling for treatment. Without counting the cost, they took him to the most famous professors. But Reckmiel didn't like the whole business; he was lost in this great foreign city. He wandered aimlessly about Mandel's restaurant all day, not wanting to go out in the streets and full of complaints.

'Where have they brought me? There isn't a Jewish face to be seen, only clean-shaven ones. One would almost think – God forbid – that there isn't a Jew in the world. God preserve me from the sin of melancholia,' he complained bitterly. Every time he was taken to the professor, he had to be persuaded anew to pull himself together. They begged him to wear his trousers pulled out over his high boots and to hide his fringes.

'Don't be so old-fashioned, Reb Reckmiel,' they implored him, 'you're not at home now. This is abroad – Berlin! You can't go out in those clothes. You'll make a fool of yourself.'

'You won't make me look like an infidel,' Reb Reckmiel replied irritably. 'You won't persuade me to hide my Jewishness. This is what I am and this is how you'll have to take me.'

'Gentlemen, please, not so much noise!' Mandel called to them from behind the counter. He spoke pompously, and in German, and his sharply creased skullcap quivered indignantly. 'What will the Germans say? It's no wonder the curse grows.'

And the curse had certainly grown every day. On the

surface little had altered; Germany was still Germany, and the Germans still wore pleasant smiles and said, 'please' and 'thank you'. But danger lurked in the air. The Brownshirts were raising their heads. And every day, windows in the Wertheim and Tietz emporiums were defaced with the word *Jude* smeared in whitewash. Passers-by smiled to themselves as they glanced sideways at the crude inscriptions, from which the whitewash had run in little driblets. Tombstones in the Weissensee cemetery had been desecrated, but when the finer marble tombstones in the very centre were like-wise profaned, this had indeed been a bad sign. On the Grenadierstrasse, great excitement was caused when Albert Muhsam opened a letter which he had found under the door of his cigar shop. The letter was short and to the point.

> Albert Muhsam, dirty Jew. Look out! You are on our death list. The revenge of the German people awaits you and all the rest of your accursed tribe.
> Heil Hitler!

Muhsam was a man of the old school: a pompous fellow with thick white cotton-wool sideburns and a yellow-stained grey moustache turned up in the Kaiser Wilhelm fashion. Around the dark panelled walls of his shop stood oak showcases with sliding glass doors. The solemn silence was perfumed with the delicate aromas of expensive tobaccos and cigars from distant countries. To this store came only life-long customers, well-to-do Germans as pompous and antiquated as himself. They took their time over their purchases, carefully fingering and smelling the cigars from the boxes that lay on the counter, and making their selections like connoisseurs. They inhaled the sample cigar, which Muhsam lit with deep deference, and blew the smoke in slow lazy rings from their lips.

'It's first-rate – perfect.'

They discussed politics and commerce with Muhsam and treated him as one of themselves, even though he held himself above the other Grenadierstrasse Jews and kept himself aloof from them. For this reason he was disliked, and it was even said that he was a renegade and an enemy of the Jews. But when the news of the letter spread through the Grenadierstrasse, this rift was healed, and every now and then some of his own Jewish neighbours came in to look at the letter.

The imposing quiet of the store was suddenly pervaded by a subdued but fear-stricken tension. The bell above the frosted-glass door was never at rest as Jews came and went. And the dignified Muhsam met each one with a wry and secretive smile as he furtively handed over the letter, so that Fraulein Gertrude at the cash register might not see. She was a dried-up old maid with mousey hair twisted in a tight bun on top of her head. Muhsam nodded his head in an intimate fashion, even to the 'Eastern' Jews with whom he had not wanted any dealings, and winked familiarly, warning them in mixed Hebrew and German against Fraulein Gertrude, saying softly while barely moving his lips, 'Not so loudly. She's a German.'

Carefully, the Jews handled the letter with the tips

of their fingers and read it once, and again, boiling with indignation.

'This should be reported to the police,' one said. 'These Nazi hooligans should be taught a lesson. It's an unheard-of outrage.'

All this time, Muhsam mopped his forehead with a white silk handkerchief he kept in his breast pocket, his hand trembling.

The police filed a report, covering long sheets of paper. But a few days later, Muhsam's window was smashed by a stone. And not only Muhsam's. Stones were thrown at the magnificent display windows of the Jewish shops on the Friedrichstrasse and Leipzigerstrasse. The assaults grew worse from day to day. On the Alexanderplatz, pogroms began; heads were split open, knives were stuck into ribs, Jews were maimed with knuckledusters. On the streets appeared mobs of young men wearing swastika armbands and long-laced leggings. They marched to music and sang the Horst Wessel song. Every time they passed along the Grenadierstrasse, the Jews hurriedly closed their shops.

For hours afterwards, the street breathed fear; an ominous stillness hung in the air. Although nothing then actually happened, the terrible fear remained. Full of apprehension, the Jews felt that this was the beginning of a dreadful inferno.

But when the ranks of the Nazi marchers swelled with stolid middle-aged Germans with fat bellies and thick well-fed necks over their stiff high collars, the Jews grew even more afraid. These men marched in a heavy plodding fashion on legs as thick as blocks of wood, trying to keep in step with their youngsters while constantly mopping their sweaty bald heads with big check handkerchiefs.

With hoarse beery voices they shouted, 'When Jewish blood drips from our knives, that will be our lucky day!'

Even Franz Hulka, the quiet, harmless stamp-cutter who lived next door to Mandel, began to rub shoulders with the Brownshirts. He was a little shrivelled man, with untidy thin hair resting like down on his head, and he wore wire-rimmed spectacles on the tim of his nose. Every day after lunch he came to the door of his mean little shop to get some fresh air. Behind the narrow panes of his window stood an enormous dummy stamp from which the red paint had faded, showing the white wood. With his hands behind his back and the breast pocket of his overalls filled with tools, he stood in the doorway and looked over his glasses at the busy noisy street. His pale watery eyes were flat and squashed like those of a herring. As he sucked the remains of his lunch from his teeth, he obsequiously nodded his head to every passer-by and grunted, *'Mahltzeit! Mahltzeit!'*

Mandel, like all the other Jews in the street, took Hulka for a simpleton and disregarded him. But every time Hulka greeted him with his polite German mealtime salutation *Mahltzeit!*, Mandel felt uneasy, as though he was being put under an obligation. No matter how often he tried to get in first, Hulka was always ahead of him with his ingratiating whining greeting, *'Mahltzeit*, Herr Mandel, my best respects.'

But now that Hulka had become a Nazi he was a different person. He gave himself airs and held himself erect so that his stiff neck made a double chin. He blew himself up and tried to look important. He had shaved the scanty down from his head and his naked skull between his narrow hunched shoulders looked hard and heavy like a cobblestone. The wire-rimmed glasses he had discarded for pince-nez with big round lenses like those he had seen Himmler wear in *Der Stürmer*. When he stood in front of his shop, he no longer greeted anyone, but with his arms folded and a swastika in his lapel, he insolently scrutinised all passers-by. Through his Himmler glasses, his watery eyes looked twice their usual size. If a Jew passed without keeping at a respectful distance, his taut face quivered and he screeched in his cracked voice, 'Keep your distance, Jew! *Donnerwetter!*' And when Hitler came to power he really began to show what he could do. Dressed in a brown shirt with a Sam Browne belt across his chest, he became quite a somebody among the Nazis. He strutted down the Grenadierstrasse with a gang of SS hooligans and pointed his bony finger, as crooked as a bird's claw, at Jewish shop windows where stickers were to be put. But the *Jude* stickers were not enough for him. He would go from one Jewish shop to another, breaking every window pane. He had developed a special technique for smashing even the thickest plate-glass with a single blow from his sharp engraver's hammer. When the owner came running into the street, alarmed by the clatter of broken glass, Hulka would laugh in his face, a shrill neighing laugh, 'He … He … He … He …'

No sooner was a new plate-glass window put in than the stormtroopers arrived again and posted new *Jude* stickers. And then Hulka had another window to smash. If it occurred to someone to leave the window broken, the Gestapo arrived and took the owner to the Brown House for spreading atrocity propaganda by drawing attention to the broken window.

Mandel was distracted. His hotel was empty for there were no more guests from Poland and he was living on the savings he had managed to accumulate in the good old days. Every few days he had to spend money on a new window, but how long could that last? And after all, he would still fall into the hands of the Gestapo. He wandered around the empty rooms of the hotel and a deathly silence arose from every corner. The tables around the walls of the restaurant were empty and redundant, and the large counter stuck out awkwardly. Under its unwashed glass top there were only a few stale egg loaves and a jar in which a single herring lay soaking in a mouldy green liquid. Mandel didn't know what to do with himself and he lived in perpetual fear. In the silence, he kept hearing Hulka's laugh; in every shadow that fell on the window he could see him; at every sound, he thought that Hulka had returned with his destructive little hammer. The man's laughter constantly rang in his ears and ate into him.

And later, when he was deported with other Jews to Zbąszyń in a sealed freight wagon, he could hear the neighing laugh in every rattle of the wheels and in every whistle of the locomotive. He heard that little laugh above the moans and cries of the wives and children packed into the stark stinking wagons and above the shouts of the stormtroopers who drove them with bayonets to the borders of Poland.

That laugh followed him from country to country as far as Shanghai, where he presented himself to numerous refugee committees, pushing himself forward in the long queues outside a welter of consulates until, finally, after great hardship, he obtained a visa for Australia.

But even in far-off Australia, Hulka's laugh haunted him as, deep within him, still lived the terror of the Grenadierstrasse. When he opened his restaurant in Rathdowne Street and saw for the first time the word 'Jew' scribbled in chalk, his heart missed a beat.

It's started all over again, he thought, and bowed his head in resignation. He had worked so hard to arrange the restaurant so that it would not look Jewish. He had put a potted plant in the window and hung out a menu card that advertised only Australian dishes: ham and eggs, roast lamb and plum pudding. He had decorated the tables with paper flowers, he did everything just as he had seen in Australian cafés. At the door he placed a cardboard figure of a smiling blonde waitress in white cap and apron, holding a sign that read: 'Dinner now served'. And when the first customer arrived, a tall, long-faced Australian in starched collar but without a tie, Mandel was delighted. He had really captured the Australian style. He would be able to work up a sound business, unlike the one on the Grenadierstrasse.

His customer seated himself at the table and slowly ate every dish that Mandel courteously placed before him.

With every bite the man's Adam's apple remained unmoving for a while in his naked neck and he cocked his head to one side like a rooster. Mandel, dressed in white jacket, anxiously watched the man's every gesture.

His guest caught his anxious gaze and nodded his head encouragingly. 'Very nice, it's a good dinner,' he said.

But Mandel never saw him in the restaurant again. Somehow he couldn't keep his Australian customers, no matter how he hovered over them in his white jacket and served them with fullest deference. Instead of the Australians, it was the German refugees who increasingly began to appear. Dressed in long European overcoats, they carried portfolios under their arms, solemnly ate the English puddings, corned beef and steaks, and spoke English with guttural 'r's and lisping 'l's. They were overjoyed at Mandel's deferential treatment and began to drop a German word or two. Further, they even took to ordering Wiener schnitzels and sauerkraut, so that, one by one, Mandel dropped the English dishes from the menu. Increasingly, they turned to speaking German and behaving at Mandel's just as they had done in the cafés back home. The painter, Felix Hindermann, who wore a soft stitched Viennese hat and a loose artistic tie, drew caricatures on the serviettes just as he had in the Viennese cafés. The others crowded around his table with total amazement and patted his back admiringly: 'Wonderful! Neat work! So artistic!'

Even the two former cantors, Herr Ashenbuher and Herr Pinkus, who always sat at a table in the far corner of the room, with heads bent over their musical manuscripts, quietly chanting subtle passages from the festival prayers and conducting with their forefingers, would raise their heads to examine the artist's work.

'The Viennese has talent. He's a real artist,' they said, raising their eyebrows knowingly.

Soon some Eastern European Jews began to appear in the restaurant. At first they shuffled in quietly and held themselves aloof from the Germans. But it didn't take long for them to make themselves at home. They began to drink Russian tea with lemon and ordered *lockshen* and chicken soup and chopped chicken livers. The German Jews followed their lead and ate less schnitzel and sauerkraut. They ordered Jewish dishes, too, and often enjoyed a dish of stuffed sausage and sweet carrot. Gradually they discarded their proper German manners and began to take part in lively discussions about the war. They sighed over the fate of the Jews and the ruin that Hitler had brought to the world. They even dropped everyday Yiddish words into their speech – '*Goles*', '*Chas ve sholem*', '*Kapore*'. As the restaurant became noisier and more homely, the decorations disappeared. There were no more paper flowers on the tables and the tablecloths were no longer as white as they had been. Mandel removed the dummy waitress by the door after some little larrikins had drawn a moustache and beard on her face and an obscene remark on an unmentionable place. No longer wearing his white jacket, he hovered around the tables with a damp dishcloth over his arm and chided his guests just as he had done on the Grenadierstrasse.

'*Mein Herren*, not so much noise!' he admonished them

in German as he waved his cloth angrily.

But when the hateful, evil inscriptions began to appear on the door and window, his spirits fell and he became silent. Slowly and heavily he shuffled around his customers. He never had a word to say in the spirited discussions that raged around the tables and he scarcely took any notice of Sergeant Ben who was an important personage in the restaurant. The diners were all proud of Ben and they made a great fuss of him whenever he appeared. They listened eagerly to his stories of the war; everyone invited him to sit at their table and a crowd gathered around as soon as he began to tell his tales. They drank in every word. He pushed his Digger's hat with the white puggaree well back on his head, and sprawled at ease in his chair at the head of the table while he talked in a loud voice.

'Yes, the Japs are good fighters all right,' he said in his strong Australian accent. 'But we taught them a thing or two. We gave them a real hiding in New Guinea. Sure they caught it. When we were up in Burma, I was in a patrol sent to reconnoitre the Jap positions. We were stealing through the jungle when I saw a movement in a palm tree. Without wasting time, I fired. It was a Jap sniper all right! He fell from the tree and lay stretched out on the ground. We ran towards him but he was still alive with a grenade in his hand. It was too late to take cover but I kept my head. With one leap I was beside him and kicked him fair in the head. The grenade fell from his hand and exploded with such force that I thought my end had come.

'Here you are,' he added, pulling a metal fragment from

his trouser pocket. 'This is a piece of the grenade. I keep it as a souvenir.'

The fragment passed from hand to hand and all shook their heads in astonishment as they examined it. Mandel felt it with his fingers and looked sideways at Ben.

'They're not so wonderful, those Japanese,' Mandel said, shrugging his shoulders with contempt. 'Anyone can be a hero against them. You wouldn't have been such a hero against the Germans.'

'Don't you believe it, Mr Mandel. We also taught the Huns a lesson in Libya. I was in El Alamein too, in the very thick of it. That's where I got my stripes. I was a sapper, and one night a company of us Aussies infiltrated behind Rommel's lines and mined his positions. You should have seen the wreck! When we advanced I saw easily two hundred Germans without heads and legs.'

'That's not so wonderful,' said Mandel. 'Against mines no one has a chance. Not such a great feat to use mines! Bah! Tell me, how many Germans you killed with your own hands?'

'What do you mean, with your own hands? Don't mines suit you, eh?' Ben smiled pityingly to the crowd. 'Mr Mandel doesn't hold with mines. He's a new strategist.'

'Of course I don't hold with mines,' Mandel replied heatedly. 'It's too easy a death for them. They should be slaughtered with knives, skinned alive. They should be made to feel something of what they gave us at Dachau and Lublin.'

Ben waved him away with his hand. 'But you're talking

nonsense. We had to win the war; that was the main thing. You can't do that with a knife.'

'No, I want a knife!' persisted Mandel. 'Only a knife! To get hold of a German and plunge a knife into his belly so that his foul, unholy blood spurts over your hands. That's what I want!' Mandel's voice was thick and hoarse and his mouth was twisted. 'If only I could get a German in my hands, I would cut pieces off him and cool my blood.'

Mandel caught his breath and stepped towards Ben to speak directly into his face. 'Oh, if only a German fell into my hands … If only a German fell into my hands!'

He spoke in a breathless excited whisper, looking around the crowd that sat silent, their own eyes fixed upon Mandel who stood with his mouth open, searching for words.

Then, unexpectedly, he laughed.

'He … He … He … He …'

His laugh was demonic and neighing, just like Hulka's had been.

Horrified by it, Mandel caught his laughter in his throat, himself shocked by the horrendous sound that had torn out from him.

He stood helpless and bewildered, blinking and choked by that laughter.

—Translated by Judah Waten
*Collected Writings* (1949)

# THE SELLING OF JOSEPH

IT WAS AFTER DINNER one Friday evening that I noticed my mother and father whispering together. They were looking over to me and I understood that their secret had to do with me. As always in such cases, I played dumb and buried my nose more deeply in the Fenimore Cooper novel I was reading just then.

Meanwhile, I watched carefully what was happening around me.

The house was bathed in the lovely peace of Friday evening. The Sabbath lights in the silver candelabra were about to burn out; the little flames rocked piously to and fro and thin curling lines of smoke rose up from them. Father sat silent, twirling his trimmed, pointed beard and nodding knowingly to my mother. He looked across to me several times, smiled into his beard, and eventually he said, 'No doubt you would be up for it, to see the story of *Joseph and his Brothers?*'

For a moment I didn't catch his meaning, and Mother, smiling kindly, jumped in to explain, 'We are going to take you with us to the theatre tonight. *Joseph in Egypt* is playing.'

'But remember, you have to behave!' Father said, adding emphatically, 'At the theatre you have to behave properly, not mess about the way you like to do.'

My joy was unbounded. I had never been to any kind of theatre at all, and now suddenly – I was going to the theatre! I shut the Fenimore Cooper book with a bang and, jumping to my feet, I began to dance and sing – 'Hurrah! I am going to the theatre, hurrah!'

'Just look who I have to take to the theatre,' said my father, shaking his head as if he was cross, while mother smiled fondly and gave me a peaceful, loving look.

Today I can remember nothing at all of what I saw in the theatre. What I do remember very well though, is that the very next morning I told all the children in our courtyard about it – with the result that we decided to stage a performance of *The Selling of Joseph* with bells and whistles – just as in the real theatre.

My friends seized upon my plan. As soon as the Sabbath was over, we got to work on our performance. We scraped some funds together and bought shiny coloured papers, sticks and ribbons. With the papers we made all kinds of hats and jackets, while from the sticks we carved out swords and played and banged away with them; and when everything else was ready, we started on the tickets. 'Tickets,' I, as the theatre person, explained to my friends, 'are at the heart of theatre. Without tickets nothing happens at all.' As Father's business was conducted at home, it was easy for me to lift a packet of his visiting cards, which I had previously stamped with his Russian business stamp, *J. Goldhar*,

*Sales Rep. for Curtains and Velvet products.* Now I numbered the cards and put a price on each one, from one to three kopeks. Then I divided them among the group for sale. We had calculated that we should take in up to eighty kopeks for them, enough for a feast after the show, something to remember forever.

However, selling the tickets turned out to be difficult. While plenty of people were interested in seeing the show, no one was eager to pay money for it. We managed to sell just one ticket, which was purchased by Józek, the son of the Gentile caretaker of our building.

Although he wasn't Jewish, Józek spoke Yiddish as well as any of us. All his friends were Jewish, since not just our building but also the whole street was thoroughly Jewish. Józek had grown up with us, playing all our games: Palent, Dumplings, the King's March – in the course of which Józek had not only picked up our language but also our customs and even our idiosyncrasies. He never came outside with his head uncovered and on the Sabbath he was never in bare feet. He even used to take the oath 'as I am a Jew'!

Józek carried this ticket around, which he had bought for one kopek, like a treasure. For the poor child of a care-taker, a kopek was something, and not a day passed without Józek pestering us and asking when the show would take place. 'It cost me a kopek, I want to see something for my money,' he would whine, sniffing with his sharply upturned little Polish nose.

We were constantly putting him off from one day to the next, so far as the show was concerned, for all of us thought that at least a few tickets would be sold, enough to get back our expenses for the sticks and coloured papers. However, with the tickets we made no headway at all. We lowered the price – to one grosz a ticket – and it made no difference. And here comes Józek on our heels, he wants his kopek back if we don't let him see the show. We had frittered away his kopek long ago and had no other to give him. So there was no choice, and one afternoon we all came together and called for Józek, and up we all went to the attic, wearing the coloured hats and with our swords, to put on a play for him. We had no choice!

In the attic we found an old half-broken washtub that we turned upside down to make the stage. The group donned the hats and girded their swords and assembled in a ring on the upturned tub. These were the sons of Jacob displayed for him. As the leader of the group, I stood over to one side and led the action, calling out their names one after the other – Rueben, Simon, Levi, Judah …

As each name was called, one boy after another came forward from the circle and performed some kind of trick. Each had his specialty. One made himself cross-eyed, the second crowed like a rooster, the third stood on his hands.

Józek was absolutely delighted with our performance. His fast-moving, deeply-set little eyes shone brightly, and he could hardly stand still. He, too, wanted to show what he could do and he began whistling so loudly through two fingers that the whole attic was ringing.

But he turned silent when I, as Joseph, wearing my paper many-coloured shirt, approached the bathtub and said, in a sorrowful voice, 'My brothers, Jacob our father has sent me to you!'

Making an incredible din, the group began to push me away from the bathtub. They waved their wooden swords menacingly at me as they yelled out, 'Off with you, away from here!'

'Throw him in a well! Feed him to the snakes!'

Józek watched the play open-mouthed. There were tears in his eyes and he pleaded, his voice breaking 'Don't do that, it will hurt him! It's not allowed ...'

This encouraged the company all the more and their shouts became louder: 'Let's sell him! Let's sell him to the Ishmaelites!' – and they began pulling me about and tore off my paper shirt.

And here the play came to an abrupt halt.

Suddenly the group realised that there was no one to play the Ishmaelites. What was to be done?

'Let Józek play an Ishmaelite!' – one of the group came up with this idea.

Everyone liked this suggestion. Józek was called over and we set him up with a paper hat on his head and his coat turned inside out, so that the lining was showing. Józek was in seventh heaven and began whistling through two fingers as before.

'Stop whistling!' he was told. 'Don't whistle, just ask for Joseph's price, and then buy him!'

'I don't want him to be sold. I feel sorry for him,' replied Józek, blinking.

'You are an Ishmaelite now, you have to buy him!' we

coached him. 'It's stated clearly in the Bible.'

'I don't want to be a *Shmaelite*. Someone else can be *Shmaelite*,' said Józek angrily, and showing off, he dug in his heels.

'Who else but you can be an Ishmaelite? Can't you understand, an Ishmaelite is a Gentile, you Gentile head you!' – and all of us turned angrily upon him.

'I am not a Gentile head! I don't want to be *Shmaelite*! I don't want this kind of theatre! Give me back my kopek!'

Józek began to cry and, throwing off the paper hat, he ran from the attic.

A silence fell upon us. The long deep attic, always such a delight to us in its peaceful, secretive dimness, had become strangely sinister. We were feeling sad now, and one after another, in silence, each of us followed Józek down from the attic.

—Translated by Andrew Firestone

*Collected Writings* (1949)

# THE PIONEER

WITH HIS BOOT, Sandy O'Brien shoved a heap of bloody rabbit skins towards the frames where he was about to hang them to dry. The lean Irishman's chin bristled with a moss-like, grey-yellow stubble. He was working in a narrow room knocked together from raw planks which, despite the chinks in the walls, was dark and reeked with a butcher-shop steaminess that clung to everything like slime. O'Brien inhaled deeply and, with a deep grunt, rose from an upturned wooden box. Slowly and deliberately, he braced his hands at the nape of his neck, stretched his long lanky body to its full height and, with a contented yawn, sauntered towards the window.

It was twilight. The overcast Australian autumn day had begun to fade. Cold rain had drizzled since morning and thick clouds hung low over the mud-black paddocks. In the distance, thinly scattered farmhouses seemed to hunch their shoulders protectively and the galvanised water-tanks beside them glowered like rusty sentries. In the distance, too, a flock of sheep like a wad of fallen cloud swayed in tight formation. A few solitary eucalypts with scrawny branches

Original illustration for 'The Pioneer' by Noel Counihan

wavered to and fro under the low sky and, against the rain, the landscape appeared as if viewed through a shimmering screen.

O'Brien frowned for some time at the window. 'Filthy weather,' he said, wiping the mist from the glass with his firm, heavy-veined hand. 'Looks like it'll keep up like this all night too.'

Behind him, beside the fireplace, staring dejectedly into the flame, sat Sam Rothman. 'All my land's under water,' he said hoarsely.

The reddish glow highlighted his hard sharp-boned features and his dark bushy eyebrows. Rothman was a Jewish farmer and O'Brien's neighbour.

'Well, that's hardly any wonder, Sam,' said O'Brien with the chastising tone of a prophet. 'I've been warnin' you all along. It's no good plantin' anythin' in this place. The land's too low. It can't help but get flooded.'

'It's not that, Sandy,' Sam cut in. 'I knew that, too. All those hours of work I've wasted, they're nothing. I can make that up. What's really getting me down is something else.'

'I know! I know!' replied the Irishman with a mocking smile. 'Don't tell me. You got this mad fantasy into your head. A wild fancy if ever I've heard one. But sooner or later, you'll come to your senses, never mind.'

'There's nothing mad about it and it's not wild either!' Sam cried out heatedly. Hundreds of families can be settled around here. It could all be made into good property. The soil is rich, it's fat and fertile, but all going to waste, all of it almost through to Adelaide taken up by sheep. Move those sheep, transfer them to the north and you will then have room for a great farming district. And if more farmers like myself were to come to put this area to good use, then somebody would see it properly drained.'

'Could be done, I s'pose,' remarked O'Brien reflectively as he crossed towards the fire and poked life back into the embers. An orange flame rose, briefly dissipating the dimness creeping into the room.

'That's why I'm here in this God-forsaken hole, the only reason. Let me have just one fair crop and a bit of cash left after paying off the loans and I guarantee that practically all the Jews in that settlement near the township would come running here. I won't be satisfied until that happens. You ought to know: after all, tell me, what sort of land do they have there? Red sand! That's all it is, which would cost a fortune to fertilise before they could as much as scratch a living from those little holdings. The only reason they hold on to it is that the train passes through it. Lucky for them, they think. There are crowds of people there, so the land's expensive. Every acre's being worked by someone or other. There's no room to spread out. But were they to come out just three miles further! There are acres galore here; good, fertile land, all of it pretty cheap, and yet it's all wasting away. If just a handful of Jewish farmers would strike it rich here, then the rest would follow. Give me just one fair year, and I'd have half that settlement here in no time.'

O'Brien gazed at Sam quizzically. 'Why do you bother 'bout the Jews at the settlement? In fact, why do you bother? They'll do what's best for themselves without you. Whose business is it what they do?'

'Whose business?' Sam flared, his voice rising like that of a Talmudic disputant, bizarre and out of place in the Australian bush. 'Listen! Not only would those settlement Jews come running, but city people as well. We could develop a district with a few Jewish farms around. There's certainly no shortage of land.'

'City people, huh?' said O'Brien with a shrug.

'Stop it, Dad! Don't talk like that!' It was Jean who had interjected, O'Brien's nineteen-year-old daughter, who had been sitting knitting quietly in a comer near the fire. Her tone to her father was surprisingly direct.

'You shouldn't talk to Mr Rothman like that,' she went on. 'He wants to achieve something. He's a pioneer, a true Australian pioneer. And you ought to be doing your best to help him and not discourage him as you are doing.'

'Haw, haw, haw, you seem to be on Mr Rothman's side a bit too often,' laughed O'Brien, winking at Sam. 'It's lookin' suspicious, you know. But don't take it the wrong way now, Jean. Mr Rothman knows I'm his friend. He's dinkum, and that's the way to be.'

'Funny the way you like people, Dad,' Jean went on, more mellow now. 'When you do, you always criticise them. That's how you were with Mother when she was alive. That's how you are with me, too, most of the time.'

'Shuddup, girl!' O'Brien growled mock-sternly. 'She wants to teach me, she does.'

Then, after a few moment's silence, he added more genially, 'Will you put a lager on the table, Jean, and we'll drink to friendship, eh? What do you say to that, Mr Rothman? A word spoken in truth must have a dash of salt in it, don't you reckon? Just like a good glass of beer, isn't that so, Sam?'

Jean went out to fetch the beer. O'Brien, smiling after her, nodded. 'True Irish blood in that girl, there is,' he said. 'She won't stand for any injustice. She'd cut her own throat for anyone if she thought he was in the right. I'm a bit that way meself.'

Jean brought in the beer together with three glasses that O'Brien filled. He then raised his own. 'The best of luck to you, Sam! Here's to a good harvest on your farm. For your sake, may a thousand Jewish farmers come rushin' to settle the land about us. Long live Ireland!'

He gulped down his drink and stretched his legs, but did not relax entirely. He kept a wary eye on his visitor, trying, it seemed, to make out what made Sam Rothman tick.

'Funny people, you Jews,' he said. 'You're never at ease. Always got some problem on your minds, always up to somethin', always so earnest about things and out to get better than face value on everythin'. Why don't you simply take life as it comes? Take yourself, for instance. You've chosen to become a farmer. Fine. That's perfectly all right. Be a farmer with my blessin'. But what a fuss and a half you're makin' with the couple of acres you have out here. Together with those acres comes a whole scheme for a settlement; somethin' that makes your actual farm work look like a sideline, a sort of hobby to turn your hand to every so often and ...'

He stopped in mid-sentence. Jean had just then thrown an accusing glance at him. In that pause, O'Brien poured himself another beer and swallowed it even faster than the first. He then wiped his lips, looked alternately between Sam and Jean and, after quiet reflection, turned more squarely towards his neighbour.

'Listen, Sam,' he said. 'I have a proposition. Be me partner. Come into business with me right away. It's an exceptionally good year for rabbits. There's a pile to be made from them with no worries. You won't have to supply anythin'. Just your labour; helpin' to trap, skin and all that. We'll go fifty-fifty. Winter's only just set in and we could have a good few hundred pounds by summer. What do you say?'

Sam looked perplexed.

'I'm ... I'm not too sure ...' he hesitated. 'I can't decide right now. I'll ... I'll ... I'll think it over ... This is ... This is very sudden, really.'

He moved as if impatient to leave. However, the Irishman caught him by the wrist. He looked over his shoulder at his daughter. She noticed and coyly lowered her head. O'Brien's eyes lit up with fatherly sympathy and he gripped Sam's wrist still more tightly.

'Come on, me boy!' he coaxed. 'Say yes and she's a deal on the spot. Just cast your eye over everythin' in this room and half of it is yours – frames, knives, traps, the whole lot. You're gettin' a really fine chance here, mate.'

'I'm ... I'm not sure ... not sure what to say,' murmured Sam confusedly. 'I can't let you know for a good while what I'll be doing ... I mean ... I'd have to give up my farm and it'd be a pity after all the effort and planning I've put into it. You know it yourself, I just couldn't pack it all up and go rabbiting. I'll … I'll need to think it over.'

O'Brien released Sam's wrist. The quiet in the room became strained. The host glanced at his daughter again but she averted her gaze. She had clearly fallen head over heels in love with the Jew, no joke. But what about him? Who could tell what went on in a Jew's head? His offer looked like coming to nothing, while, at the same time, he was only embarrassing the girl.

The prolonged silence unnerved Sam. 'I must be off,' he said guiltily. 'I'd better go milk the cow. She's waiting to be fed. She's bound to be hungry waiting all this time.'

O'Brien, for his part, also rose and said over-hastily, 'Look at me, loafin' all this valuable time away. Reckon those dingoes and foxes'll be tearin' me rabbits apart in the traps pretty soon if I keep on gasbaggin' here much longer. Let's go, Sam.'

'In any case,' Sam said, 'Thank you for your offer, Sandy, and for your friendship. I … I will give your offer serious thought. I promise you, I will.'

'Any time you like, Sam, I'll be orright,' O'Brien replied. 'And, believe me, I stick by what I say, mate.'

The trapper took down a saddle from the wall, slung it across his shoulders and slapped his neighbour on the back with his free hand.

'You're a hard fellow to make out, Sam,' he said, banter-ingly. 'But you're an honest bloke, at least, and that's the main thing I suppose.'

He then turned to his daughter. 'Cheerio, Jean! Have me meal on the table for when I come back, eh? And a beer.

You won't forget that, will you?' he asked with an awkward chuckle.

The two men walked outside. As Sam stepped out, he could not resist turning back his head. He saw Jean watching him with sad eyes.

\*

Sam was disgusted with himself. He stood before the sole window of his humpy, watching the rain. His was a slapdash little building constructed mainly of galvanised iron sheets. The interior was drab and, without any inner lighting, it looked like a stable. Night had fallen since his return and was it not for the glow coming from the primus stove where a pot was being heated, the place would have been consumed by total blackness. The rain, meanwhile, pounded metallically on the roof and the walls that did nothing to keep out the biting cold. He watched the night thicken at his window.

Soon after, he lit a lamp from the flame of the primus. The room at once filled with smoky yellow light. He began to pace about the room heavily, thinking the while of Jean. Her face was vivid, her eyes betrayed longing, her lips trembled and he heard her say, 'Sam, Sam.'

He wanted to drive her image away.

'What the devil's got into me?' he spat in self-rebuke. 'Look at me, me, a pioneer, the creator, the founder of a new Jewish settlement, suddenly playing love games with an Irish girl, a *shikse*.'

He grew more agitated with every step. His farm must

be thoroughly Jewish, warmly, homely Jewish, he insisted, nothing less! Otherwise, the whole business of coming here was not worth the trouble. Had he so separated himself from other Jews simply to catch a local girl? Hardly! What was needed was greater effort on his part. He must be harder on himself, he must discipline himself more firmly. Only then, and with similar willpower, would his vision succeed.

He thought then of Rosa Sallmann back at the Jewish settlement. Rosa, the smart, level-headed girl. Against her, what was Jean? What had Jean but a few girlish attractions that were at present so unnerving him? Admittedly, Rosa was not beautiful; but she was a fine Jewish girl with whom he could have a true Jewish farm, bring up Jewish children, and, in that way, give his work a purpose and justify his struggle.

That Rosa was fond of him, he was certain. She always smiled when she saw him and her talk was always friendly. Whenever they sat together, she would take his hand in hers and blush with genuine Jewish charm. And yet, he could not quite understand her. Somehow, she repeatedly contrived to slip through his fingers; she seemed to have set up a barrier between him and herself, which he could not circumvent. Clearly, for all her affection, something about him bothered her. Perhaps she was waiting for some sign. But what? He had tried at times to be direct and tell her how serious he was about her. He was not one for sentimental courtships, he would say, but what he would give her was honest full-blooded love. Rosa, however, would not let him get as far as discussing the matter, wriggling out of any such conversation with half-promises.

Had he known whether Rosa's parents thought well of him, he would have been more forthright; he would have asked Rosa, 'Yes or no? Is it on or off?' and get it over with. But their impressions of him were hard to gauge. There had been a time when they had asked Reverend Goldman, the ritual slaughterer, to act as a kind of matchmaker between him and their daughter, but nothing had come of that. On Sam's last visit to Rosa, Sallmann had paid just sufficient attention to him to say a few casual words. Mrs Sallmann was quite the opposite: she smothered him with kindness as if to assure him they were still good friends.

These thoughts depressed Sam. He walked towards the stove, lowered the flame and emptied the meal from the steaming pot onto his plate. He pecked at the food. Its warmth made him drowsy; the stillness about him, coupled with his solitude weighed heavily upon him. Not succumbing to the torpor of it all, however, he stood up with a grunt and took down a crystal-set from the mantelpiece. Adjusting the ear-muffs, he heard queerly muffled music humming along the wires as if emanating from some other planet. The sound merely accentuated his loneliness, causing pain to well in the pit of his stomach.

Once again, he recalled Jean, conjured up pictures of her and saw her profile and inviting eyes, which roused in him desire. Angrily, he threw off the earphones and resumed his pacing. He clenched his jaw, his fists; he contracted his eyebrows; his steps resounded with echoing thumps on the earthen floor. He tried to drive away the vision he had of Jean and, late as it was, he resolved to go to the Sallmanns there and then. He must have it out with Rosa, one way or the other. The uncertainty of not knowing where he stood with her was wearing down his nerves to a frazzle. If he had to stay on his own, then so be it, whereupon he would defeat loneliness with work, work. He would run the farm himself. The farm would be his mission. He might well be the laughing-stock of all those around – his fellow Jews, the Chinese, the Australian farmers, even of his Irish neighbour, the drunkard O'Brien, but in spite of them all, he would yet establish a farm here, he would, even in the midst of sheep and dingoes and undrained land. For, as Jean had said, he was a pioneer, a Jewish pioneer, and he meant to fulfil his task, realise his goal.

These intentions cheered Sam. He began to dress hurriedly, but took his time over brushing his thick dark hair and rubbing the soap well into his black-haired wrists and hands. He searched carefully through his creased stock ties till he found a fairly bright one. He also did not neglect to fold a handkerchief into his breast pocket before setting off to the Jewish settlement in the nearby township.

A lively party was in progress to celebrate Mr Sallmann's appointment as beadle at a Melbourne synagogue. The family's friends were giving him a send-off. People were chattering gaily, cheerful interjections and jokes were thrown about the room, a number of them smoked, while others drank tea. Dumpy, quick-eyed Mrs Sallmann kept weaving her way through the gathered crowd, proffering well-laden plates as she pressed upon this one and that, 'Do have some of my cakes. Try this lovely sponge with the tea. Please taste this, if only for me ...'

Mr Sallmann sat at a table. He was already the city gentleman, dressed in stiff collar and buttoned vest. A solid watch and chain were in his fob-pocket. In a soft, measured voice and satisfied smile, he was explaining how he had obtained the post.

'Getting that position, I can tell you,' he said, 'almost gave me an ulcer. It's not as easy as you may think to work your way into a position as nice and responsible as that. Now don't go thinking that I had to plead or get under their skin. Good Lord, no! But what one needs is technique, style. You have to know how to deal with people who sit on synagogue boards and the like. They have no time for crawlers and they cannot stand people who try to wangle things their own way, you understand. Least of all, they don't like doing favours, no matter who you are. Well, I just mentioned a few times how nicely I was doing on my farm out here. I also let on how I'd saved a good deal of money. So what was I doing there looking for a job in the city? For my children, I said. And what won't a man do for his children's sake, I ask you? That's how I reasoned with them. And in the end ... Well, you can see for yourselves, everything's turned out for the best.'

Thin-cheeked Reverend Goldman here added his bit.

'Luck!' he said. 'You must have luck. If you're not lucky, then all the brain-power in the world won't help you. This good fortune, Mr Sallmann, was fated.'

Another guest, a red-headed Jew who was chewing pensively on a pipe, caught the reverend's words. 'Good fortune is putting it mildly,' he said in a gravelly voice. 'To be employed by a Melbourne synagogue is an honour!'

His tone, however, changed to irony. 'It's far easier, though,' he went on, 'to plough the land with your nose than to earn a living working for a temple.'

After whom, a third man around Mr Sallmann gesticulated with outspread arms. 'Do you want to know what I think? A farm is wonderful, yes, don't you all agree, dear Jews? But, frankly, I could live without such marvels. A farm! For a Jack, for a Jim, a farm is just right. For such as he, it is beautiful, it is excellent. Five days a week, he works his head off. Then comes the weekend and he can soak or drown himself in beer. What else would he want?'

Mr Sallmann drew attention back to himself with something of a sneer. 'How can you even begin to compare? A farm, on the one hand, a fine job in the city, on the other? I'd gladly do a thousand acts of penance to avoid dependence on a piece of land. Apart from food to *fress*, what else does a farm give you? So, you stuff your belly. After that, what? Surely a man does not live by bread alone? For a Jew, there is more to life than merely sitting on a farm all his days. There is, for him, just as surely, always something better to reach out for and achieve.'

A dog outside barked just then. Mrs Sallmann paused

to listen and then turned to her husband.

'Someone else is coming,' she said. 'Go and welcome your guests.' Reluctantly, he left his seat, but even before he had got very far, the door opened and in walked Sam Rothman, bringing with him a draught of cold night air into the cosy room. Raindrops glistened on the shoulders of his coat and on his hat. Having just entered from the darkness, he stood there blinking, then seemed surprised at seeing so many people gathered there.

'A visitor! Welcome!' Mrs Sallmann greeted him with exaggerated cheerfulness. 'Rosa! Rosa!' she then yelled into the kitchen. 'Bring a chair for Mr Rothman! He's just arrived!'

She turned to Sam.

'Isn't it amazing how news travels? That you should hear about this out there on your farm! Amazing! Still, good friends have their ways of hearing news, isn't that so, Mr Rothman?'

'What news do you mean?' asked Sam with a questioning glance at Rosa, who had just brought in a chair.

'Don't you know?' she said, averting her eyes from him. 'Father's been appointed to a synagogue in Melbourne. We're leaving the farm by the end of the week. How lucky that you dropped in; you're just in time to say goodbye.'

'Please take a seat, Mr Rothman,' said Mrs Sallmann. 'Do join us. Would you like a cup of tea? You've come such a long way that a cup of tea would do you a world of good.'

Sam sat down and continued to cast surreptitious glances at Rosa, hoping to receive at least some sign from her, even a wink. But she remained impassive and stern, and, in the end, took herself back to the kitchen without returning him a single look.

Of the others, none bothered with him at all. He might as well have been a stranger, some invisible intruder, and they simply went about their talk as before.

'If I could get only half a chance to go to the city,' one of the guests said with a sigh. 'I know straightaway what I'd do. They say shirt manufacturers are having a record season, raking in as much money as their hands will take.'

Mr Sallmann cut in deprecatingly. 'Shirts!' he said. 'You can't do better than shirts? Hah? That's child's play, shirts. But take socks, for instance. Now, that's a different matter altogether. Since they've placed a tariff on imported socks, the locals can't turn out enough of them. You can produce socks all day and all night and still not meet half the demand.'

'That high tariff they've imposed isn't such a bargain,' a grave voice spoke out. 'It only helps the big shots, the mass producers. The small manufacturer prefers prices to be low. How else can he compete with the larger ones? By having less overhead, he can trim his prices to the bone. As long as he can put out the cheapest product, nothing else matters.'

The rurals talked on and on about the intricacies of the world of commerce, their debate growing ever livelier, their cheeks burning, their eyes alight. The topic found them all with something to contribute. They discussed Jewish factory-owners, middlemen, bankrupts; they related how acquaintances were amassing huge fortunes;

how ship's-brothers were faring; and they talked about who was starting up his own business, and what articles seemed to be selling well; and exports, imports, loans, and stocks and shares. They totally put out of mind their farms on the settlement. Their more customary talk of paddocks, fences, cows and feed was wholly bypassed. They found themselves instead in the world of business, recklessly throwing their money about in tandem with the merchants of Melbourne and Sydney. Even the glum red-headed Jew gave vent to opinions in a high-pitched treble. Stabbing at air with his extinguished pipe, he let forth a string of anecdotes about past friends who had worked their way up from nothing, to become 'allrightniks' now, all of them wallowing in money.

'Who'd believe it? That Steinberg! Came to Australia on the same boat as me without a penny he could call his own. He took up dealing in rags. Rags! I treated him as a big joke. Fancy going into rags, into *shmates*, of all places, here! You'd think this was old Warsaw! Go on to the land, I told him, that's where you'll make the money. Well, the joke was on me. I kill myself working like crazy on this farm and he sits like a king on a throne in his big flourishing knitting mill, him, a one-time Warsaw rag-picker who today takes baths in my cows' milk!'

'And what about Segal? And Frenkel? And Levine?' added another guest, groaning as he counted off each name. 'All of them in the big time, all in the city, all having worked their way up to being something, and not only something, but somebody as well! Not like me, fool that I am, a Jew on the land, stuck on a farm!'

Sam sat through the animated discussion in silence. He felt alien in the company of Sallmann's guests while they, for their part, and Sallmann, too, totally ignored him. As if to add salt to his wound, Rosa did not appear. He looked towards the kitchen from which emerged a continuous clattering of dishes, and he came to imagine that the noise was a deliberate attempt by Rosa to indicate her displeasure at his coming. He was on the verge of leaving several times, but felt so ill at ease that he could not bring himself to move.

'Better sit and wait till they leave,' he thought. 'Don't want them to think they've upset me in any way.'

He began even to contribute a few comments of his own, clearly so that Rosa should hear him, and once actually broke into laughter to show her that her hostility troubled him not at all – to show her how he could not care what she did! Nonetheless, a deep-seated sense of emptiness prevented him from unreservedly joining that boisterous company. The high-flying talk made him withdraw into his shell. He thought again of his isolated farm and flimsy home. Its tranquillity drew him back with a strange appeal – that very home, steadfast proof of his idealism, serving as an act of defiance against them all.

When the party began to disperse, he almost rejoiced. With exaggerated verve, he tendered to Sallmann his best wishes for a happy stay in Melbourne. Sallmann, in turn, looked him over patronisingly and replied, 'If ever you're in town, drop in to see us. We won't mind.'

Rosa came out from the kitchen. Sam extended a hand,

looked squarely into her face and said, 'Well, Rosa, I wish you all the best.'

Hastily she withdrew her hand. She fixed a cold stare upon him and pursed her rounded lips, but said nothing. Sam stood before her in patent embarrassment, till he drew himself up and said in a clipped and formal tone, 'Goodbye, Miss Sallmann,' to which Rosa, with what Sam sensed might be a tinge of regret, answered softly, 'Goodbye ... Goodbye.'

*

On his way home, Sam felt that his face had been whipped. He had never conceived that his project would so abjectly fizzle out. He turned his anger upon himself and murmured in imitation of the way he had earlier said, 'Miss Sallmann, Miss Sallmann.'

He strode firmly along the dark deserted road. It had ceased to rain; the sky had cleared; a crescent moon glittered like a dagger of pearl between the curtains of cloud. Beside the road, the eucalypts were a reflected white, gaunt stony giants with upraised arms.

A slow steady rumble of wheels came from the distance. Its source was a heavy wagon driven by an Afghan who hummed an eastern chant as he passed. In his white turban, the driver swayed drowsily to the rhythm of his song and, soon enough, the wagon disappeared, leaving behind it an eerie silence.

Sam continued walking in the night. Its vast quietude breathed restfully upon him, his bitterness subsiding in its wake. He even let himself become carefree as, before him, he made out a tiny vermilion light blinking in the blackness. The light, he saw, belonged to the Chinese market gardener who, dressed in loose-hanging garments and holding a lantern in one hand, was just then turning the sodden soil around his vegetable beds. Sam cupped his hands around his mouth and called out amiably, 'Hello, John!'

'Hello, boss!' replied the Chinese man in a reedy voice without lifting his head.

Soon Sam was on the point of leaving the main road to take a shortcut to his farmhouse when he heard his neighbour O'Brien call him beerily. Sam shuddered. He was overcome by a premonition. He stopped and waited, as O'Brien rode up to him on horseback. Lying across his body were a score of rabbit furs at all angles, shreds of torn red flesh still protruded from the carcasses. 'Why, it's a night of purest gold, Sam, eh, wouldn't you say?' he bellowed cheerfully.

'Have a good catch?' asked Sam.

'The rabbits are crawling into me traps like a charm,' said the Irishman with a hearty laugh. He untied a dead fox from his saddle and swirled it around in the air for Sam to see. 'A beauty, this one, don't you agree?' he beamed. 'It'll fetch a pound at least. Say, what about comin' over for a little visit. We'll drink to this fine fox's health. A creature like this is well worth drinkin' to, eh? What do you say?'

'Bit late,' Sam demurred.

'Oh, come on, be a sport!'

The Irishman dismounted and took Sam's hand, leading his horse behind him with the other.

Together they walked into the rabbiter's yard. The door was open. Jean appeared on the threshold. 'Hello, Dad,' she called out brightly and ran forward to take the horse's reins.

'Brought along a visitor,' O'Brien said. 'It's a trifle late, but he's a good sort of bloke.' He pointed at Sam standing at a slight remove behind him. 'A guest, I hold, belongs to the lady of the house,' O'Brien went on. 'Go, take him inside and make him feel at home. I'll take the saddle in meself.'

O'Brien led the beast to the stable. Sam remained in the yard with Jean. He approached her, his heart heavy. 'Well, Jean,' he said, his voice a low whisper.

She faced him, a faint smile playing on her face. Even against his will, Sam found himself reaching out for her hand. Jean did not move, except to bow her head. But he did feel her quiver at his touch, and this excited him in turn.

'Sam,' she said. Her eyes, to Sam, shone like sapphires.

Nearby, O'Brien's boots pattered on the damp earth. Jean retreated a step and tried to free her hand. But Sam held her hand still more tightly and drew her back. O'Brien, on approaching, stopped dead. Enshrouded by darkness, with his saddle slung across his shoulders, he watched Sam with his daughter. They stood together, their separate forms merging into one silhouette.

—Translated by Joshua Goldhar.
*Australian Yiddish Almanac*, vol. 1, 1937,
as 'On a farm', *Dertzeilungen* (1939),
*Collected Writings* (1949)

# OFF TO *CHEDER*

'AS SOON AS HE begins to go to *cheder* to study Hebrew and religion, will I tell his Rebbe a few things about him! On my life, you mark my words ...'

This was my Aunt Dina's oft-repeated threat as she inspected me through the glass of her pince-nez that was held by a black string. Her circular eyes loomed large and flat behind the glasses, like pennies.

This aunt was the family tycoon. She was always dressed to the hilt in her black silk dress with a white heart and a high fishbone collar, even on ordinary weekdays. Her double chin and goitre looked like a bag of flour hanging over her collar. She spoke with a deep, gruff masculine voice, dotting her speech with Germanisms: *Also was, jawohl, aber wo ...* I was only allowed to address her as *Tante*.

Whenever my parents took me along to visit her on a *Shabbes* or *Yontev*, I was forced to kiss her hand. I would try and trick her by only putting the point of my nose on her hand and making a smacking noise with my lips. She refused to be cheated out of the honour due to her and would push her hand, which was cold and heavy like a dead thing, under my nose. Refusing to surrender, I licked her hand so that she would not have her way. But she kept pushing her hand even more determinedly to my lips, bossing me around with her deep voice.

'Is this how you kiss your aunt?'

Thus was I compelled to give her a real kiss, which made her smile, wink at my parents and say with pride, 'A gutsy boy, you mark my words …'

My parents would then melt with the glow of parental pride, even though I knew that they disliked her as much as I did, while I stood vanquished and too ashamed to look them in the eye. They referred to her by the nickname, Reb Dinele Tsats. Whenever my father had to ask her for a favour such as a loan of a few coins, he felt as if his world was about to collapse. He paced agitatedly through the house, tugging his beard and begging my mother, 'Will you go instead of me? It would save my life, she drives me crazy, I can't stand her!'

But my mother would reply, 'Don't pass your Dinele Tsats on to me! After all, she is *your* cousin, *your* high and mighty family, not mine!'

'Please, I will sell you the entire value of the family if you go,' my father would then retort angrily, setting off the usual arguing and screaming at each other, until my mother grabbed her black *Shabbesdik* shawl, threw it over her head and set off to see our aunt.

'Oh, woe is me that I should have to face that mongrel,' my mother groaned on her way out while I would be overwhelmed with pity for her. In my imagination, I could see my mother at my aunt's door, having to look right into her eyes, not permitted to drop her own even for an instant, and see, too, my aunt's goitre wobbling mercilessly as she spoke in her masculine voice, 'But still, but still…'

But, back to my story: as I said, my parents would melt with parental pride, my mother standing, smiling and gently smacking her lips and my father glowing as he rubbed his hands while I felt an overwhelming desire to cry out, 'Reb Dinele Tsats!'

But my aunt's heavy voice and round bespectacled eyes stifled my own voice and, even later, when we sat down to a table covered in the finest *Shabbes* fare, I was still afraid to let a squeak escape from my mouth. From a distance, there winked at me the stout gleaming samovar that stood on a separate table by the window from where it threw sprays of gilded splinters onto the walls and the ceiling. I loved looking at its ever-gleaming roundedness in which my face became elongated and my nose resembled a *krepl*.

The entire house, with its dark, ostentatious cupboards and heavy dressers, loomed strange and clumsy when reflected in the samovar. Everyone looked gross and awkward, things appeared to be hanging from the ceiling and I imagined that the cupboards and the dressers were looking down from the samovar and laughing at me, 'Hee, hee!' I was dying to go up to the samovar, but I knew that I would get quite a bawling-out from my aunt if I moved towards it. She loathed me making faces at the samovar and whenever I so much as approached it, she would angrily cry out, 'Away from the samovar! I have never in my life seen such a scamp … a boy making such a fool of himself, twisting his face as if he were a baby.'

Oh, well! What choice did I have? So I abandoned the samovar and turned my attention to the grand chandelier with its glistening triangular crystal glasses. Small rainbows shimmered in each crystal, their colours changing through red, green and blue, the rainbows that they made springing to life whenever I turned my head. If one looked through those crystals at the sun, then the entire heavens would light up into bright coloured flames. If only I could reach up to take just one crystal from that chandelier, I would be the king of the world. I would spend all my days looking into the sky, making rainbows to my heart's content.

But what was the point of my dreams when my aunt sat directly opposite me and when, as soon as I cast my eyes upon the lamp, I was confronted by her large flat eyes that stared sternly at me through her pince-nez, certain that she could read my every sinful thought. Thus I remained rooted to the spot, not daring to move a muscle, thereby pleasing my aunt.

'Now, that's what I like to see, a boy sit at the table like a grown-up,' she said, passing me a bowl of nuts. I took the nuts without a word, but even though I was well aware that I had to thank her and felt her eyes fixed upon me in waiting, I totally ignored them and remained silent in spite.

'*Nu, nu!*' she began to press, 'what do you say when your aunt gives you something?'

'Say "thank you very much",' my mother urged me, too, in a softer pleading tone.

But I merely hung my head and refused to reply.

'Why do you sit there like some idiot? Why don't you thank your aunt?' angrily butted in my father.

Still, I remained silent. My throat constricted. I felt that if I so much as opened my mouth, I would burst with a deadly scream. Biting my lips, I summoned up all my strength to control myself.

But my father took to me more firmly. 'We are talking to you, don't you understand? Why are you silent? Just say "thank you". Enough of this already!'

'I ca … ca … can't,' I barely managed to stammer out with effort and with tears sticking in my throat.

My aunt's face became distorted. She shook her head, piercing through me with her hard bespectacled eyes.

'*Nu, nu*. As soon as he begins to go to *cheder*, will I tell his Rebbe a few things about him! On my life!' threatened my aunt.

The mere mention of the word *cheder* filled me with dread. I had heard the word so often that the very notion of it was fearful. Even when the wonderful Reb Mechel 'Klap', whom I adored, dropped the word *cheder* from his lips, I became overwhelmed by fear. Reb Mechel was a frequent visitor in our home, coming to play chess with my father, as he did soon after this occasion.

Reb Mechel. He was a tall bony man with a scraggly beard spread in separate clumps on his chin, cheeks and front of his ears. Above everything, he loved to talk – which was why he was nicknamed 'Klap' – and it was whilst he played chess that he was most talkative.

Not for a moment did his mouth cease moving. He

held an entire sermon with every move of his pieces, speaking with the lilt of a *Gemarah* tune.

'Oh, so this is how you play the game, if you can't go over, you go under … If I move my rook, I know that my opponent will meet me with a queen … Rashi says don't go poking your head where it does not belong …'

My father would then hurry him on.

'Come on, let me see you make a move or this game will never finish …'

But his urging was in vain. He could just as well have been talking to the wall. Reb Mechel went on as he pleased.

'Don't be caught out, if you get caught, you will get it,' he continued in his singsong tone, as he moved a chess piece with a fingertip.

He then released a deep groan as if he had just completed a difficult task. He raised his head and looked around the house with dreamy eyes as if he had never been there before. As soon as he saw me, he broke out into a big smile and all the little clumps of his beard smiled along.

'Come here, my dear friend, come closer, come closer to me,' he gestured with a finger, accompanied by a wink. 'Look into my pocket. I have something special there for you.'

I dipped my hand into the pocket of his long gabardine, searching for the treasure. The pocket was deep and damp and full of sticky crumbs. My hand, moving deeper and deeper, reached beyond my elbow until I finally felt a thick block of Vedel chocolate that had already melted from the pocket's warmth and was covered in old crumbs.

'Reb Mechel, may you remain healthy and strong, what

are you doing?' my mother called out when she saw streaks of chocolate on my cheeks. 'You are spoiling the child. He will get an upset stomach.'

'Don't worry, don't worry,' Reb Mechel said, waving a hand. 'Let him enjoy himself before he goes to *cheder*. He is still only a child, he deserves a treat, it is his special time ...' and he winked.

I, however, was suddenly filled with dread. Here they were – talking about *cheder* again – first Aunt Dina and now Reb Mechel.

The visit to us by its hunched little Rebbe sprang back into my mind. He had come to visit and sat whispering secrets with my father whilst throwing darting looks in my direction with his half-closed red eyes. He had sat forward on the very edge of the chair, twirling a thick stick between two fingers. He was saying something to my father in a hoarse, pressured voice.

'So, this is your boy, *kayn ein harah*,' he said pointing to me with his stick, while he tilted his head in my direction. 'Come here, my boy!' he called to me. 'Come here to your Rebbe, don't be frightened. What is your name, young one?'

'Pinchas.'

'Mm, Pinchas ben Eliezer ben Aharon HaCohen. An impressive name, right out of the *Chumash*. Do you want to learn *Chumash*, do you want to come to *cheder*?'

'No!'

'Hee, hee, hee, you will go anyway,' he laughed quietly in his hoarse voice, with his eyes narrowed to a mere two slits.

His laughter did not allay my fears. It only continued long to ring in my ears and whenever I heard the word *cheder*, his hunched image with his thick stick pointing at me, accompanied by his hoarse laughter, swam before my eyes.

'Hee, hee, to *cheder* you will go, hee, hee.'

One morning, when I was still eating breakfast, there presented at the door a tall youth dressed in a man's cloth dustcoat and a pair of thick boots on his feet. He stood in the doorway, looked around the room with a pair of bright, whitish-yellow eyes and said in a loud, official tone, 'Good morning, I am the *belfer*, the assistant teacher!'

'Oh, the *belfer*!' my mother called out cheerfully. She began to fuss about me, cleaned my face with a wet towel, straightened my cap on my head and kissed me on my brow. 'You are going to *cheder*, my child, to learn the Holy *Torah*,' she said in a reverential tone.

'I don't want to go to *cheder*, I'm scared!' I cried out, trying to escape from my mother's arms. But it was to no avail. The *belfer* approached and grasped me with strong hands that extended beyond the sleeves of his dustcoat, which were too short for him. Before I even realised it, I was already on his shoulders being carried out of our house. He held me firmly while I felt small and pathetic on his broad strong frame, with the stale sweaty smell of his body filling my breath and irritating my throat. Trying desperately to break out of his hold, I writhed this way and that and kicked my legs and screamed with distress every step of way, 'Help, save me! They are taking me to *cheder*!'

But no one gave me even a second glance. People kept

walking in the streets, moving about as if nothing was happening, my cries for help seeming to disturb anyone. Only one round, pock-faced, wide-bearded man, holding a wooden stick in his hand, paused before my tumult. With a shake of his beard and a tickle under my chin with his stick, he said in an open pleasant way, 'Feh, it's not nice for a boy to act like this. One ought to go to *cheder* and love to learn,' and continued on his way.

This set off more screams from me. I was overwhelmed with such helplessness and bitter despair that the screams that emerged from my throat were beyond my control; until just when my sobbing began to use up my last reserves of strength, we came upon a Christian woman with a golden cross upon her chest, a large straw hat on her head and a white veil across her face.

'*Co to znaczy? Biedne dziecko!*' 'What is the meaning of this? The poor child!' the woman screamed in Polish, angrily waving a red sun umbrella in front of the *belfer*'s face.

The *belfer* let me down immediately and looked at me with his distressed eyes.

'*Dziecko do cheder,*' 'The child is going to *cheder*,' he stammered helplessly, half in English, half in Polish, speaking in a soft pleading voice similar to the tone my mother used when addressing Aunt Dina. His large, muscular body shrank suddenly, drawing in his shoulders.

'Go ahead, go, run like the wind!' was the first thought that ran through my mind. However, I did not move. I remained fixed on the spot, just like the *belfer*. I kept staring at the woman who continued screaming, her face burning and still madly waving the umbrella. Her cross swung on her chest along with her fury. The *belfer* stood hunched up before her, gesturing dejectedly with his hands. I continued to stare at her, unable to tear my eyes from the cross when she stretched out her hand to stroke my head.

I stepped back quickly and snuggled up to the *belfer*. I grasped his hand and whispered, '*Belfer*, I'm scared! Let's go! Quickly!'

The *belfer* moved away from the lady with short stealthy, steps. Then, as if he were being pursued, he began to sprint quickly while I clung to his hand, clutching it for dear life right beside him as we ran towards the *cheder*.

—*Collected Writings* (1949)

'The Cheder', Noel Counihan

# IN A QUIET STREET

BY THE END of their working day, the Jewish steam-pressers at Levi Hosiery Mills hadn't the strength to stand. Thick scorching smoke billowed relentlessly from the oily black steam presses. The pressers were soaked in perspiration. They worked wearing only their singlets. Ceaselessly, their sweaty bodies stretched the socks over moulds, moving them through two searing metal plates. The presses seemed never to rest, working constantly throughout the day. The presses ripped the heavy moulds right out of the workers' hands, never letting them catch their breath. The steam never let up, getting hotter and thicker as the day moved on. It billowed chimney-like over the pressers' heads, then slowly descended lower and lower. A sticky brown fog covered everything in sight. Presses and pressers were so totally engulfed that they became invisible.

With a troubled heart and a worried glance, Mr Levi the boss frequently looked out of his office window into the pressers' corner. The view from his window allowed him to see into every corner of the factory. He could remain in his deep comfortable armchair that enveloped his small thin body so completely that he almost seemed to vanish, and still he had a clear view. He only had to raise his eyes to the open window in order to see all that was happening in every nook and cranny of the factory. The sock machines were lined up in straight rows, their elegant heads shining and turning in a rhythmic pattern, hungrily devouring the many different coloured threads in their sharp, spiky teeth. The slim powdered gentile girls wandered around, holding open their scissors that cut the finished socks one after another from their machines. Mr Levi was a small shrunken man, just skin and bones, with a bald head jutting from his narrow angular shoulders. All of his employees, on the other hand, were tall and thin. Their build somehow made him feel more important. Through his office window he liked to watch the tall statuesque girls buzz around the machines. Their white girlish hands fluttered like caged birds in the maze of threads.

The entire factory worked at a rapid rate, the radios emitting a constant loud stream of prattle. The machines roared and shook, as if in a steady hurry. All this belonged to him. They were hurrying for him, for Levi Hosiery Mills.

Whenever his gaze wandered towards the pressers' corner, however, he became more perturbed. The thick smoke hid everything from view; he could see nothing, and imagined that these workers were not working but standing around with their arms folded. How could he trust a Jew? One could enjoy eating *kugl* with another Jew, but that was all! When the war ended, he would get rid of all of them. He did not need a synagogue in his factory. Mr Levi twisted and turned in his chair. He could not sit still for a moment.

He rose to go to the pressers' corner to check what they were doing. With light swift steps on his short thin legs, with his well-pressed trousers swaying to and fro, he proceeded to the pressers' corner. He suddenly stopped in his tracks. He felt as if all his staff were watching him.

'See the boss going to his friends, to the other Jews.'

He went no further. He raised his eyebrows and looked haughtily over the whole factory. Just then, Jim, his foreman, materialised beside him in a white work coat with two thick red pens tucked above his ears.

'Well Jim, is everything all right?' Mr Levi said, throwing a glance over the whole factory. He turned his bald head to face Jim, who was so tall that Mr Levi only reached his chest.

'All right,' said Jim, shaking his head of pomaded blond hair that glowed like a brass globe.

'Hmm,' said Mr Levi as he glanced sideways in the direction of the pressers.

Jim gave him a playful wink with his laughing blue eyes, immediately understanding the boss's hint, and headed straight for the presses.

'Hurry up, boys!' he shouted into the thick smoke so that Mr Levi could hear.

Shortly after, when Mr Levi had returned to his office, Jim called to them in a softer, more playful tone: 'Hey Jerusalem! Heil Hitler!'

'Anti-Semite! Go to hell!' the pressers replied.

'Blind' Sam despondently shook his head. 'And they

call this a factory. Oh, what a bitter exile!'

He removed his glasses, which were fogging up with steam and wiped them with a dry sock just off the press. In his pale delicate fingers, he held them up to the overhead light and gave a deep groan. He always groaned when he cleaned his glasses. The motion somehow always reminded him of the good life he had had back home. He had been a collector for *Mizrachi*. He had walked about with a leather briefcase under his arm. He had been considered an important person.

'Samele, do you believe in this country? I tell you, it really is some country,' said his friend, Charlie the actor, with a mischievous grin. He was a bigwig in the Yiddish theatre that staged performances on occasional Saturday nights at the Carlton hall. Charlie liked to show off his little artistic tricks at work. Screwing up his flat meaty nose and rubbing his hands together gleefully, he breathed new life into the tired pressers.

'Charlie's going to start his tricks. We'll be able to catch our breath for a minute.'

They pointed at Melekh who stood some distance away from them next to a large ironing table, sorting the freshly ironed socks. He worked there all day without uttering a word. They all knew he was constantly thinking about his wife who was caught in Hitler's Warsaw. They forgot all about him for most of the day. Only at the end of the day, when they could hardly lift their hands because of the weariness that had by now overwhelmed them and they felt they could not see the long work day through, did they remember Melekh. They turned to look at him and Charlie's eyes lit up with cheer.

'I'll show you something different today. I thought I might play a trick on Melekh, hmm?'

He put down his iron and called out in a woman's voice with a Warsaw accent. 'Mailoooch! Mailoooch!'

Melekh suddenly looked up as if he'd been burnt. He quickly spun around and looked madly into the brown steam. 'Ha?'

'Hee, hee,' Charlie laughed. 'He's dreaming of his little wife in Poland, she must be a beauty, I betcha.'

'What a performance! It was worth buying a ticket for,' said the other pressers, immensely enjoying Charlie's pranks, and even the ever serious Reb Eliah could not suppress a small chuckle and grinned into his grey goatee beard. The pressers called him 'Reb Eliah with the papers' because of the pile of newspapers he always carried. During lunch breaks, he would spread the papers around him and read aloud the latest on the war to his fellow workers in a trembling, disheartened tone. The English words came slowly and painfully. Every few minutes, a broken cry left his lips: '*Oy Gotenyu*, Oh father!'

He would read on, shaking his head every time Hitler's name was mentioned. He looked up at the crowd gathered around him. His eyes would glaze over and he would say with a booming voice, '*Imach shemo vezachro!* May his name and memory be blotted out.'

To which all the pressers answered, 'Amen!'

Tall Melekh remained alone in his corner, also listening

to this news. His eyes never left Reb Eliah, his head constantly moving back and forth, back and forth. Only when Reb Eliah finally finished reading and the pressers returned to their work did Melekh quietly approach him. In a quiet, muffled tone he asked, 'Reb Eliah, is there any news from Warsaw?'

'Why do you ask about Warsaw? Don't you know it's a slaughterhouse, my dear friend? Our Warsaw no longer exists! What news can we get from there now?' said Reb Eliah, spreading out his hands.

Melekh silently lowered his head and returned to his ironing table. Reb Eliah watched him, stroking his goatee beard. He felt a strong pity for the young man and when Charlie and the other pressers made fun of him at his expense, he approached him, affectionately placing his hand on his back. 'They're just a pack of empty-headed clowns, Melekh. Don't take any notice of what they say.'

Melekh murmured something under his breath, turned around and continued pressing the socks that lay waiting for him. His calloused hands flew over the table, moving between the socks. He kept shifting his weight from one foot to the other, remaining standing on one spot for scarcely more than a minute. Everything kept falling out of his hands. He barely managed to complete his day's work when the foreman Jim called out to the workers, 'Right, everyone! Time's up!'

Melekh wasted no time. He quickly threw on his jacket and scurried out of the factory.

Once outside, he stopped for a moment to wipe his

sweat-soaked face with a dirty handkerchief, then hurried on his long legs towards home, not bothering to wait for a tram.

He took no notice of anything that lay before him. He kept bumping into people. As he approached his street, his steps slowed as they became heavier. From a distance he recognised the red-tiled roof of his house. He had been ready for his wife's arrival since the outbreak of the war. But he was still waiting for her, and waiting. He looked at the house from a distance and slowly dragged his feet. He had come close to a standstill.

'Idiot, what are you running for?' he said to himself. 'What are you going to miss? Is there some great reception waiting for you?'

His head hung. He dragged one foot after another down the quiet street. A soft shadow, like a piece of velvet, cut the street into two distinct halves: the light and the dark. The red tiled roofs of the two rows of houses on each side of the street shone as if glazed by the fiery reflection of the sun already setting over the roofline, with just one flaming segment still cooling in the cold low evening sky. The street was restful, even sleepy. It could even have been daybreak. Every house was surrounded by a neatly trimmed sparkling front garden – sleepy houses, the blinds in the front windows drawn. There was not a soul in sight. Melekh's steps resounded on the concrete footpath with a sharp, tinny echo. He approached his house, which looked like an orphan protected by the curved head of brown curly hair brushing lovingly against his veranda.

A profound hollow silence emanated from the closed windows and doors as if no one lived inside. He opened the wire door and looked around to see if anyone had been there.

Everything was the same as in the morning before he had gone to work. The only exception was the dry bread left by the baker. Melekh looked into the letterbox but it was empty as usual. He knew only too well there was no one to write him a letter, nor was there anyone who would come to him. Regardless, every evening when he came home from work, he looked around with a pounding heart. One never knew … The whole day, when he worked at the ironing table, he could not help feeling that something was waiting for him at home, something unexpected had happened, and his heart burned with this secret hope every day as he approached his quiet, lonely house.

He unlocked the door and it opened with a thin rusty squeak. The dark house greeted him with a deep silence. The light-coloured furniture glowed in the dark room, appearing as if brand new. The air was filled with the smell of old dust. The entire house was covered in a grey layer of dust that had settled during the day. Melekh opened the windows and doors to air it out. He had a quick bite to eat then started wandering through the house, wiping the dust from the furniture. He turned on the electric lights in every room to make the house feel cosier, even though it was still light outside. The light illuminated the furniture. It brightened up the light wood and ran its thin golden threads along the length of the room. Melekh dusted the furniture, wiping off the tiniest speck of dust so that all the furniture looked as if it had come straight out of the shop. If his wife ever had the chance to see the house he had prepared for her, she would have taken joy in exploring every nook and cranny. She had so longed to *have* light-coloured furniture. Whenever he walked with her past Shcherbinski's furniture store in Krulevske Street, she could hardly tear her eyes away from the display window where a bedroom of light-coloured furniture was exhibited. Her eyes would light up whenever she looked upon the exhibits.

'Melekh, look how beautiful,' she would say, as she peered with longing into the display windows, her beautiful head of brown curly hair brushing against her shoulder. 'It really is something special. A sheer joy to look at. I would give anything in the world to own such furniture.'

'You will get your light furniture and it will be much nicer than this. Gutche, you can rely on me,' he would respond.

Ever since the moment he first met her he had been promising her splendid gifts. He painted castles in the air for her. She was an elegant Warsaw lady, the daughter of Reb Mordechai Izhbitski. Melekh was a poor simple youth, a boy from Konskevolye, the son of a working-class family, who had won her with his sweet talk and his promises.

If not for his promises, she would never have paid any attention to him, even though he was a regular visitor to Reb Mordechai's house. Reb Mordechai was distantly related to Melekh's mother; they were cousins a few times removed. Melekh's mother was very proud of this family connection. She even used to refer to Reb Mordechai as 'our Warsaw Uncle Mordechai'. In earlier days Reb Mordechai had owned a large tailor shop on Gensha Street. He was a wealthy man. Then suddenly his popularity with the Poles waned. The economic downturn and the heavy taxes turned him into a pauper. He had nothing left from his booming business, so he became a vendor of lottery tickets, selling them door-to-door to his old customers. Melekh's mother in Konskevolye only knew him as a wealthy man, a tycoon. He was her claim to fame. In difficult times she would always say, 'I will hold out my hat and write a letter to Uncle Mordechai in Warsaw. He will help me out. I only have to let out a little squeak and he will come running to help me.'

Somehow her pride never allowed her to ask for his help. When Melekh expressed the wish to leave Poland to seek his fortune out in the great big world, she refused to hear of it. She did everything in her power to ensure that Melekh only went to Reb Mordechai in Warsaw.

'Why should you go roaming around the world when you have such close family in Warsaw? Do not forget your Uncle Mordechai! You will do well in the arms of such a family. Why look for riches in unknown places?'

Melekh's mother convinced him to go to Warsaw. His first step was to find Uncle Mordechai. He lived on Praga Street in a third-floor apartment. Melekh entered a dark narrow home, filled with heavy, dark, old-fashioned cupboards and chests with lions engraved on their doors. Everything had the appearance of glamour long diminished. An elderly Jew with a pair of dimmed, tired eyes, wearing a worn-out velvet skullcap, sat at the table. He was bent over, intently studying Talmud, while at the same time stirring a strong cup of tea with a thick slice of lemon. This was Uncle Mordechai. He summed up Melekh with a sideways glance. He noticed his stiff tight-fitting provincial suit, then asked him, 'Well, young man, what news do you bring?'

Melekh was unnerved by Reb Mordechai's tone of voice and by his judgmental glance. With a nervous uncertain tone he told Reb Mordechai who he was. Reb Mordechai looked him over once more, chewing a strand of his sparse, long pointy beard as he knit his forehead. 'Now I know,' he acknowledged, 'I think I remember your grandfather, Melekh Ber, may he rest in peace. I also seem to remember that there was a daughter somewhere, if I am not mistaken?'

'Yes, yes, I was named Melekh after my grandfather,' Melekh replied in his warmest voice.

Reb Mordechai held out his soft fingertips to shake hands and welcome him. He then sighed, sat down once more and became engrossed in his learning.

'Sit!' Reb Mordechai said to him, not even taking his eyes off his page. He then called out into the next room: 'Gutche, bring us a glass of tea!'

Gutche brought in the same strong tea with the same thick slice of lemon which sat next to Reb Mordechai.

'He is a relative, just arrived from Konskevolye,' mumbled Reb Mordechai with his eyes still lowered.

Gutche lightly shook her head of brown curly hair. She hardly looked at Melekh as she silently placed the glass of tea before him. He wanted to thank her, but his voice felt so strangely thick and heavy that he was unable to utter a word and, before he knew it, she had already left the room with her small, elegant and dainty steps. The loud clear ring of her high-heeled shoes could be heard from the other room, reverberating in big-city tones.

Melekh felt devastated when he left Reb Mordechai's home. He had not expected a welcome like this. Nonetheless, he returned just a few days later. He felt drawn to Reb Mordechai's house. He could not get Gutche out of his mind. Her gentle face was always before him. He kept seeing the sparkle in her beautiful eyes. No one paid any attention to him. When he came, no one uttered a word. Still he could not control himself and would often find himself sitting quietly at Reb Mordechai's table, drinking the scalding tea Gutche silently brought him. After a while they became accustomed to him and he became a frequent visitor. Reb Mordechai occasionally asked him how he was managing in Warsaw. Things were not going well for Melekh. He was finding it impossible to find a job in his trade, boot-making. He would occasionally find a day's work at half rates in a poor factory. He hardly earned enough to keep himself alive. No matter how hard he scrimped and saved, he still had to dip into the little money he had brought from home. In front of Reb Mordechai he pretended he was earning vast sums of money. He discussed French leathers, expensive Belgian suede worth thousands. Reb Mordechai listened to him with great envy as he slowly stroked his beard.

'It is very important to have a good trade,' Reb

Mordechai would say. Touching his breast pocket he sighed deeply as he sat in his chair. He appeared to be concentrating on something of great importance. Then he would pull out an old, battered bag stuffed to overflowing.

'How about buying an eighth, Melekh, an eighth of a lottery ticket,' he said, opening up the bag.

A torrent of multicoloured lottery tickets poured forth.

'It's no big deal to me, I can even buy a whole page!' he would say very loudly so Gutche could hear him from the next room.

Reb Mordechai lifted his brows with astonishment. He had never before sold an entire page to his tailor customers. It was even difficult for him to sell a miserable eighth. He could hardly believe his luck, and who should be the bearer of this blessing but a dumb provincial.

'Well, well, a quarter will be enough for you,' he would say, waving his hand. 'It is not good to buy too much at one time. If the One Above helps you, you can also be very lucky with a quarter.'

He very carefully pulled a ticket out of his satchel, held it between his fingers, then looked out at Melekh from under his glasses. He gave a sideways glance into the next room where Gutche was sitting, then back at Melekh. He repeated this motion a few more times.

'Who can understand God's hidden ways?' he sighed deeply under his breath. 'We will see what will be!'

Melekh persevered. He survived by eating a piece of dry bread and brought the rest of his earnings to Reb Mordechai to buy lottery tickets. Reb Mordechai became very friendly towards him. He invited him to a Sabbath lunch. He began to feel close to him, started treating him as one of the family. Gutche also seemed to warm to him. She started calling him 'cousin' and, whenever he bought a lottery ticket she would help him choose a lucky number.

'Cousin should pick a number with a seven, it's lucky.'

She, herself, would pick a ticket out of her father's bag. She would blow on it with her warm young breath. 'Pe, pe, it should bring you luck.'

Melekh picked up the ticket, carelessly shoved it into his breast pocket, saying loudly to Gutche, 'There's no point in making such a big deal about a quarter ticket. After all, I'm not poverty-stricken. If I lose, I lose. No big deal,' he said. 'Money is like mud to me.'

Gutche's warmth gave him courage, and so he began to seriously court her. Reb Mordechai immediately agreed to the match. He had no dowry to give her. He could see the boy was crazy about her and prepared to take her without a penny. He felt it was a match made in heaven. How else could he explain that this unknown relative had suddenly appeared from nowhere, had come all the way from Konske-Volie, and was a grandson of Reb Melekh Ber's, may he rest in peace? Reb Melekh had been quite a simple man, simple but religious with a strong fear of God ... his grandson was just fulfilling the will from above.

'You see, it was divine providence, it was meant to be,' he said to his Gutche, who turned her nose up at the match. She was not interested in this country boy from Konske-Volie. Melekh, however, refused to leave her alone. He did everything in his power. He promised her the moon and the stars served up on a platter. He did all he could to make her change her mind, until she finally gave in and the wedding ceremony was held.

Straight after the wedding she realised she had been cheated. The wealth Melekh had promised her turned out to be an impoverished existence. Melekh gave her every penny. There was hardly enough to buy even a piece of stale bread. He was still unable to find a permanent position. He still ran around like he had done before the wedding, knocking on the doors of every little factory and work-room, trying to get some work. Gutche carried her burden quietly. She never raised her voice. Melekh could see how she was devouring herself. She became sadder and sadder with each passing day. Her big glistening eyes turned darker and darker, with the glimmer of a tear constantly in the corner. This glimmer stung Melekh. He could not look into her eyes. Sometimes he took a few złoty of his hard-earned money and gave it to Gutche. 'I earned this extra money, take it, Gutche, go and buy something for yourself,' he said with false light-heartedness.

She would buy pretty vases with this money, china figurines to decorate their poor, single-room home. 'I love pretty things so much. They give me so much pleasure.'

She constantly played with her ornaments, cleaning them, dusting them. When she was occupied with them, her eyes shone with the deep, warm glow of old.

'I will give you the most beautiful and the best things

there are, all that your heart desires! The time will come, don't you worry.'

He kept making the same promises as he had before the wedding, big, hopeful promises. He was becoming more depressed within himself. The times had become even harder. It was nearly impossible to get even a single day's work. Their poverty became more intense and Gutche walked around the room like a shadow. Yes, she was simply devouring herself. His world closed in around him. He once more started thinking of venturing out into the world to seek his fortune.

In Warsaw, the new country on everyone's lips was Australia. People said that gold lay in the streets. He had heard the most amazing stories about this new country being discussed at the Leather Union Building. The other unemployed boot-makers said that in Australia a boot-maker is worth his weight in gold. They are snatched up as soon as they arrive. Every person has his own car and a house fit for a lord.

He told Gutche all he had heard. He spoke with such enthusiasm, as if he had himself seen this with his own eyes. Gutche also became very excited with the idea of the new land. She did not waste a moment. She sold all their possessions. She even sold the diamond left over from the good times when her father had been wealthy. They scratched together enough money to pay for Melekh's fare. She was as anxious as he was for him to reach the golden land as soon as possible.

But as the time of his departure approached, she suddenly became very frightened by the vast distance to this land. She was to remain in Warsaw, alone and impoverished. Who knew how long she would have to stay that way, she cried to Melekh, looking fearfully into his eyes.

'Don't be a baby,' Melekh said, trying to encourage her. 'I will send you a ticket and papers before you even know I've left. I'll have the money to bring you in no time at all. After all, they say you simply gather money off the streets. Money is like dirt.'

Melekh did not find any gold on the streets in Australia. It was true, he, along with all the other Jews who travelled with him, was well received when he arrived in Australia. A welcoming committee came to pick them up in large, bright and shiny cars. An ample figure in white trousers, tight about his large waist, said he was the President of the Jewish Welcome Society. He looked after the immigrants for whom he completed the required documents and collected their baggage. He asked about each one's origins and professions.

'If you are a tailor, you will do well,' he told all of the immigrants in a peculiar sing-song that few could understand. But if one were not a tailor, he could be a hawker around the country.

'I am a boot-maker. A Warsaw tradesman,' Melekh said, pushing his way towards the man, believing the man would be impressed.

'Good, well, another hawker,' the other quickly replied without looking at him.

He received the same response whenever he ran to the Welcome Society, in the hope that work would be found for him. He was repeatedly asked the same questions: How old was he? Was he married? Had he any money? His answers, too, were always the same with minor variations. But, whenever they asked about his trade and he stammered back, 'A ... a ... a boot-maker', he would be returned the customary reply: 'It's fine that you are a boot-maker, but we don't need any boot-makers here.'

But, on one occasion, when he was reduced almost to tears, pleading, 'My fellow Jews, I have a wife at home!' and refused to be yet again dismissed, he was given an introductory letter to Levi's Hosiery Mills, which he was advised to give directly into Mr Levi's hand.

'Mr Levi is one of our members, you understand?' he was informed.

But Mr Levi refused to accept the envelope in person. Glancing at it from a distance, he shook his head with anger and said, 'I don't need anybody, I have enough workers!'

'I left a wife at home,' Melekh pleaded to him, too, pushing the Society's letter into his hand. 'Please give a fellow Jew a chance,' Melekh begged.

Mr Levi leapt up from his chair, his bald patch turning a flaming red as he set upon Melekh in a frenzy and raising his thin bony hands, which he waved madly in the air.

His small frame appeared even more withered before Melekh's manly build. He became still, caught his breath and scrutinised Melekh with his sharp, penetrating eyes.

Melekh was in turmoil. His arms hung helplessly. He

still clung to the letter from the Welcome Society.

Mr Levi thought for a moment, wiped his head and said slowly, measuring every word, 'Doesn't matter. Drop in another time. I may have something for you then, you know!'

So Melekh frequently returned to Mr Levi, who sized up Melekh from head to toe every time, forever wiping his own head, saying, 'I might have taken you on, but you know I only pay full wages. So I don't like monkey business.'

'I don't need full wages. I have a wife at home,' Melekh, too, replied every time.

Mr Levi shook his head, understanding.

'Well, I guess one should help a fellow Jew. Come in again and I'll see what I can do for you.'

It took Melekh many visits before Mr Levi finally gave him a job in his factory. He worked industriously at the ironing table next to the presses. The days wore on slowly in the thick sticky steam and, as he worked on, himself like a machine, he lost track of the days. He lived only for Fridays when he would receive his wages in a closed yellow envelope. He was careful with every cent and did not spend an unnecessary penny. He saved the money for Gutche's fare. She was always in his thoughts. He kept dreaming about the day when she would finally return to him.

Meanwhile, he looked about for a little house, a pretty house with a front garden. He bought furniture on credit. He bought expensive furniture made with light, golden-coloured wood, the sort Gutche loved so much. He went into debt over his head. He did not know how he could make ends meet. He decided he would take a little longer to send the ticket. As long as Gutche had not arrived, he could continue to keep his belt tight. Even though he longed for Gutche and each day that he was separated from her was like an eternity, still he was prepared to wait so that she would have something to arrive to. he buoyed himself with the thought of how happy she would be. When she saw the lovely house and furniture she would be stunned. She would not believe her eyes on seeing the spotless rooms, the carefully-selected furniture he prepared for her, and how she would light up with the joy on full sight of it.

'See, Gutche, all this is yours,' he would say as he would lead her by the hand from one room to the next. 'All this is for you!'

But it was not to be Gutche's fate to experience this joy. He lost time in sending the ticket. He put it off from one day to the next. And then, war broke out. The pressers in Mr Levi's factory had already been talking about the probability of war for some time. Reb Eliah, with the papers, waved away all their speculations. He would look up wisely, stroking his goatee beard.

'Mud! That's what they will make of him. He will be beaten up into kreplach meat in a flash. May his name be blotted out! Thinks he can take the Jews to task. Thank God the world is not going to stand by with folded hands. He is only threatening, may his name be blotted out. It is no more than an empty threat, believe me!'

'Of course, it's just a threat,' all the workers agreed with him. But Melekh began to speed up the process of getting the necessary papers. He borrowed money left and right to buy a boat ticket. But before he completed the task, the news arrived that Hitler had taken Poland. News of the war only reached Melbourne on Friday night. Melekh was fast asleep at home, exhausted after a hard week's work when a noise awakened him. Loud voices rang out from the street that was usually completely quiet. Doors were banging, people were running in the streets. Melekh woke up in fear and jumped out of bed, pulled on a pair of trousers and ran outside.

A dishevelled boy was running down the street with a huge bundle of papers under his arm. 'Extra! Extra!' he shouted.

Melekh bought a paper. The word 'WAR' glared out in giant letters. Melekh was disoriented as he looked at the paper. He could not get a hold of himself. The street was suddenly aglow with brightly lit windows. Lights shone from every open doorway, spilling onto the dark pavements. Half-dressed dishevelled sleepy people gathered in groups, distributing papers that appeared as if by magic along the street. People spoke loudly amongst themselves, their voices echoing in the stillness of the night. A barking dog ran wildly about. A restrained girlish laugh rippled through the air. Melekh stood alone outside his house. He wanted to approach the other people, to speak to someone. They appeared so distant. Their voices seemed to be carried from somewhere far away. He stood helplessly alone, as though he had wandered there by accident. One dour message kept recurring in his head, 'Everything is finished! Everything is finished!'

The pressers at work were obsessed with the war: such a disaster, such a tragedy! They bewailed it, as they did any Jewish disaster. They cried about the Jews who were still caught in the old country. Reb Eliah gathered together all the papers during the lunch break and read to all the workers about the war. He read slowly, noting every word. Whenever he came upon an unfamiliar English word he would raise his glasses to his forehead, look towards Charlie and address him.

'Charlie, you are the great English specialist here. Come, look at this, what does it mean? Don't show off. Only tell us the truth. This is a matter of life or death.'

Charlie tightened his trousers and nimbly skimmed the newspaper: 'Extermination … destruction … annihilation …' He read word by word while Reb Eliah achingly shook his head.

'Extermination, destruction, woe upon us! To our poor fellow Jews who are trapped there. We should go out and scream in the streets. All they feel they need do here is write about the destruction and that absolves them.'

Melekh listened to the news silently with a throbbing heart. He felt that every word Reb Eliah read out was about Gutche. She was incarcerated in the ghetto, being starved and beaten, poisoned by noxious gases. His own world, too, was being destroyed. At work the heavy thuds and hisses of the irons seemed to call out her name, 'Gutche! Gutche!' as he stood all day at his ironing table enveloped by the steam. The image of her face shone before him through the smoke, then blurred swimmingly out of view. No matter how hard he tried, he could not summon back a clear, living, breathing image of her. He tried to close his eyes.

Closing his eyes in the attempt to retrieve her in his imagination, even here, she remained elusive, unclear.

Then, unexpectedly, he would hear Charlie's voice call out: 'Melekh!'

A shudder would shake him from head to toe. He could no longer remain in one spot. His work fell out of his hands. He despaired to return to his quiet house. Everything stood prepared for Gutche, waited for her in the quiet of his little home. A deep longing lay in the gentle glow of the light-coloured furniture. When the things he had prepared for her surrounded him, he felt closer, more connected to her. After all, everything was for her, it was hers. He had had her in mind whenever he bought any item for their home. Devotedly, had been caring for everything in the house. Every evening when he returned from work he cleaned and polished the whole house yet again so that everything remained fresh and new, in the pristine condition of his promise, his source of deepest comfort.

After he finished his cleaning he would walk slowly and carefully from one room to another, taking great pride in how nice everything looked. His favourite room in the house was the bedroom. The room was an exact replica of the show window of Shcherbinski's on the Krulevske Street. The wide double bed had a tall headboard; a golden bedspread covered the bed. There were two night tables, one on either side of the bed on which two night lamps glowed cheerfully. The light shades were made from the same golden fabric as the bedspread. The glow of the lamps was reflected in the ornate mirror resting on the dressing table, accentuating the warm sheen of the light-coloured furniture.

The whole room was bathed in a golden hue. The only things missing from the display at Czersbinski's were the two small rose-coloured lamps that should have stood on the dressing table.

'I will get the rose-coloured lights. I will not deny Gutche anything!' Melekh said aloud as if speaking to someone. He suddenly felt a load lifting from his heart. He busied himself wandering around his immaculate home. Everything was spotless. It shone with a festive spirit under the glow of the electric lights. As he savoured the beauty of his home, the thought that Gutche was so far away never entered his mind, nor that she was caught in Hitler's clutches, suffering all the pain that Reb Eliah read out daily from the newspapers. He had a secret idea that she had somehow escaped the scourge of the war. She was actually on her way here to him. She would arrive any day now.

A deep silence enveloped the house. Melekh trod very lightly and quietly, as if he were afraid to disturb the silence. He looked about at the beautiful things. He stroked a chair, a cupboard. He felt loving warmth towards everything he touched, as though he were touching something precious belonging to Gutche. He was filled with warm thoughts and memories of her, vivid, clear, almost tactile and within his reach.

All of a sudden, he caught his breath and became lost in the silence. The slightest noise stirred in him a tremor, a burgeoning expectation that she was coming, that, at any moment she would be stepping from another room.

And everything glowed for him, glistened with that expectation. He kept imagining that he heard her steps; her high heels sounded loud throughout the house. Then, late at night, when he was already on the verge of sleeping, Gutche's image loomed before him. He saw her precisely as she had been that first time he had stepped into Reb Mordechai's house, distant and proud, with a faint smile on her delicate lips, with a head of thick brown curly hair. He tossed and turned, unable to fall asleep. The entire house was awake with nocturnal scratching and wandering. Sounds came from the walls, from the furniture, from every corner of the house, as if someone were walking around there.

Upon which, in the darkness around him that, with the thickness of tar, poured from one room to another through the open doors in a flood, there pounded in his ears Gutche's footsteps waking him from sleep.

—Translated by Tania Bruce
and edited by Pam Maclean
*Tsustayer Zamulbukh* (1944),
*Collected Writings* (1949)

# NEWCOMERS

HYMAN JACOB had not seen his brother Yossel since leaving home, which had been thirty years before. In those days, Yossel was, he recalled, a gawky youth, his arms and legs growing too quickly. His eyes had looked tired but shifty and usually focused upon the ground. In fact, he had been called 'Yossel Zombie'. He hardly ever spoke and seemed to be in a daze wherever he went, displaying as much initiative as a spoilt cat on a cushion. As for work, he simply moped and lounged around his father's small leather-goods business – what he had called 'helping Father in the shop'.

Their father was a religious Jew with a carefully trimmed beard that looked like a small mat of cotton on his chin. A fire smouldered in his deep-set eyes as he worked carving out leather shapes with a narrow cutting instrument gripped in his hand. He watched the workers as they glued and tapped the leather onto shoes with their blackened crooked fingers. To test their hardness, he would sniff each piece of leather, then bite it with his teeth.

'Bird-brain, you're making rubbish of my goods!' he would snap when dissatisfied and frenziedly tear the leather from the craftsman's hands. At the same time, he kept a hawk's eye upon Yossel who frequently happened to be roving around the cash-box.

'Don't be such a watchdog over my money, Yossel Zombie,' he would say irritably to clear Yossel from the workshop. 'Just kindly do me the honour of leaving here in peace and quiet.'

When Yossel contrived to avoid being watched, he never left the store empty-handed. If he were not to be seen near the cash drawer, then he was snooping around the shelves. The next thing you knew, he had pulled out a large strip of leather that he soon palmed off at half-cost to some buyer down the street. With the money in hand, he went straight to the good-time ladies promenading in the vicinity of the Iron Gateway, a Warsaw landmark.

Somehow his thefts never went smoothly. His father knew the exact sum that should be in the till and, moreover, kept count of every bit of leather in stock. It was obvious from the way he acted when he came home that he always knew what had happened. His pale thin fingers drummed on the table till he eventually stormed, 'He's robbing me, that zombie! He's driving me to the grave! Time for him to leave this house altogether!'

For some time after that Yossel would not dare show up at the business. He loafed about from one room to another, gaping drowsily at the walls, while Hayim, his elder brother, would shake his head and ask repeatedly, 'Well, Yossel, what's going to become of you? It's up to you, so let's hear what you want to do.'

Yossel lowered his head in annoyance, then casually

threw a sideways glance at his brother, as though he were too tired to lift his head fully, then droned in a heavy voice, 'Lend me a few guilders, Hayim. I'll pay you back.'

'There you are! That's all you need,' Hayim would pass him a shilling. 'Don't think we begrudge you a little money.'

'Arr, a shilling!' Yossel said as he snatched it up with his chunky fingers, sniffing his nose contemptuously. He dribbled out of the place as though he were a stranger and not one of the family at all.

'I'll travel overseas. I'll go wherever the wind carries me, that's what I'll do,' he said as he deliberately stopped in the doorway, his back still to his brother. He turned back then to face him with a look that chilled the blood in Hayim's cheeks.

Events, however, turned out the opposite way. It was not Yossel but Hayim who set off to wander abroad. He had to undergo the indignity of starting afresh in different lands while Yossel stayed home, continuing to filch from his father and throwing the proceeds at the women of the Iron Gateway. After Hayim's departure, his brother went completely to the dogs. His father wrote how Yossel was causing him no end of trouble and reducing him to a pauper in his old age.

Mr Hyman Jacobs never learned what became of Yossel. When the war broke out, letters ceased and little news came of any kind. At one time, he did learn of his father's death but then he lost all touch. This rarely bothered him. He had problems enough without worrying about others. He married, launched several business concerns and became such a busy man that he seldom spared a moment's thought about his old home or family.

Yossel Zombie's fate then left his mind altogether, but if ever a memory of his brother did arise, Hyman swiftly disposed of it and grimaced with the thought, 'A lot of good it does thinking about that fellow! Huh, some brother!'

Then, unexpectedly, a letter came. It was not addressed directly to him, but care of Rabbi Levi. One day, the rabbi himself came to him all out of breath. He was rubbing his soft hairy hands and his eyes shone excitedly. Clearly, he. was proud of himself and exclaimed in a flutter, 'Congratulations, Mr Jacobs! I have great news for you. I bring you greetings from your brother.' He blurted it out in one breath in his cantorial voice, whereupon he handed him Yossel's letter.

Very gingerly, Mr Jacobs took the letter. It was written with Yiddish words but in German characters. In a long-winded introduction, Yossel presented himself to his 'dearly beloved and esteemed brother', continuing with a remarkable list of good wishes and salutations from their many uncles and aunts, nieces and nephews and first and distant cousins. Finally, in very courteous terms, Hayim was requested to prepare a welcome for his brother, who would be most honoured to come and stay with him. Mr Jacobs turned the letter about in his fingers as though it reviled him to touch it. As soon as Rabbi Levi had gone, he tore it into minute fragments.

'Arr, what a nuisance!' he thought. 'Yossel 'Zombie'

now wants to dump himself on me, does he? He's all I need to top things off!'

But Yossel persisted. Letter after letter arrived via Rabbi Levi, after which they began to flow regularly directly to him. Their tone grew more pressing. Yossel was in dire circumstances, visas must be sent to rescue him. To remain where he was had become positively dangerous. It was a matter of life and death. Each letter ended with the same flourish:

> Till we meet again in the very near future.
> Yours in eternal gratitude,
> Ignace and Mathilda.

The German script and the 'Ignace' drew him back. Why all of a sudden 'Ignace'? It was not so very hard to imagine what this 'Ignace' was like since he had emerged from Yossel 'Zombie'. But Mathilda? Who on earth could she be? Could Yossel have ever married anyone – that Yossel?

Mr Jacobs ripped each letter into shreds and wrote no reply. So Yossel turned once again to Rabbi Levi who would bring these letters to Mr Jacobs. The rabbi carried out that task with a face so flushed with sanctimonious anger that Mr Jacobs realised he would never escape from Yossel. Although heavy-hearted about it, he posted not only visas, but also passage money and some extra to spend on the excursion. Yossel gave his oath that he would pay this back with gratitude and interest. So he had written in his last letter.

And now, Yossel and his wife were here.

In Mr Hyman Jacobs' lavish lounge room, the table gleamed; silverware and expensive wafer-thin porcelain were set on a spotlessly white tablecloth; the large crystal chandelier with every globe glittering brightly pierced the eyes with its blaze. Nevertheless, Mr Jacobs felt that his lounge room was still too dark for his liking.

He glanced apprehensively at his brother Yossel who was standing beside his wife. Her slim, still girlish figure was dominated by her eyes and hair; the latter was bleached blonde, while her full rounded eyes shone softly. Yossel and his wife were just off the boat a mere hour or so in the country.

Yossel was a well-built man. His cheeks were fleshy and there was a manly sort of knobble about halfway down his prominent nose. It was not long before he seated himself and crossed his legs. From the big armchair his deep voice came: 'Nice to be seeing you, Hayim. It's been a long time, my word it has.'

The sound of his original name had a queer ring in Mr Jacob's ears. He cleared his throat, sighed, then answered vaguely, 'Well, you know … the years hurry by …'

Mrs Jacobs was a thin, solemn woman with greying hair parted in the middle and combed into a bun at the back. She moved about the table with a soft smile, arranging the cutlery and plates, while her sister-in-law, Mathilda, stood behind her, tying a red silk ribbon around her bun. Then Mathilda moved ceremoniously to face her and pinned a large bright flower on her dress, starting up a homely chat and keeping on smiling with her full glistening eyes at Mrs

Jacobs. Most unexpectedly then, she embraced Mrs Jacobs and kissed her. Mathilda's hug and kiss took Mrs Jacobs totally by surprise. Abashed, she lowered her head and coyly began to finger the ribbon in her hair ill at length she said through closed pursed lips, 'Oh, Mathilda … please!'

Into the room came Suzy, the Jacobs' only daughter. She was in her twenties. Her eyes were so big that they looked hungry while her neck was so thin that it was only by a freak of nature that it could hold up her sharp face. She had not wanted to be dragged to the port to welcome her relatives, having fiercely resisted all attempts to make her do so. Instead, she had spent the afternoon playing tennis. She had returned bathed in perspiration, having extended herself to exhaustion. A brief pair of shorts revealed two ugly knees in the middle of scrawny legs that looked like welded pipes.

Yossel leapt from his seat and extended his hand. 'So this is her, your beautiful daughter?'

He glanced at Hayim, but without waiting for a response, he at once approached and embraced her in his arms. She, in turn, stared at him, aghast.

'A real sports girl, just how I like them!' his manly voice resounded through the salon. Patches of crimson rose to her angular cheeks. Despite her efforts to free herself, he drew her all the closer to his chest and looked her in the eye. One hand ran through Suzy's hair with a fluid motion while the other gripped her wrists tightly.

'Come on, Ignace, acquaint me also with my niece,' his wife now said in a lilting tone.

'You're jealous, you darling cook of mine, ha, ha, ha!' Yossel boomed and winked at her. His laughter grated in Mr Jacobs' ears. He watched anxiously as Yossel petted his daughter and looked to see how his wife was taking it. However, a beaming smile was lighting her face and she had taken out her shawl and draped it around her head as though it were a special occasion.

'Let's all have something to eat,' Mr Jacobs said drily to break the suspense.

They sat around the table but Yossel contrived to sit next to Suzy. He kept stroking her hair and playfully patted her cheeks.

'Just the image of her mother, yes, bless her soul, your little Suzy!' he addressed his brother without taking his eyes off Suzy.

'I suppose … she does take after the wife's side of the family,' said Mr Joseph lamely.

The situation was becoming intolerable with Yossel sitting so close to Suzy. Mr Joseph took a close look at Yossel. He seemed contented now; his face was well rounded and his chest was solid. His tailor-made suit was the latest in style and a silk handkerchief peeked smartly from its breast pocket. There was no trace of the old-time dishevelled Yossel 'Zombie'. Perhaps in his eyes there did lurk some of the former 'gipsy' in him but it had an added quality of cunning. It was the sort of drowsiness that put people on their guard.

He made himself at home. He sat back comfortably in his chair and savoured each of the delicacies in a leisurely manner. Every bite appeared to please him as he kept smacking his lips and, nodding his head, he said, 'Ah! Of course, the English! They know how! Even back there in Europe they value English cooking, *comprenez-vous la cuisine anglaise?*' He leant across to his wife and winked at her with his sleepy eyes.

Several guests arrived – members of the family and some good friends, all of them Jewish and each a wealthy person of social standing. They came wearing fixed smiles as each dutifully offered their fingertips with their genial '*Sholem aleykhem*, how do you do?' to Yossel. As for Mathilda, each simply nodded with a smile in her direction.

Mr Silver, a cheery little fellow with restless eyes twinkling behind his gold-rimmed spectacles, went straight to the table and sat down. He grabbed something to eat, but stopped suddenly as if something was wrong. He fixed his eyes upon Yossel, measuring him up and down with an imperious air. 'Wooh, how do you like this country, ha?' he asked, rubbing his hands as he ogled at Yossel over his glasses.

Nearby stood a wealthy jeweller, a Mr Newman. His flabby ears shook every time he moved his bear-like head. He placed his septically clean hands on the table and turned their palms upward, their pallor visible to all. 'You see these hands, Mister? That's now, you see! Yes, in this country you have to work really hard if you want to get somewhere.'

'Certainly, my dear Herr! To work makes the life sweet,' Yossel shot back. He exuded confidence. He then inquired how business was in this country, asked about the

Government, about import and export and nodded with the air of one who did not need to be told which end of the fork to hold. His slow eyes looked shrewdly from side to side as if he were thinking, 'This is kids' stuff, simple … I've done bigger deals than that.'

The discussion of business brought the gathering to life. They mentioned politicians and the high price of wheat and retailing as Yossel listened, alert to every comment. He even threw in a few words of English, unfolded his handkerchief gracefully and replaced it carefully. The guests around the table, these gentry, took well to Yossel. Their conversation moved on to various topics but paused frequently to ask for Yossel's opinion.

Mr Jacobs sat silent. The animated chat and the clattering of dishes and cutlery had kept him distant. As he watched, Yossel seemed to be seen as a business tycoon.

But suddenly Mr Jacob burst out loudly and related a long story about a wool contract he had 'practically signed with a Japanese agent'. Although he stood to earn quite a few thousand, he had pulled out of the deal at the last moment. Actually it was over a trifle. Prestige was involved and they had quibbled. He spoke with studied deliberation and removed his glance from Yossel who sat vaguely chomping with his front teeth, scarcely showing interest in his brother's story. Mr Jacobs came to the end, coughed thinly and then exclaimed for all to hear, 'Well, you know, business with Japan is hardly my line. It's too easy, really. I leave that to others. Anyhow, a couple of thousand this way or that doesn't trouble me.'

'Yes, of course!' remarked Yossel coolly, reaching for a cigarette from the silver box on the table, which he lit after sniffing it and finding it to his satisfaction. 'What does a few thousand matter to a businessman?', upon which he screwed up his nose, saying, 'A Dukes! ... Is this all you smoke here, this Dukes stuff?'

He then leaned his head back and surveyed the luxurious dining room whose walls were painted in a silver hue that reflected other colours from the lights of the gaudy chandelier. Yossel ran his fingers over his chin as smoothly as if they had been dipped in fine oil. Dreamily he shut his eyes and let out a thick cloud of smoke through his nostrils.

'Not a bad place you have here, Hayim. A lovely room, quite tastefully done up, but still lacking something, shall we say, an artist's touch, some drops of imagination. My own inclination would be something different, more in the European style. That would really be a place worth seeing. Ah, yes, my Mathilda has a talent for work like this, *comprenez-vous*?'

'Oh no, Ignace!' Mathilda's large eyes lit up as a weak smile settled upon her face

Mr Jacobs knit his eyebrows. His face fell and his lips quivered. An ensuing silence reigned in the room. Mr Jacobs' eyes wandered towards Mathilda's girlish face. She was evidently still a young woman.

After several moments' thought, he looked solemnly at his own wife, then at Suzy who still watched her uncle with the same redness in her cheeks and her eyes shining. It struck him that Yossel must have been all of forty-eight since he was two years younger than himself. His dry hands passed nervously to his face and felt the deep wrinkles between the bones. In a subdued voice, he said, 'You'll be all right, Ignace.' The name Ignace came off his tongue, sounding as if it had been whistled.

'Do you call this "all right"?' Yossel roared out and laughed. 'Ha, ha, I'll show you "all right". I can be really somebody, just wait till I get started properly. You'll see something then. If I were here already thirty years like you, I'd be looked up to, aha, yes! Millions I'd be playing with, tens of millions, *entendez-vous!*' he said with a broad wink at Mathilda.

More guests came, including Rabbi Levi and some younger people, Suzy's friends. The dining room became rowdy. Everyone seemed to be revolving around Yossel and Mathilda and wanted to meet this 'charming and intelligent couple' – that was how Suzy had proudly introduced them to every guest. Mrs Jacobs' mood grew almost festive. Smiling sweetly throughout the proceedings, she circulated amiably around the visitors and frequently pressed her way through to Mathilda, having always something intimate to whisper into her ear. Meanwhile, Yossel stood smoking a fat cigar in the midst of a group of elderly men engaged in earnest discussion, sagaciously nodding his head at appropriate moments. Once, like a good fellow, he flicked a dust particle off Mr Newman's suit. Rabbi Levi kept within Mathilda's presence, beamed piously at her and, at intervals, scrutinising his nails.

Mr Jacobs kept wending through the crowd, not

speaking to a soul. No one appeared to notice him. He was like an outsider. Suzy was the only exception. Several times she approached him, flung her matchstick arms about him and kissed him on the cheeks. Her embraces startled him. Glumly, he asked from the corner of his mouth, 'Well, how do you like your new uncle?'

'What do you mean, Dad? Isn't he your brother?' she muttered rapidly and quickly departed.

'My brother, hmm …' Mr Jacobs murmured to himself. 'The star of the show, Yossel "Zombie", now a big shot! Not happy unless he's playing with millions!'

It was not till very late that the last caller left. The ornate reception room lay in a hush of emptiness. The crystal chandelier still glittered splendidly. Mrs Jacobs sat blinking from the sharp light. Her chair was near the wall; now she let her usually well-arranged hair straggle in thin strands.

Suzy had not yet overcome her excitement. With her red blotches suffusing her face, she kept marching about the room. Mr Jacobs himself was slumped over the table. His head was whirling. Traces of fatigue were deeply etched into his lined face, but something held him back from going to sleep.

As for Yossel, he stood in a corner whispering to his wife. From time to time he threw anxious glances at his brother. He seemed disturbed.

His large manly face was a little drab now. His fine Roman nose jutted forward like a gloomy rooster's beak.

Mathilda drew near to him, burying her head in his chest. Her dyed blonde hair curled like a clump of cotton wool, making her head resemble that of a doll.

Mr Jacobs furtively observed their confusion. As he watched them, his desiccated fingers grazed over his chin. 'Ignace and Mathilda. Poof! Just a couple of newcomers. Greenhorns like the rest of them! And him, he's going to fiddle around with all the millions and millions. Big shot, huh!'

He sniggered. Then he rose and with a loose but friendly grin, walked over to them.

—Translated by Joshua Goldhar
*Australian Jewish News*, Supplement,
*Literary Journal*, Sep.-Oct. 1938,
*Dertzeilungen* (1939)

# COMPATRIOTS (*LANDSLAYT*)

## 1

WHEN THE NEWS of Zharnev's destruction reached Henekh Bootcher, he was devastated and unable to utter a word. He just slowly raised his head, his wide forehead glowing and his high cheek-bones profoundly tense.

'*Nu*, I always felt that it would end like this,' he finally said in an emphatic tone. 'Did you think I did not know?'

This was a quirk of his nature. He felt that he had to know everything before it happened. He was a slow, heavy man but very influential. He never undertook more than he could manage, nor ever became over-excited, but clung to his beliefs, saying, 'I always knew that it would end like this. What do you think, I did not know?'

His wife, Faige Tzirl, was small and thin with a narrow lanky face shaped like a bulb of garlic. She had swift, mobile eyes that refused to stay still for as much as a moment. She would often complain to people about her husband.

'That husband of mine has a white liver, he's cold as ice, nothing bothers him, nothing moves him,' she would bewail him pitifully, sucking her thin bloodless lips.

Henekh's son, Sam, had brought him the news about Zharnev. He had read of the tragedy in the English newspapers. He came by in the evening after dinner, during a spell of blistering heat that penetrated through the window as a hot wind blew with parching dryness that made the inside curtains billow out widely and, in its coursing outside, shook the heads of the palm trees to wild unruliness.

Henekh sat at the table, his braces lowered, drinking scorching tea, one cup after another, believing that this would cool him down. He was sorting his bills with his daughter Sadie, a girl of some fourteen years with a bright red-cheeked little face and a head of dense hard hair that was constantly falling into her face. Large beads of perspiration caused by the tea formed on Henekh' s face. They had only just finished the supper and its fatty odours still engulfed the room. He was puffing with satiation, turning the much-worn pages of his ledger with his large meaty hands.

'Sadie, write this down,' he began to dictate in a weary voice, as he wiped the perspiration from his face and thick round butcher's neck. 'Mrs Kaplan – three pounds top rib and a liver and lung, two and a half shillings.'

This set him to whingeing.

'Some people just can't help themselves. Three pounds of top rib and a liver and lung. They are filthy rich, wealthy beyond belief and what do they eat? Liver and lung. Like paupers, always scrounging.'

He threw a swift dismayed glance in Sam's direction, squirmed uncomfortably on his chair and glanced at his wife who was in the kitchen washing the dishes and the cutlery. Her narrow, angular shoulders heaved and dropped as if she were fighting with someone. Henekh glanced at her a few more times, and then pushed the account books away.

'Sam,' he called to his son, 'are you sure you read it right, was it really Zharnev?'

'I'm sure it was Zharnev!' he said, raising his head. He was sitting peering into the newspaper as he picked at the red sores that covered his face. He passed the paper to his father and pointed with his finger, saying, 'See, here it is, Zharnev. The Nazis have destroyed it completely, they bombed it. You see?'

His maturing deepening voice that still had its juvenile residues was almost choking with emotion.

'See … shmeee … good on you!' Henekh erupted at Sam with an angry murderousness so out of character for him.

Fayge Tzirl ran in from the kitchen when she heard his flaring of temper. Still clasping a dripping pot in her hands, she was frightened as she looked from husband to son with flickering eyes and asked in alarm, 'Henekh, why are you so suddenly screaming? What happened? Say something, you bandit, you!'

'Ask him, that brat of yours!' Henekh replied, angrily throwing his head at Sam.

He took the paper in his hand, even though he could not read a solitary word, and stared the spot that Sam had shown him for a long time. He groaned and without a word, carefully folded the paper and placed it in his pocket.

Henekh guarded the paper with his life. He often

touched his breast pocket where he had put it and spread it out on the table at every quiet opportunity in the butcher shop and stared at the undecipherable script. Whenever he opened it, the word Zharnev that Sam had pointed out to him sprang before his eyes. It looked warm and familiar in the midst of the surrounding mass of other foreign letters. The ship-like shape of the 'z' reminded him of the Zharnev church with its high, pointy tower. The 'A' recalled the house of the town tycoon, Reb Bunim Aychner, with the red roof that covered its porch. The 'W' at the word's end brought to mind the Kruszczyński's pharmacy with its glazed double doors and its wide display windows down which large waterfalls rained down in coloured waters, red, green and blue. He stared mutely at the paper and whenever one of his own, a Zharnev *landsman*, a compatriot, entered his shop, he gave her a prolonged tragic look from beneath his brows and pointed at the paper, moaning, 'Have you heard the news? There is no more Zharnev, Zharnev is finished …'

'We've heard, we've heard,' the women joined in his laments, shaking their heads in sorrow, their mien transforming into pious tragedy. Their sorrow broke Henekh's heart. He felt even closer to the women as he looked at them with his familiar smile widening under his moustache.

Mrs Kaplan was one person who had not heard about the disaster. She entered the shop in her usual manner, puffing and panting and dressed to the hilt in her expensive fox collar that kept slipping down to her high bosom, and wearing a fashionable red suede hat. As soon as she entered the shop, she began to inspect the meat that hung from metal hooks around the walls. She could not remain in one place as she dug her dainty manicured nails into every bit of flesh. She was the same determined Malkele that she had been back home. Even though she had worked her way up in the new country to become a real lady given to wearing perfume and lace, she was still unable to control her old habits of bargaining over every penny, every piece of bone that she demanded for free. She still loved bargains as in the past and bought spleen, liver and lung that, pound for pound, were the cheapest meats to be had.

Henekh, in the inner recesses of his heart, bore a long grudge towards her. Sometimes, when she poked too long around the carcasses or kept insisting on bargaining, he felt like swiping her across the face with a cut of meat in a rough butcherly manner. But the main reason for his anger was that he felt her to be somewhat responsible for destroying the match that he had been trying to bring about between Mr Phillip Hayman and Temerl, Reb Bunim Aychner's only daughter. Bearing that resentment towards her, he never looked at her when she entered the shop, nor wrap her order, but angrily threw her regular purchase in her direction.

Never did he have a pleasant word to say to her.

This time, however, he withdrew his newspaper from his breast pocket as soon as she entered and looked at her out of the corner of his eyes. He slowly spread the paper on the table and, with a strained voice, spoke as if into the void, so that she, Mrs Kaplan, should not think he was addressing her.

'Zharnev has been wiped out! Zharnev no longer exists!'

Mrs Kaplan froze, her arms extended as her fox collar slid from her shoulders to the floor.

'What? What do you mean?'

She fixed such large frightened eyes upon Henekh that it melted his old tough heart.

'It fell into Hitler's claws; everything has been destroyed, not a stone was left unturned!'

Henekh kept talking into the void, but his tone became softer, less remote.

Mrs Kaplan continued to scrutinise him with her gaping eyes, unable to come to herself, then suddenly clapped her hands and let out a wail.

'I can't believe my ears! My Zharnev! My poor Zharnev!' She sobbed, her tears large and rounded like beads.

Henekh came out from behind the counter, bringing a chair for Mrs Kaplan. He took her by the hand and helped her to sit down. His resentment towards her waned. Bending over her and looking into her teary face, he said, 'Mrs Kaplan, my dear Malkele, this tragedy was preordained. What can we do?'

## 2

From that time on, Henekh's opinion of Mrs Kaplan improved dramatically. He now always greeted her with a broad warm smile and when she entered the shop, he treated her as an honoured customer. He forgave her for ruining the match, even though its success had been of considerable importance to him. He had had his heart set on this match from the day he had arrived in Australia, from the time he visited Mr Phillip Hayman, who had brought him regards from home. Mr Hayman had a three-storey clothing factory in Flinders Lane and was a force to be reckoned with. Nonetheless, he made a point of making Henekh very welcome. He received him in his office, made him feel very important and asked him everything about their old home in Zharnev. Was the old pump with the rusty lion's mouth still standing in the middle of the market? Did Vove, the town idiot, still run around the village every morning, flapping his arms like wings, and crow in his shrieking voice, 'Kookerikoo! Help! Save me! They want to slaughter me! Kookerikoo!'?

'Well, well, well, it seems that our Zharnev still looks exactly the same as it did in my time,' said Mr Hayman happily, rubbing together his white hands whose fingers were dotted with black hairy cushions. His eyes, behind thick-rimmed glasses, shone with a slimy sheen as if they were swimming in oil. The phone on his wide green writing desk rang every few minutes, disrupting their discussion. Mr Hayman picked up the phone absent-mindedly and spoke a few words in English in a thick, soft voice. His large desk and authoritative way of speaking made Henekh feel out of place. He was constantly about to rise from his deep leather armchair and, coughing in a guilty way, said, 'I am probably disturbing you, no? I see that you are busy. I should come back another time.'

'Never mind, Reb Henekh, sit yourself down! The business will not run away.' Mr Hayman waved his hand and smiled cordially at Henekh.

Henekh remained seated, his smile tense and askew, his cheeks ablaze. He kept meaning to tell Mr Hayman that his father, Berish Shneider, was deathly ill. He had spent the entire winter lying in his bed, spitting blood, and when Henekh had gone to say goodbye to him prior to leaving, he did not recognise him, he had aged so much during his illness. One could barely see him within his mound of soiled bedding while his face with its matted grey dishevelled beard, like the wings of a dead bird, was yellow, like putty.

On that last visit, shaky and in discomfort as he straightened his *kippah*, Mr Hayman's father had asked in a barely audible voice, 'So, Henekh, you really are going? May you have luck and good health. It is always warm there, a pleasure, imagine, no winter, that's what my Fishl writes. I could perhaps be revived there, what do you think, Henekh?'

'Don't worry, Berish. I'm sure it will soon be your turn to come. I will talk to Fishl, don't worry, you can rely on me,' Henekh had promised him.

Berish's older son, who was then also with his father, countered him with bitter contempt. 'Yes, I'm sure you will find in Fishl a man filled with great pity. He will really take his father's illness to heart, that old scab head.'

Berish's son had been sitting on the sick man's bed, cutting his nails with a peasant's clippers onto paper, so that, God forbid, no fragment of it should fall to the ground.

He kept pushing aside his beard with his sleeve as it kept getting in the way. He had deserted his own store since his father had fallen ill. He spent whole days by his father's bedside, waiting for help to arrive from Fishl. He had written long letters to his brother, begging him to show some concern for his father and send money to heal him. But no replies arrived from Fishl, not even a few words. Fishl had vanished off the face of the world.

Henekh could not find the strength to burden Mr Hayman with the news about his father's illness and the family's poverty. He could hardly believe that this was the same Fishl Scab, as he was nicknamed, that he had known back home. He remembered him as a hunched frightened boy, wearing his greasy cap pulled over his ears so that his filthy head could be hidden. Even though Berish was just a poor tailor, he was a learned man. He had travelled to the Voker Rebbe and he had his heart set on his boys finding more lucrative means of livelihood than tailoring. He did everything to introduce them to merchants and other businessmen. Fishl was the only son whom he had trained to follow in his footsteps, only to tear angrily at his beard as he watched him hunched over the sewing machine with his hat over his ears, leading him to mumble, 'How can I make a success of him with all that rot in his head?'

Henekh could not take his eyes off Mr Hayman. He stared at his big full face, at his shaven cheeks, his confident gestures and the perceptive gaze behind his thick-rimmed glasses. He felt himself inadequate and did not want to bother him with the litany of woe which he had brought with him. He remain humbly seated, his throat was tight and he did not know where to put his red sweaty hands, which jutted out like pieces of raw meat from his cheap, old-fashioned jacket.

Henekh felt dejected. He left Fishl with a heavy heart. He could not forgive himself for not having mentioned anything about Fishl's sick father and how they waited for him back home to save his life. He was annoyed with himself for having been so overawed by Fishl's wealth that he was too inhibited to open his mouth. The image of the old Fishl in Zharnev was still vivid in his mind, especially his hunched tailor's shoulders, the greasy cap pulled over his ears and the way that whenever the Zharnev *landslayt*'s talk turned to Fishl, Henekh would wave away his importance and insist on referring to him by his nickname, Fishl Scab.

'Why are you making such a big deal out of him?' Henekh would complain. 'Those of us who know him know also what he's really like. He's a nothing. A scab will always remain a scab.'

'All Jews should be cursed with such a scab,' the *landslayt* would say amongst themselves as they proceeded to exchange tales of his wealth and about his business. They told each other of his high esteem, how he was a welcome visitor to some of the richest homes, and of the most beautiful and wealthiest girls having been proposed as matches for him. Yet he just snubbed them all, a person in his position being wholly free to pick and chose.

'Don't you know that he already has a sweetheart, is having an affair with a Malkeleh Fliak?' butted in Mr Max, twirling his thick Stalin-like moustache between his fingers. He was proud of his locksmith's trade and liked to show off with his thick workman's hands.

Between himself and his *landslayt*, there was never any peace. He was always at odds with them and, to spite them, insisted on referring to them by their former names back home and nicknames. He invariably found a way of riling someone, which incurred comebacks of their own.

'You'll get it all back, don't you worry,' they threatened him. 'Comrade Stalin is not asleep, and when our time comes, he will know what to do with you.'

Despite the *landslayt*'s grudge towards him and their tendency to avoid him, on this occasion, his wonder tale of romance so fascinated him that they even egged him on.

'Yes, it's real, passionate love,' he told them. 'If not for Malkeleh, Fishl would have been married long ago. But he is so besotted with her that no one else even has a chance.'

Henekh did not give this tale of romance much credence, although he did admire Fishl for his daring. After all, he himself had not been such an angel before he had married. Once his son would be introduced to his true match – the real thing – he would surely leave Malkheleh and their passion romance for dead. He, Henekh, was an expert in the field. He tried to imagine how Fishl would react to a truly good match from home with Reb Bunim Aychner's only daughter. True, it was a wild impossible thought – so incongruous was it even to imagine that Berish Shneider and Reb Bunim Aychner could ever be related. In fact, it could even be a joke; and how he regretted that there was no one with whom he could share it. Yet, it was the very unusualness of this match that, refusing to let him rest, kept weaving through his mind. And, if it did come about, what if the match actually succeeded? One could not be sure of anything in this day and age. Reb Bunim Aychner was not the tycoon that he had once been, even though he was still very comfortable. When he walked along the street in his reserved rich man's way with his blond well-groomed beard and dressed in expensive fur, he was greeted warmly from all sides. Yet, despite the admiration in which he was held, he, for his part, would look upon those same poor, expectant, impoverished people with patent nonchalance, mumbling into his beard in a German dialect he acquired in Karlsboder, '*G'moien, g'moien.*'

There were rumours rife in the town that things had not been going too well for Reb Bunim lately. His tannery that once provided the livelihood for half of the people in the town had become quiet, while Koletskin, the fat *komornik*, the bailiff, was seen there far too frequently. The people were saying that he had lost many thousands of złotys in Warsaw; he had lost so much that he was now unable to present the dowry that he had promised for Temerl, thereby having to sever the match that had been made for her with one of the finest boys in Radom.

Henekh could hardly stop thinking about the match and the more he thought, the more he felt that it was a distinct possibility. He did not waste any time.

He was at Fishl's door the very next day to offer his

proposition. Fishl received him this time a little more coolly, devoid of any exuberance. He scrutinised him with a long, slow look from behind his thick-rimmed glasses as though Henekh was a stranger. He sat at his spacious green writing desk absorbed in assorted papers. He uttered just one brief word: 'Well …'

Without waiting for a reply, he returned to his papers, turning his full shaven neck constricted by his stiff collar to Henekh. After Henekh had made his proposition, Fishl gave him a few sidelong glances, coughed lightly and faced him more directly.

'You are talking about Reb Bunim's daughter,' he replied with a strained laugh, 'the one from the tannery? Well, well …' he said with a deepening blush.

Fishl's reaction encouraged Henekh. He saw that this match appeared to have hit the proverbial nail on the head. He seated himself on the leather armchair in a friendly familiar manner opposite Fishl and began to talk enthusiastically. 'What would you be thinking? That I should come to make a match with just anybody? This match is really something! Reb Bunim Aychner's daughter, his only child, so adored and worshipped. Think of the fine family, its heritage …'

Fishl listened quietly with a quickened pulse. He remembered the tears back home when his father would take him along whenever he brought a newly made suit to Reb Bunim. He would stand and wait with his father in the dark entrance hall where the furniture was covered in fine sheeting and from where he would peek into the rich, luxurious house with its large rooms and giant credenza. The house always smelt of lightness, brightness and festive holidays. Sometimes, Temerl would float through that brightness with light, nimble, feminine steps, her golden braided hair shining like a crown upon her head. He had never been able to see her face, but whatever he did see of her imprinted itself sharply in his mind.

He swallowed every word that Henekh spoke, his face having coloured more brightly. But his newly-found wealth and pride held him back from agreeing to the match. He stroked his chin pensively, coughed and said, 'Well, I really will have to think about this and give you my decision later.'

3

Fishl did not need to think long. Henekh sent a letter to Reb Bunim Aychner within a few days. He wrote about Fishl's wealth and indicated what a most suitable match he would be for Temerl. With Fishl, she could have anything that her heart desired. He wrote the letter on Fishl's company's letterhead that pictured his three-storey wide-windowed factory in Flinders Lane, its name, inscribed in large fancy script, reading PHILLIP HAYMAN INC. CORP.

Meanwhile, Henekh advised Fishl to send a goodly sum of money to his father Berish to give the town really something to talk about.

It did not take very long before he received a reply from his family thanking him for the money, including regards from Reb Bunim who had been asking many questions about Fishl, wanting to know everything down to the finest detail. Henekh felt that the letter had brought very positive tidings and clapped Fishl on the shoulder in a friendly manner.

'Fishl, things are really moving, what did I tell you? Didn't I always know that it would go so well?'

A little while later, a letter arrived from Reb Bunim in person. He had written it in an angular merchant script, his real thoughts concealed behind business-like expressions. He wrote Henekh how difficult it would be for him to send his only child out into the world. But since that was the way that matters had been decreed, then it was probably for the best. There was, however, not one word in the letter that referred to Fishl or to the possible match, this causing Fishl to be resentful, although he was heartened by Temerl's personal touch in English, 'Greetings from Tamara Aychner.'

'She is all right, she knows,' said Fishl as he pored over Temerl's thin and delicate script with a tender smile broadening on his lips.

'Of course she is all right, what did you think?' encouraged Henekh. 'Did you expect a daughter of Reb Bunim not to know?'

After reading Temerl's words, Fishl left immediately to arrange the necessary documents, as well as send her a first-class ship's ticket. He did not scrimp in any way. The match was the keenest topic of conversation among the Zharnev *landslayt*.

On Temerl's due date of arrival, everyone turned out at the port to greet her ship. Even Mr Jack Knester, who had come to Australia many years earlier and considered himself a complete Englishman, showed up to greet her. He was a small lively man, sportily dressed in a red striped blazer and green sunglasses that sat proudly on his beak-like nose. He smoked a bent old-fashioned pipe at the races and was an expert in all sporting matters. He spoke only English in a thick, slow, hoarse voice. Even the profession that he had chosen for himself was wholly Australian in nature. He owned a pub in some outlying area where not one Jew could be found. He did not make much money from the pub, for he kept selling his beer on credit like a good sport. Hence he remained a pauper. Yet, he still felt that he was an important man. He surveyed his *landslayt* with measured looks. They were such greenies; what a racket they made at the port as they stood chatting and pointing at the ship that, on approaching, bobbed up and down on the nearer side of the horizon.

Henekh could not take his eyes off the ship. He stood slowly rocking with a gentle expectant smile and saying to whoever would listen, 'What a small world this is, hey! Reb Bunim Aychner's daughter will soon also be in Australia. Just think, we have lived to see this day. It won't be long before we see Reb Bunim himself here too. You can rely on me.'

'Sure, no one worth a pinch of salt will stay behind in Europe. Everyone is bound to leave sooner or later, believe me!' responded Mr Knester with his deep bass voice, looking around his *landslayt* from beneath his glasses.

As the ship neared, like a slice of mountain drifting in

from the sea, it loomed larger by the minute while, on the decks, its passengers were seen increasingly to be pushing and shoving, waving their kerchiefs and hats enthusiastically and calling ever louder towards the shore. In the midst of the excitement, Mrs Kaplan suddenly realised that she had to re-tie the bow in her little girl's hair as she stood clutching a large bouquet of flowers in her thin little hands.

'Netishe, darling, you will remember to say, "Welcome, Miss Aychner", won't you? Don't forget, now, will you?'

And, in the hold of that same excitement, with her fingers fumbling, her daughter's satin bow was knotting up in her hands.

Fishl stood apart from the fracas. He was dressed up in his festive best and wearing a hard new hat. He stood to a side, next to his sizable blue automobile, carrying on an earnest discussion with a long-faced port official to whom he offered cigarettes from his golden cigarette case, as if the forthcoming event that so directly involved him was of scant consequence. He did not move until the ship had come to shore and had anchored. He looked around in slow motion, like one emerging from some dream, and only then parted from the port worker to join his *landslayt* with light even steps. The crowd around him itself now set to shoving, each his own way, desperately eager to get aboard. Only Fishl did not hurry. He did not proceed until all the others had ascended and, only then, with hat in hand, did he too mount the steps.

He spotted Temerl instantly, even though she was barely visible in the tight crush around her. She, in turn, stood bewildered, smiling at everyone, but nervously transferring the bouquet of flowers that little Nettie had presented to her from one hand to the other. At last, Fishl approached the conclave around her, whereupon Henekh, ceremoniously taking him by an arm, led him to Temerl herself.

'Now then, you don't need me to tell you what to do from here, hee, hee,' Henekh said with a bright happy smile as his wife, Fayge Tzirl, looked at Temerl with such deep emotion that tears welled up in her eyes as she recalled how she had once worked in her family's house.

'Oy, my dear friends,' she said in a stifled voice. 'I remember her when she was just a slip of a girl and I used to hold her in my arms!'

Fishl felt restless beside Temerl. His customary confident manner had crumbled. He felt constrained by the numerous questioning eyes that surrounded him. Temerl was short and chubby and her roundish face was bright and flushed. She looked at him with a shy, confused and embarrassed smile. A loose lock of blonde hair had slipped from beneath her tropical straw hat that she must have bought on her journey.

Fishl, as tense as a board, extended his hand to her.

'Temerl Aychner,' she introduced herself in the familiar old-home fashion and her small, soft and cool hand seemed to melt submissively into Fishl's wider warm palm. With that, Fishl's confidence returned. He sized her up with one swift glance and addressed her in a quiet, cordial tone, but evidencing assured self-importance.

'How do you do?' he said. 'Pleased to meet you.'

'What do you mean?' said Temerl in her mother-tongue, looking at him questioningly, not having understood a word.

Fishl's face froze. He scanned her once more, replying curtly. 'It's all right.' His tone and the expression in his face revealed quickly to Henekh that something was wrong. This was not how events had been meant to unfold.

A silence fell over the *landslayt*. No one uttered a word. Only Mrs Kaplan seemed oblivious to the sudden tension, her eyes fixed more upon Temerl's baggage.

'What have you here, Miss Aychner?' she asked, pursing her red painted lips as she pointed at an old-fashioned basket covered in fabric. 'I haven't seen such an odd basket in ages, since I left our old home.'

'It's bedding,' answered Temerl. 'A feather doona.'

'You brought bedding? Who needs feather bedding here?' Mrs Kaplan went on, screwing up her face as if she smelt something burning. She then looked at Fishl who, with an enigmatic smile, stood speechless, his hat pulled lower over his forehead.

Henekh intervened, approached Fishl and, in an affable confidential tone, asked him, 'So how do you like our Temerl? A delicate soul, no? Not like the scatterbrains we have here, hey?'

Fishl rubbed the tips of his fingers as if they had been soiled with dirt and turned his back on Henekh.

'A homely little kid, a greenie!' he said.

Nothing came of the match. Not for Henekh's lack of trying. He was forever running to Fishl, trying to persuade him to reconsider. He ran to the *landslayt*, too, pleading with them that they should not allow such a fine Jewish girl to be so humiliated, what's more, a girl from such a distinguished family. Try as he might, he was unable to move the mountain that Fishl had become. The widely held view was that Mrs Kaplan was partly responsible for this state of affairs.

Fishl insisted that he had been deceived.

'She is not for me,' he insisted. 'She is old-fashioned. She brought me a dowry of feather bedding; she does not speak a word of English; she is a complete greenie, and had the cheek to write to me in English. She wanted to trick me. No one tricks Phillip Hayman, no sir!'

Temerl, for her part, was completely beside herself. She could not stop weeping. She would visit one of the *landslayt* after another, sobbing bitterly, wiping her swollen red eyes with a fine lace handkerchief, lamenting her ruined life. She was talking about the good life that she had had back home, bemoaned Australia as a desolate hole, the end of the world where a person loses self-respect and self-worth and gets swallowed by a deep chasm. Yet she refused to hear about returning to Zharnev. She felt that she would become a laughing-stock there, unable to lift up her head for shame. She would rather do anything, anything else in the world than return home.

'My *tateshi* and *mameshi* would be devastated,' she cried into her handkerchief.

No matter how hard the *landslayt* tried to reassure her, promising that they would find respectable work for her, she refused to heed their words. She insisted on becoming a maid since her life was already ruined. There was no point in pursuing any other course.

The *landslayt* comforted her to her face but laughed behind her back. They ridiculed her for calling her parents *mameshi* and *tateshi* and for settling for a life of servitude. She began to appear strange even to Henekh. If he had not known her back home, he would never have believed that she was really Temerl Aychner, the only child of such a wealthy family. In his heart of hearts, he felt a hint of sympathy for Fishl, understanding why he did not wish to go through with the marriage. He felt that he had no one to talk to, she was incapable of discussion, she just kept on weeping. He began to resent her for wanting to be a mere maid as his wife Fayge Tzirl had been in the Aychner home. He became angry at her and stopped trying to persuade Fishl to proceed with the match. He lost the will to keep trying on her behalf.

Since he had heard the news that Zharnev had been razed in the war, his thoughts returned to the match. His mind was constantly filled with images of their destroyed town. He could not come to terms with the notion that Zharnev no longer existed in this world. He kept visualising himself back home, home on that narrow muddy street that had been his, lined with its tattered old houses that snuggled so closely together, their mossy rounded roofs on top of each other and looking like roast chickens laid out on a festive table. The dark narrow windows looked out upon the pitiful overworked and overburdened Jews, amongst them the young wives in their matted wigs over their smudged wrinkled foreheads. He recalled the Fridays, overhung by dark, dense clouds that shrouded the sky; the bleak autumn rains that would fall, but still not diminish the excitement of approaching *Shabbes*; the scents of cinnamon and the freshly-washed and pressed celebratory clothes; and the clatter of fish-knives against the fish-boards in preparation for the coming meal.

Then there was Zanvel Feldsher's barber shop, crowded with young men having their cheeks shaved and their hair trimmed for *Shabbes*, their talk loud with exuberance and laughter, interweaving with the constant 'Kookerikoo! Kookerikoo!' from crazy Vovo, Zanvel's weekly *Shabbes* guest, and Reb Yedidah, the wine merchant, on his round to distribute his Kiddush wine to all the better homes, who, whenever he passed the barber shop, would spit to the side and tighten his dustcoat about his neck to conceal his scarred, otherwise heavily bearded chin, at one time a luxurious object of pride, resulting from an assault upon him by thugs with razors, in this way also protecting it from the Evil Eye.

Henekh groaned. He was deeply disturbed. He could not get his Zharnev out of his mind. Along the full length of the wide sprawling Lygon Street with its stretch of low tropical awnings, where he had his butcher shop, a persistent hum discomfited him. He became consciously overwhelmed by the street's strangeness, by the foreignness of the Italian fruit shops with their mountains of bananas alongside their open doorways, and by the Greek fish and chips shops with their large display windows lit up by their blinking iridescent signs in the darkness of night where, amidst the greenery around them, lay assorted fish, their dead mouths weirdly gaping.

Everything appeared to Henekh astonishingly bizarre as if he was seeing it all for a first time. His sudden sense of the alien feel of the place attended him even in his own butcher's shop and fell upon everything around him: the high white-tiled walls, the polished meat-hooks, the scales, the electric refrigerator that droned without cease ... All of it was like some fantasy, some dream, a vision that had him recall once more his impoverished butchery in Zharnev, the street of butcher shops tended by others whom he counted as friends – sturdy, strong, but slow – their necks always smeared with animal fat, with feathers in their beards and wearing work-coats coats stiffened by hard congealed grease.

Those same friends thought him mad when he decided to leave Zharnev.

Melekh 'Kishke', who owned the butcher shop opposite him, turned him into a laughing stock. Melekh was wild and strong; it was said that he could flatten a bull with one slap of his hand that was missing half of its middle finger. His strength made the town tremble; no slaughterer dared to render any of his animals *treyf*, unsuitable for Jewish consumption. The women of the more pious households never stepped into his shop. He did not make a particularly good living, tending more to wander around forlorn and angry at the other butchers in the street, refusing to be a member of the Butchers' Club. The Club made a *Melave Malke* every

Saturday night, drinking a barrel of beer provided by Chene Shenker. Every *Shabbes*, after the *cholent*, when the large barrel was paraded down the street and carried into the butchers' clubhouse, Melekh would appear shortly after, carrying a barrel of beer on his shoulders and a metal beer stein under his arm. He would place the barrel down next to his bed and, seated in his underwear, would slowly drink the entire barrel, one glass after another, permitting no one else in the house even to sip of it until he collapsed in a stupor onto his bed. He was unconscious until morning, was in a furious mood and would then stand before his shop, his black eyes blazing, swearing at all the other butchers and accusing them of bad-mouthing him to his customers.

Henekh was the butcher who had borne the brunt of his anger. Melekh would stare at Henekh's shop with fury and, whenever a customer entered, he would begin a tirade of curses in his thick beer-laden voice against him.

'Look at him; he thinks he is so great. May he rot in hell! He touches up the women, that's why they all run back to him!'

When Henekh was about to leave, Melekh had come into his shop, put his hands on his hips, looked him up and down and set about deriding Henekh's preposterous plan.

'What's got into you? Why are you running away to who knows where, you great big idiot? Who ever heard of this Bestralie? You call that a place? You are making a big mistake, Henekh! Listen to your good brother. We butchers have to remain in one place. Let them, those light-headed wormy tailors, wander around the world, but we must stay put!'

What a fine piece of advice that had been from Melekh 'Kishke'. He had wanted to remain, he had thought himself so clever. But what would have happened to me if I had heeded him, that hotshot! Henekh tried to comfort himself, but his own words brought him little comfort. He felt guilty, guilty about Melekh and guilty about the entire butcher street, as if it was *his* fault that the town had been destroyed. He also began to feel even more guilty about Temerl. Her tragedy gave him no rest; it pressed heavily, like a weight upon his heart.

One day, when Mrs Kaplan came into his shop and there were no other customers present, he had said to her, 'Mrs Kaplan, we ought to do something for Temerl, we ought to get her married. We have a responsibility to look after her!'

'What can we do?' replied Mrs Kaplan, shrugging her shoulders and sighing. 'Mr Hayman is is very particular. He is an expert in love and Temerl does not appeal to him. It's his business.'

'What do you mean it's his business?' Henekh countered firmly. 'Don't we have some say in this? Can we afford to disregard people in this day and age, let alone our own people, people from Zharnev. We must remember who we are and the responsibilities we have in our world.'

Mrs Kaplan did not reply. She stood confused and disturbed, unable to look Henekh in the eyes, then, without a word, quickly turned and made her way out of the shop.

Henekh did not see her again for some time and re-gretted having said anything about Temerl. But some time afterwards, she returned, wearing a suede hat, her face flushed.

Even though the shop was crowded with women cus-tomers, she burst out, barely able to breathe after her haste.

'Reb Henekh, it's all right! Mr Hayman agrees to the match!'

Great excitement erupted among the women. They surrounded Mrs Kaplan, all speaking at once and question-ing her from every side. Mrs Kaplan was so thrilled and talked so quickly that she appeared to be swallowing her own words.

'I told that Phillip like it is!' she said, highly elated. 'I let all my thoughts and sorrow out on him – that since the Zharnev tragedy, I had completely lost my head; I have kept dreaming about our home, that, in my dreams, Zharnev and Australia get mixed up; that I just don't know where in the world I belong anymore; and that, in my dreams, too, my mother, may her memory be blessed, keeps coming back, always wearing her black *Shabbesdik* shawl over her head and holding a blue lid in her hand. And why on earth is she carrying a lid? I have thought and thought about the dream and I was suddenly overcome by fear and palpitations.'

Mrs Kaplan caught her breath, wiped her lips and sighed.

'I am completely beside myself, believe me! I am terri-fied of my dreams, my life is useless. I began to wonder if this had something to do with Temerl. Who knows if she has not been orphaned, if she still has a mother or father in this world? We dare not hurt her in any way, I told Phillip. I told him also to have mercy on me and remove this pain from my heart by marrying her. I feared that we were sinning against Zharnev. And I cried before him like a child. I would suffer because of it and all the guilt would be laid upon my head.

'And poor Phillip, he was squirming like a worm. But I refused to release him. He will now do anything for me, anything I say. He is a puppet in my hands, that big Mr Phillip Hayman. Convincing him was hard work, but my goal has been achieved: we will have a wedding!'

'A wedding!' repeated Henekh after her, overjoyed. 'And it will be no ordinary wedding! It will be a real Zharnev wedding with all the flavour of home, you can rely on me!'

### 4

Henekh became totally absorbed by the wedding between Temerl and Phillip Hayman. It was to be a lavish wedding held at the grand Victoria Hall. Fishl felt uncomfortable. He wanted to shy away from such excess. He did not have the head for extravagance of this kind. After all, the world was at war. He would have been happier to settle for a *chuppah* in a regular synagogue, followed by a reception for a small group of close friends, something quieter and more intimate.

Henekh, however, refused to heed his plea. He was determined, as if his life depended on it, that the wedding should be opulent, grand and, more important still, that every Zharnev *landsman* should be invited.

'Fishl,' he cautioned, 'don't you dare to shame even one of our *landslayt*! Whom do we have left in the world, if not for these few people from home?'

And so he prevailed upon Fishl, watched closely over the preparation of the golden invitation cards lest, God forbid, even one person be overlooked: even Mr Max, over whom Fishl shook his head, refusing so much as to hear the very mention of his name.

'I can't stand that man!' he protested. 'I will have nothing to do with him! He is the last person I need at my wedding! I don't want that kind of embarrassment there! He is incapable of being among people. He is contemptuous of everyone, he insults everyone he meets.'

'But he is still a *landsman*,' Henekh countered. He will be one of your in-laws, same as everyone else.'

In the dispute between Henekh and Fishl over Mr Max that followed, Henekh remained so forceful that, in the end, he won out. But when on the night of the wedding, he saw the proud, widely disputatious locksmith Mr Max enter the gracious Victoria Hall with his assured broad rocking gait and Stalin-like whiskers on his heavy face, he came suddenly to regret his insistence on having him invited. For, in the midst of the surrounding festivity in the bright golden glow cast from the splendid chandeliers, Mr Max proved exceedingly ordinary. 'Don't you know that he already has a sweetheart, having an affair with a Malkeleh Fliak?' butted in Mr Max, twirling his thick Stalin-like moustache between his fingers. He was proud of his locksmith's trade and liked to show off with his thick workman's hands.

As for the other guests, the men were festively dressed in smoking jackets over cut-away vests and sparkling stiffly starched shirts, while the women wore collared evening gowns and diamond pins in their sparklingly coiffured hair, all mingling colourfully, their presence filling the hall with a joyous hum and the scents of perfume and silk under the bright luminescence of the lights.

Mr Knester, the Zharnev *landsman* who had come to Australia long before and considered himself an Englishman, and was now dressed in top hat and white gloves, wandered about, ensuring that the function met with the protocols of English etiquette, fussing over circular frock tails and greeting each guest with cheer.

In his circuit, he approached Mr Kaplan, who was sitting at the head table near the bride and groom and heartily chewing on a fat cigar that he kept moving from one corner of his mouth to the other. Every time he inhaled, he broke out in a light cough with a shaking of his round shoulders up and down as his face with its double chin turned bright red. Mr Kaplan rarely attended social functions. He was forever undergoing medical treatment or travelling from one sanitarium or clinic to another. This did not, however, seem to interfere with the running of his business. From wherever he was, he would phone his workers, boss them around and keep himself aware of every detail there.

Meanwhile, people would make fun of him behind his back, for Mrs Kaplan's many flirtations were well known and the talk was that she led him by the nose. In public, however, he was honoured. People milled around him, eager to rub shoulders with him. Even other prominent guests, in the main well-to-do manufacturers also seated at the head table, were keen to mingle with him and clung eagerly to every word that issued from his broad meaty mouth together with the blue circles of smoke from his cigar.

'Fat, you know, you have to be careful of the fat,' he cautioned with his raspy voice as he pushed away the plates with the delicacies. The people listened with genuine earnestness and respectfully nodded in agreement.

Mr Max had been standing for some time by the open door leading into the hall. No one took any notice of him while he, for his part, was surveying the guests with a slow, roaming critical gaze as he twirled the corner of his moustache. To Henekh's eyes, he wore the expression of one who refused to be slighted and, seeing it, Henekh became afraid. All he needed was Mr Max making a scene with another of the *landslayt* and setting loose a lashing of his tongue, as he was so often wont to do. To play around with Mr Max would be to bring about an explosion. Henekh wasted no time. He rose from his place, pushed his way between the people and made a beeline straight towards Mr Max. He took him by an arm and led him to his table where he made a place next to him.

'I wonder what I'm doing here,' Max grumbled from beneath his whiskers. 'I stick out like a sore thumb. Zharnev has certainly worked its way up in Australia. Are you proud of your *landslayt*, Henekh, ha?'

'What can one say? This is all that's left of Zharnev. Nothing more. But it's good to be amongst your own. Don't look upon their good fortune, Motl, and let yourself enjoy the occasion. After all, it's a Zharnev wedding! Enjoy!' urged Henekh warmly, addressing him affectionately by his past familiar Zharnev name, wanting to create a bond of brotherliness.

'Eat something, Motl, taste a real Zharnev poppyseed cake. My Fayge Tzirl baked it, it tastes of home,' he went on, placing a plate of cakes before Max.

While passing the cakes, however, the plate struck a densely placed assemblage of crockery and glassware that rang out loud, in chaos. Everyone in the hall looked around at the source of the sudden commotion while Henekh fumbled with the plate and the cakes fell around him. Fayge Tzirl, who sat nearby, leapt up from her chair and began to straighten the fallen dishes. Her lively black eyes shot arrows of fire at Henekh.

'Oh, you men, you men, you're still just like children, you are!' she berated him.

Henekh felt insulted, embarrassed. He did not even taste the delicacies that were continuously being served up to the tables by the young English waitresses who wore white stiffly-starched head-dresses.

As the guests ate, the cutlery rang out actively and tunefully while the wine bottles popped upon the removal of their corks. Mrs Kaplan, wearing a short jacket over her gold silk dress, was excitedly moving between the laden tables, bossing the waiters around with a waving of her little diamond-studded fingers. After all, as she was the one who had successfully managed to bring about the wedding, she felt she had a personal stake in its outcome. She roamed around with exuberantly red flaming cheeks and her eyes shimmered with a festive glow. She lightly danced over to Temerl every few minutes and, with a fine laugh, whispered some secret into her ear, the while wagging a finger at Fishl.

'You naughty boy!' she said, smiling at him.

Temerl, throwing her bridal veil over her shoulders, snuggled against Fishl, straightening the white rose that was pinned into the satin lapel of his frock coat, her round face blushing lightly.

After some time, Mr Knester loudly struck his glass with a spoon and pointed towards his hat to indicate that the men should cover their heads as, in his deep drawn-out voice, he called out, 'Ladies and gentlemen! Order please! The rabbi will now recite the *Birkat hamazon*, Grace after meals!'

The men hastened to cover their heads, seizing whatever they could find – a handkerchief, a serviette, anything. Only Mr Max did not so much as move a muscle. He remained seated, his shoulders tensely raised as, angrily, he viewed the proceedings. Henekh nudged him with an elbow, winking at him, but, alas, to no avail.

'Say whatever you like, but I don't believe in it,' he sneered. 'I won't bow down to them!'

The rabbi coughed lightly into his palm and with his white chubby hands pulled forward the skull cap that had crept towards the back of his head, invisible there behind his thick lavish hair. This rabbi was no fanatic. He was at all times immaculately dressed and moved freely and easily at social gatherings, an easy welcoming smile always on his lips above which sat a thin and trim black moustache, as if to say, 'Well, as long as we understand one another, not so?'

He sang the grace in a deep, melodious voice, sounding each word in a full cantorial tune, his eyes joyfully scanning the hall until his glance fell upon the bare-headed Mr Max, whereupon the force of his singing waned. From then on, his prayers quickened and he increasingly swallowed his words, while his smile remained as before. He deemed it not worth making an issue of the matter and thereby disrupting such a fine, opulent, festive evening.

At this, all the guests turned to stare at Max and quiet murmurings were heard from every direction.

Henekh did not know where to look, he was so ashamed.

'Motl, don't drain my blood! Put something on your head! Be a good brother, do it for me!' Henekh appealed to him softly.

Max gave him a dark, sideways glance and mumbled under his nose, 'Know that I am doing this only for you. About them, I don't care!' as he placed a paper serviette on his head.

When the rabbi finished reciting the Grace, he adjusted his skullcap as before, stood up, pensively studied his nails and began to deliver his speech. He spoke about the holy forefathers, Abraham, Isaac and Jacob and about the greatness of the Jewish people who had given the world such important people. He then spoke about the groom, Mr Phillip

Hayman. His speech was interlaced with many verses and quotations from the Torah, lowering his eyes whenever he uttered its holy words. He also threw in thoughts about the war, recalled the names of King George and Churchill in a deep fiery tone and dismissed Hitler without mentioning his name with a wave of the hand, referring to him instead as 'the paper-hanger, you know'.

'Hear! Hear!' Mr Knester interposed with a clapping of his hands. The guests enthusiastically joined the clapping as Mr Kaplan in his hoarse voice called out, 'Sure, a paper-hanger, dat's all!'

He turned his head to every side, his flabby cheeks wobbling loosely over his stiff starched collar and white bow tie.

From his seat, Henekh scrutinised his *landslayt* from beneath his eyebrows.

There was Fishl at the head table, wearing his spanking new top hat slightly tilted to one side, his brow knitted as he listened attentively to every word of the rabbi's speech, with his back turned to Temerl, like one already married for many years whose wife was no longer of particular interest. On the other hand, there was Temerl herself, snuggling up to him, uncertainly seeking his gaze with a tense smile on her lips. And there were many others too.

But Henekh, sighing to himself, could not tear his own gaze from Temerl. With her head dropped, she sat completely still with her veil falling over her face. Secretively, she wiped her face with the veil.

Henekh's face suddenly lit up. 'The bride is weeping!' he said quietly to the people at his table, rubbing his hands.

No one around him responded. With his elbow, he lightly nudged Mr Max who sat miserably, the serviette on his head having slipped over an ear.

Where the other men had already long before removed the coverings from their own heads, Mr Max straightened his own and left it on.

'Motl, look at the bride,' Henekh prodded Mr Max again. 'She is weeping. So what do you think of Zharnev now?'

But Max, too, said nothing in reply. Quiet descended over the table. The rabbi's voice flowed widely throughout the hall and the air trembled under the sharp light that flooded down from the chandeliers.

—*Second Australian Yiddish Almanac* (1943),
*Collected Writings* (1949)

# THE CIRCUMCISION

JACK SILVER was completely astonished when wife Katherine agreed to the circumcision of their child. He knew that Katherine was deeply religious and that she had been secretly visiting the church. He noticed, further, that she had become increasingly devout during the last few months of her pregnancy. He had seen her sneak quietly out of bed in the middle of the night to spend hours on her knees in fervent prayer. He had wanted to mention circumcision on a number of occasions since she had returned from hospital but he had not been brave enough. She had been wandering around the house in a pensive mood. A strange uncertainty seemed to dwell in her gentle blue eyes. It was obvious that she was going through an inner battle – she had to reach a decision but was unable to do so.

On the fourth day after her return from hospital, late at night, just before going to bed, she turned to Jack and told him in a trembling voice, 'Jack, I know that you are tortured by your wish to circumcise our boy. He is our first child and I am prepared to give him totally up to you. Do what you want with him. He belongs to you.'

Jack's heart pounded so hard he was at first too

overwhelmed to say anything. He approached and embraced her with shaking arms and said with a tremor, 'My darling, I will never forget this.'

Jack did not close his eyes that night. He got up first thing in the morning, went to Katherine's bed where she slept with the child and looked at them both with great joy. He could not control himself; he bent down and kissed his wife on her forehead. She opened her eyes, the candid blue eyes that he loved so much, gave him a sad but friendly look and said, 'Never mind, Jack,' as she stroked his arm.

Jack spent all day preparing. He ran around to all those friends who had not abandoned him for marrying a Christian, told them about his great happiness and invited them to the ceremony. He found a *mohel* to perform the circumcision and bought wine, fruit and sweets. He ordered a lavish dinner from a kosher restaurant and came home in the evening, glowing with happiness and joy.

'We will make a circumcision,' he boasted to Katherine, 'that will be the talk of the town. We will make a ball fit for a king. And you know what we will call our son? "Ben Zion". A real Jewish name.'

Katherine responded to him with a gentle and loving smile. Her smile hurt him and he suddenly felt guilty about her. He wanted her to be happy with him, to share his joy. But she just looked at him with her smiling, sad eyes as if she was sacrificing herself for him.

On the day of the circumcision, Katherine felt weak. She did not rise from bed and Jack could not help but be a little pleased. He did not want his guests to meet her as they entered the house. He imagined the circumcision would have more of a Jewish atmosphere, be more *haimish* if Katherine was not present.

The *mohel* was the first to arrive. He was a tall thin Jew with a sparse pointy beard and a shrill high-pitched voice. He moved about awkwardly and heavily and immediately filled the house with the noise he made.

When he accompanied Jack to the bedroom to look at the child, Katherine took an instant dislike to him. She was frightened by his flitting black eyes, his gipsy beard and expressions that appeared so strange to her. It seemed to her bizarre that both Jack and the *mohel* were wearing hats.

Slowly the other guests arrived. Katherine listened attentively to every noise, to the chairs being moved, the plates being set, the foreign language being spoken. She heard her Jack also speaking loudly in this language and heard him laughing, and suddenly, he too appeared strange and distant. She began to imagine that the people in the next room had come to take something away from her and she clasped her baby even tighter to her breast. Her bed became unbearably hot and cramped and she was overcome by an uneasy, painful sensation. She came to resent that Jack was so cheerful and happy, and that he did not bother to check on her.

When the *mohel*, Jack and an unfamiliar fat woman with a powdered face and mawkish eyes entered the bedroom to take the baby, she was overwhelmed by an all-encompassing fear. She listened intently to the noise coming from the next room, alert to every sound. Her heart felt as if it had seized up, as if someone were squeezing it in a cold hard fist, herself breaking out in a thick sticky sweat.

Just then, the voice of the *mohel* reached her ears. He sang incomprehensible, obscure and secretive words in a monotone, immediately followed by a quickly stifled scream. Katherine began to tremble. They must be doing something to her child. She sat up in her bed and she bit her lip until it bled and remained immobile as if she were paralysed. The scream grew stronger, and became more distressed and uncontrolled by the moment. It tore cruelly through her heart. She was overwhelmed by a wild resentment and such profound anger towards Jack that made her aware, made her know, that she would never forgive him.

She wanted to leap out of bed, run into the next room and tear the screaming child from Jack's arms. She felt that the baby was crying out for her help. But she could not move; her limbs were paralysed. An intense stifling spasmodic sobbing rose from her chest while a ball-like obstruction settled in her throat.

After Jack had said his goodbyes to some of his friends, he returned to the bedroom to restore the child to Katherine. He found her sitting hunched forward in bed, her face in her hands, her shoulders convulsing as, more quietly now, she continued weeping. Just then, the bedroom became filled with happy cheer as remaining guests came to congratulate Katherine, sympathise with her, wish her comfort and offer courage.

Katherine, however, kept her face covered and writhed in silent anger.

And Jack, seeing her thus, recognised that something had been destroyed between them, destroyed, perhaps, for the rest of their lives; and only realised how distant and alien she was from him.

—Translated by Tania Bruce and Pam Maclean

*Oystralier Leben*, 13 March 1931,
*Dertzeilungen* (1939)

# THE SHOFAR BLOWER

HASKELE, THE *HULTAY*, the rascal, waited impatiently all year for the Days of Awe. *Hultay* was the nickname given to him by his father, Reb Shmelke, the kerosene merchant. Reb Shmelke was a tall but hunched Jew with a sparse beard and thick brush-like eyebrows, which almost entirely covered his small sickly-red, perennially tear-filled eyes. Regardless of whether it was summer or winter, he always wore the same old greasy gabardine, which shone as if was made of plastic and smelt of herring and kerosene. He walked around constantly, silent and distraught, worked on his accounts with a tiny pencil that he would moisten in his mouth, and was forever angry at his wife Gittele for spending too much money.

'Again already?' he would say when his wife asked for money for housekeeping expenses, 'Money and more money ... one sacrifices oneself in earning every penny, it's like crossing the Red Sea, but what do you care? You and Haskele *Hultay* will reduce me to begging.' He would then whine as he drew a money note from his bulging wallet which, like himself, reeked of kerosene.

In his shop, he was forever in a foul and bitter mood. He argued with the women who poked around in the herring barrels; they argued when they wanted more kerosene, pouring it carefully into their containers as if it were oil. Never for an instant did he take his eyes off Haskel who helped him in the shop. He did not trust Haskel with money and, as soon as he would approach the till, Reb Shmelke would be right beside him, shouting, 'Don't think that you're my son-in-law, already at my money, you *Hultay*! I can manage the money perfectly well on my own.'

Haskel was a pale, tremulous young man, with a pince-nez on a gold chain and fine thin hands like those of a ritual slaughterer. He was one of the newly enlightened; he subscribed to the *Hatsfira* and smoked the best cigarettes. Reb Shmelke smoked the cheapest, roughest and most bitter tobacco that always made him cough, and whenever he saw Haskel take out his own packet of cigarettes, he never failed to reach out his hand, repeating as always, 'Give me a cigarette' which, upon taking, he rolled about in his greasy hands, staring at it intently and would say, 'What foolishness you spend your money on.'

Haskel always had some chocolate in his pocket and he would eat it when his father was not looking. His father was quite aware of his son's habit; often he would rise early in the morning and search through the pockets of his son's gabardine, and if he found chocolate there, he would scream so loudly that the entire household could hear.

'There it is!' he would yell in a rabbinic tune, shaking the chocolate in his hand as if holding it up for the whole world to see. 'Is this where the money is going? This is how you throw away a fortune?'

But as soon as the month of Ellul arrived, Reb Shmelke turned into a different man. He had a passion other than money, and that was to blow the shofar. He was the best shofar blower in the village, maybe even in the entire vicinity. For the entire month of Ellul, he stayed away from the shop. He would spend all those days in the *Bes Medresh*, rehearsing the shofar blowing over and over. He would stow away his greasy gabardine over the holiday period and parade around in a new coat and new Sabbath boots. He would visit other *Bote Midroshim* to listen to the hoarse cry of the shofar as it was blown elsewhere, bringing together his bushy eyebrows and smiling through his sparse beard.

'Whoever has a hand or a foot is already blowing a shofar. Did you ever hear such a noise? It pierces the eardrums, but what do I care? It's not my problem.'

Haskel remained in the shop without supervision during those days. He sat regally behind the table, dressed up in a new silk tie. He was continuously counting the money in the till and would slip yet another coin into his vest pocket. He would not touch the kerosene container and asked the women instead to measure it out for themselves. He would lift the herrings delicately with the tips of his fingers, turning his nose away. He was generous when he weighed out the soap and often gave more than asked for. The women were bewildered by him; they would flirt in front of him and praise him amongst themselves: 'That Haskel, Shmerl's boy, a wonderful boy, such a golden soul! How did Shmerl ever get such a boy? So good-natured, refined and gentle.'

Shmelke, meanwhile, was engrossed in his shofar blowing. He sat throughout the day in the *Bes Medresh* practising his shofar blowing. His constant foul and bitter look yielded to a satisfied smile. In the evenings, he would boast to Gittele.

'You know that Sender came to see me again at the *Bes Medresh*? Imagine, he wanted me to show him how to blow the shofar. How can I show him when he does not have even the slightest idea how to place a shofar on his lips, and he wants to blow *Tekiah*.'

Sometimes, Shmelke would throw anxious, suspicious glances at his son. Haskel appeared a little too festive for his liking. He could smell the chocolate on him from far away as he contentedly read magazines full of coloured pictures or smoked strange cigarettes with golden lettering that must have been from overseas. Shmelke would shake his head and say, 'You are really living it up, Haskele, you thief, hey? Throwing away all your money … On chocolates, cigarettes … How much did you make today?'

'Around four roubles, I don't remember exactly,' Haskel would answer, wanting to avoid the topic.

'Around four roubles,' Shmelke said, imitating him, 'That's a pathetic amount before a holiday, what can I say?'

That night, Shmelke could not fall asleep. He kept groaning, tossing and turning in his bed until finally he rose and began to search through Haskel's pockets. Haskel had however hidden his theft and Shmelke found nothing. But this did not reassure him and the next morning, Shmelke put on his customary clothes once more and accompanied Haskel to the store. He began investigating the barrels of kerosene and green soap.

'A fine business you are running here!' he kept gnawing away at Haskel, 'The shop is empty, there is no stock, no money. All you can think about is spending money. Well, enough is enough!'

But Shmelke was unable to remain long in the shop. As soon as he heard the cantor's voice from the nearby synagogue practicing the melodious Holy Day prayers or the shofar being blown from the small alley, he became restless, looking outside repeatedly until finally he could hold out no longer and said to Haskel, 'I will be back soon. Look after the store and don't forget what you are doing.'

The nearer the holidays approached, the less time he spent in the shop, often leaving it for whole days, leaving Haskel in peace.

As Shmelke stood on the synagogue platform on the great holiday, draped in his long white *talles,* its silver border turned black with age, his face shone with happiness and pride. His bushy angry eyebrows softened, his eyes lost some of their redness and he looked at others more happily and cordially. But every now and then, when his glance fell upon Haskel, who sat by the eastern wall dressed in a new silk gabardine and brightly polished boots, his face would become clouded and his eyebrows taut and angry again.

Haskele *Hultay* seemed to him to be dressed up to the nines. 'I cannot tolerate this!' Shmelke said to himself, trying to catch his son's glance.

When, finally, he did, seeing the diamond pince-nez with the golden chain that he wore and his silk gabardine, he looked him mockingly in the eyes, as if to say, 'You can try and be a dictator but you can't change a thing.'

Distressed, bitter and full of repressed anger, Shmelke shoved the shofar into his fist and blew *Tekiah* sharply and loudly, with all the strength of his pained heart. The notes had a strange severity about them as if they were calling out a warning of retribution.

—*Oystralier Leben*, 11 September 1931

## *MA NISHTANA?* (WHAT IS DIFFERENT?)

MR DAVE ALLISON sent a telegraph to his wife in Melbourne, informing her that his business affairs would detain him in Europe for a few more weeks and he would therefore not be back before Passover. In truth, he had already completed all the necessary business and was ready to return home, but he had stopped at the *shtetl* to see his parents for a few days. They insisted that he should spend Passover with them.

'So many years have passed since we last saw you,' his mother said, with her old dimmed eyes brimming with tears. 'Let us have our fill of you, as we deserve. Oh, today's children! We raise them with sweat and blood, we give up for them the marrow of our bones and then they leave us all alone in our old age and fly away to the four corners of the world: Chayele in America, Moyshele to the Bolsheviks and now that God has finally brought you to us from the other end of the world after so many years, please let our eyes be filled in the sight of you ...' Upon which she broke down into heart-wrenching weeping.

'And truly,' added his father, 'what is your hurry to

return? When will we see each other again? We do not have many years of life left. Who knows if this will not be our last time together? It would be wonderful to have you here for Passover. We have not celebrated it at home once since Moyshele left. We have always gone to relatives for the Seder. But now that you are here, let us celebrate it at home like everyone else.

Dave could not refuse his parents' request. He knew that he was seeing his parents for the last time and he promised to remain for the festivity, even though he was already missing his wife and children terribly and his heart was longing to return to Australia. He found *shtetl* life very boring. He could not get comfortable in the small low-ceilinged rooms of his parents' home. It hurt him to see that his parents had become so helpless and feeble in their old age, appeared to him to have shrunken, and he felt alien and uncomfortable in the company of the small-minded *shtetl* inhabitants. There was no one to talk to. Everything had changed so much, it was now so foreign and distant from him.

It was Purim time. A dirty rain mixed with snow kept falling. The unmade streets of the *shtetl* turned into big sticky pools of mud. Young women in greasy dirty aprons with their wigs in disarray dragged themselves up and down the streets. The continuously overworked Jews in their small black hats and their long kaftans that resembled big black wings when they were blown apart by the wind, appeared so strange to Dave, so abnormal, so awkward. Every time he went into the street, Jews who all wanted to greet him, shake his hand and call him by his old name Dovidl, immediately accosted him. They asked him everything about the big world outside and complained about the bitter times that they were experiencing.

The *cheder* boys with their red noses and long, unwashed *tallesim ktanim* opened their eyes filled with wonder upon seeing him; they shook their fingers at him disapprovingly and referred to him as the Englishman. The water-carrier and the policeman saluted him amicably, at the same time glancing at his hands, hinting that they would like a coin or two.

After a few days, the *shtetl* became so repugnant to him that he stopped going out into its streets. But even at home he was unable to get any respite. They came to him as they would come to any good Jew, asking for help for a poor bride, for the synagogue, for the fence around the cemetery, for the school, for the Bundist library or for anything else. His mother and father were also torturing him with their exaggerated concern. They were pampering him as if he were a small child – they would bring coffee to his bed every morning, and his stomach was no longer accustomed to the greasy food or the sweet cakes that his mother prepared especially for him and was continuously pushing upon him.

'Maybe you would like a cup of tea?' she asked him frequently. 'Or maybe a glass of milk straight from the cow? Try this cheesecake. Have a bite of this poppyseed cookie, you surely don't have cakes like these in your Stralie. Take, eat, it will give you strength!'

Dave nurtured deep regrets that he had listened to his parents and allowed himself to be talked out of going home.

The constant chatter was making his head spin and each new day was drudgery. He was most agitated by a particular teacher, a short, thin young man with a squeaky voice and bad breath who was a devout Zionist. He babbled a few words in English and would nag him every day to make conversation.

'Yo-si, in Palestine, yo-si, hmm ...' he would repeat, stumped by every other word. Dave felt that the constantly mumbled *yo-si*s were puncturing holes in his brain.

A distant relative, a spinster with her pince-nez hanging from a thin black string, was another tormentor. She would hardly leave his side, purse her lips flirtatiously and continuously philosophise in a sickly sweet voice about pessimism and free love. Her speech was intellectual and she frequently punctuated her sentences with 'absolutely'. She called him by the odd pet name of 'Duptshie'.

The days stretched endlessly for Dave. He felt that he had already spent years in the *shtetl* and that he would never be able to extricate himself from there. The pre-Passover days arrived and his mother began preparing the house for the festivity. She dusted and washed, put all the old clothes and books out on the tables and chairs and pushed him from one room to the next. He did not feel like going out into the streets but also could not hang around the house, so he spent his days wandering around the dirty little yard, unhappily smoking his pipe. He found an old *Times* newspaper that had been stuck in one of his pockets, which he read and reread from cover to cover numerous times, including the Women's Page as well as all the advertisements. He kept being overtaken by anger at himself and disappointment.

Finally Passover eve arrived and his father woke Dave early in the morning. 'You have slept long enough. Passover is tonight. Get up and have something to eat before we clean out the leaven.'

The morning was bright and sunny. A happy pre-holiday spirit seemed to blow in from the street, the air carrying with it the mild warmth of spring.

Dave himself did not know why he suddenly felt light, fresh and rested like this for the first time since he had arrived in the *shtetl*. The small dark rooms that had been gnawing at his spirit were suddenly filled with easy cosiness. The whole house was suffused with the sweet smell of *matzos* and goose fat, while the broom stood by the water jug, which was covered with a sparkling white tablecloth.

As bidden, Dave rose, quickly washed himself and ate breakfast. The holiday spirit shone out of every corner, the spring air streaming in through the open window. Dave regained a sense of youth that led him to recall events of years long past. His own family, his home in distant Australia, his business all seemed to be wiped out of his memory. He imagined Moyshele coming in at any minute, still sleepy with his thick black hair squashed and full of feathers; and he appeared to hear the fresh vibrant voice of Chayele from the next room. She had always filled the house with song:

> 'All the girls are getting married,
> Only I remain alone, oy, oy, oy ...'

The day passed quickly, almost indiscernibly for Dave.

His heart was gripped by a feeling that was at once both sweet and bitter. His childhood memories rose with the immediacy of the present. Each corner, every piece of furniture reminded him of some event. There was the squat cupboard with all the dishes and the coloured glasses, the same old clock with its eroded numbers whose chimes sounded like asthmatic coughs, the same cupboard that still stood crookedly on three legs after so many years, on which he loved to climb when he had still been a child. Everything was as it always had been, not altered by a hair.

He spent the day in silence and thought as he roamed throughout the house. His mother kept watching him sighing quietly to herself. It hurt her to see him so distant, so unhappy. She sensed that he badly missed his own home and that he could not find a place for himself.

She came up to him, looked him in the eyes and asked, 'What is the matter, Dovidl?'

He broke out in a crooked smile as if he were in pain, bent towards her and kissed her on her old wrinkled cheek. 'Life is just a dream, Mama, a big long dream!'

Towards evening, however, when everyone sat down to the Seder table, he seemed suddenly to have become more cheerful, babbling continuously, telling happy stories about Australia, telling jokes and, when given a cup to make Kiddush, he was overtaken by such childish giggling that he broke into fits of laughter with every word.

His mother looked at him with beaming eyes, happily mumbling, 'The same Dovidl as ever, the same cheeky boy that he once was …'

His father, meanwhile, with earnest concentration, carefully placed the *maror*, *zeroa* and *charoses* where they belonged, seemingly angry, and agitatedly mumbling over his shoulders, 'Mina, Mina, maybe it is enough already?'

He refilled the cups once, straightened the cushions that surrounded him and asked timidly and uncomfortably, 'Nu, Dovid, ask the questions.'

Dave brought the Haggadah nearer to himself, smiled at his mother, and began reading aloud. *'Ma nishtana halaila hazeh …?* How is this night different …?'

His voice broke right after the first two words. A warm gush enveloped his heart and something seemed to get stuck in his throat. His parents sat quietly as if they were waiting for something. It was so quiet that Dave could hear the blood pulsating in his temples.

His eyes filled up with huge tears that he tried to suppress. He raised his eyes from the Haggadah and looked at his parents. He saw that his mother was sitting stiffly; she was tense, tears were rolling down her cheeks. His father was nervously picking at his beard, his head bowed. He also appeared stirred, deeply moved.

Dave regained courage and with a struggling voice resumed reciting the questions. *'Ma nishtana …?'* But his voice collapsed and he broke down into a convulsive uncontrollable weeping.

—Translated by Tania Bruce
and edited by Pam Maclean
*Oystralier Leben*, 1 April 1931

# FROM THE CARRIAGE WINDOW

THE THIRD BELL has already rung. Lethargically the locomotive begins to exhale its heavy damp breath. Words of farewell are exchanged in the last-minute crush as the train leaves the platform.

We pass the grey and smoky railway huts. The tracks wind around like skinny snakes, at times joining together, and then abruptly separating. The red-brick factories that stand at the edge of the city pass in a flash, the first splashes of green appear. The houses become sparser, smaller and more humble. The locomotive billows clouds of smoke and the train rushes resolutely forward as it leaves the city behind. We have already left Melbourne and the Australian countryside surrounds us. Miles of plains full of dry yellow stubble stretch out around us. Every now and then, desiccated gnarled bushes leap into view, as the grey thirsty land passes by. We can see solitary farmers peering from their identical rusty iron huts with their round iron water tanks sitting on land dissected by muddy dirty irrigation channels. The roads are littered with black scorched trees, their thin bare protruding branches a reminder of the last bush fires that combed the area.

The eyes begin to tire of the grey and featureless vista, flat and dry as it stretches far towards the horizon of indistinct mountain ranges. There is no view of a refreshing and shimmering silver lake to relieve the monotony, nor the sight of lush greenery. One cannot even hear the cheerful melodious song of bird life – just the loud constant drone of tractors working the land. The surroundings are vast, quiet, desolate and tragic. From time to time, someone cries out. This is the call of the local farmers, their signal that they want a newspaper thrown to them from the train.

Yet one is aware that the soul of the country is filled with dedication, commitment, an almost sacred human toil and pioneering spirit. Neat grey plantations of trees stand carefully surrounded by wire. The sparse thin trees grow in neat symmetrical lines. The area is enveloped in the devoutness of hard human toil, human sweat and of stubbornness spent in struggling to tame the inhospitable wild Australian land. The white shadowy eucalyptus with its hard jagged leaves and stripped trunk stands as a symbol for the toughness of Australia which is slowly overcoming the barren land with hard work and pioneering determination.

We are enveloped in silence, but in the silence the perceptive ear is able to pick up the song of the future. Although the surroundings are dull and unfriendly, nonetheless the narrow irrigation channels, the new symmetrical fields and orchards stand as a sign of victory for the youngest of the five continents. Each turn of the wheels, each puff of locomotive smoke brings visions of purity and simplicity, of hard labour and ongoing battle. Even the small khaki-coloured farmhouses that dot the countryside resemble the tents of a huge army conquering the continent with the sheer magnitude of the toil. The monotonous and lifeless scenes that appear through the rectangular train window weary the eyes and weigh heavily on one's heart. That feeling is soon overtaken by the sound of the powerful silent hymn of the workers. One's heart trembles with excitement as the song reverberates quietly and gently through the mighty plains of the Australian countryside.

The train rattles and screeches as it races on at 50 miles per hour. Darkness descends and night dissolves into the contours of this vast borderless land. The flatness is replaced by round mountainous shapes. We are approaching New South Wales. The hills and mountains move towards each other until they almost collide. The green trees dotting the mountains look like sheep grazing in the fields. Tall pale eucalypts stand above us and fill the air with a sharp aroma that makes the nose tingle and allows one to breathe more freely and deeply. The bush is turning lush and green. The rich freshly-dug black earth looks into the setting sun. The huge sheep stations in the distance resemble great wads of brown cotton wool in motion. We fly past small local train stations with increasing frequency. Their small electric lights momentarily chase away the falling darkness. We become enveloped in a dark damp autumn night. Suddenly the tightly-packed train carriage loses its intimate relationship

with the outside world and is transformed into a lost speed-
ing comet hurtling into the depths of the dark night.

—Translated by Tania Bruce
and edited by Pam Maclean
*Oystralier Leben*, 1 April 1932

# DRUMMOND STREET

DRUMMOND STREET, a poor, working-class street close to the centre of the prosperous noisy city of Melbourne, absorbed many Jewish migrants. Its houses are poor and old with rusty galvanised-iron roofs and peeling walls. From the open doors exude the smells of sweaty bedding and poor food. Their low windows, covered with cheap old-fashioned hangings and drab tattered blinds, look blankly but patiently onto silent sidewalks. Drummond Street is empty all day with seldom any passers-by to break the monotony. From the police station, which is half obscured by ailing trees, there occasionally sidles out a dark-uniformed policeman who disappears immediately like a clandestine shadow into one of the side streets. At the opposite end of the street is a bar half-clad in polished red tiles.

A dreary sleepy buzzing can be heard from inside this pub and from time to time the half-closed glass doors spew out a drunkard. The pattern is constant. These men wear crumpled clothing and have sickly red cheeks. Their eyes screw up against the glare of the sun as they scrutinise the street in blinking surprise. With lurching movements and staggering steps, they ponderously seem to shy away from the silence of the street.

An elderly, sweating woman sits on the steps of a house stripping green peas and half-rotten cabbage into a dish. Her face is liquor-swollen and her head covered with scraps of old newspapers into which is rolled her dirty grey hair. These primitive homemade undulations make her hair resemble a bunch of black and white bananas. A hungry cat arches itself against her legs and, from time to time, pushes its wet nose into the basin of peas.

In the middle of the street, spread-eagled with rump uppermost, sprawls a sleeping dog. The whole street seems to be governed by the leisurely peace of a long tropical day.

At sunset, Drummond Street takes on new life. Motor-bikes roar past and bicycles make soft swishing sounds in the softened asphalt of the road. Housewives, parcels in hand, hurry to prepare a quick meal for their home-coming husbands; children with sweets clutched in their dirty hands chase each other about noisily. Italian ice-cream vendors bring out a resounding multitude in response to the summons of the copper bells attached to their red-gold-lettered barrows. Through a window rasps an old waltz from a worn recording, while a local bar resonates with laughter and freewheeling fun. Its glass door is never still, perpetually fanning back and forth with the unceasing movement of its clients as the thick and cloying smell of beer emanates from it into the street. On the steps of the houses, tired working-men suck peacefully at pipes or chatter and horse around with their women-folk or, half-stripped, displaying their hairy chests and bronzed muscles in the dusk, cool the sweat from themselves in the evening breeze while, at times, a procession of the Salvation Army marches down the street, singing hymns to its accompanying band on its way to the small Salvation Army Church. And, when the street lamps flicker to life as the sunset fades into darkness, youngsters gather outside the now-closed bar, laugh and flirt and play mouth-organs. Girls in short light summer dresses wiggle their hips to the sound of the music and their passionate moist eyes shine from heavily powdered faces. The young men, chests thrust forward, strut about and ape their elders by dragging at cigarettes and bumping into the girls. Soon they pair off and disappear into dark corners and shadowed narrow passageways between the houses, and damp passionate whispers break into the late evening silence. The heavy tropical night clothes Drummond Street in silence and a soft silky darkness.

So lived Drummond Street for many years – a monotonous, hard-working, beer-swilling and earthy yet romantic life.

There was a time, however, when Drummond Street looked different. Many years back when gold fever gripped the country, adventurers from all over the world stormed to Australia. In those days, Drummond Street was a Jewish street. The first Jewish migrants to settle there were from England and Germany; they were then followed by newcomers from Tzfat and Jerusalem, by Nikolaievsky soldiers who deserted from the army and escaped exile with Jews from Rumania, Hungary, Poland and Galicia, whereupon

Drummond Street echoed to the sounds of many languages. Jewish shops and small clothing factories were opened. The street was alive. The Jews worked hard and noisily. They, their wives and their children worked and saved, had no rest and little sleep and saved penny upon penny. Good times came. The small businesses became large department stores and the little workshops, factories. The Jewish women added flesh and their large dark eyes became harder and more tired with success.

When Drummond Street became too constricted, the Jews began to spread out to other streets in Carlton; later they moved to respectable St Kilda, which had grown and expanded into a suburb of clean villas at the shore of the sea. The little factories and shops began to move to the city itself and Drummond Street began to die as factory windows were boarded up and large 'To Let' notices sprouted in every yard. Then the empty houses were sold to the new poor, to Syrian shirt-makers and Indian hawkers. From a rumbustious Jewish life were left only a few poor market stall-holders and dealers in old clothes. Like an orphan stood a little old house with a dirty window in which an all but erased sign read Hatkhiya Zionist Organization. Yet, who knows, this old half-erased sign may have been the thing that drew a new wave of migrants to Drummond Street after the war and the street came to life again.

After many years, people could again be seen with sad eyes and suffering Jewish faces. They wandered in groups with searching eyes along Drummond Street, dressed in new suits from which could be smelled mothballs and on which numerous creases betrayed their fresh unpacking from suitcases. They greeted each other with '*Sholem aleykhem*', inquired about each other's livelihood and joked about the Golden Country, Australia. From the curtained windows and half-open doors, suspicious eyes assessed the new arrivals and throughout Drummond Street could be heard the quiet buzz, 'Jews'.

—Translated by R. Z. Schreiber

*Collected Writings* (1949)

# THERE IS NO GOD IN THE WORLD

FISHL PROCHNIK was very proud of his friendship with Mr Jacob Grossly. And he had good cause to be proud. Mr Grossly was a very wealthy Jew, an important man and extremely influential. He was a Justice of the Peace, had a say in the City Council and, it was said, even had some effect on the government. He was also a committed, religious Jew, wore a golden *chai* in his buttonhole and, every Sabbath, would attend the Anshay Israel synagogue, where he was president and was *Maftir*, the last person to read from the Torah.

One just had to glance at Mr Jacob Grossly to realise that he was someone special. He was heavy and rotund with a large balding head that appeared to sit without a neck on his bulging circular chest. His face was bulky and immobile and covered by a sweaty paleness as if it had been kneaded out of raw dough with a pair of vivid agile eyes attached to it and suspended from a pair of springs. He had a strong voice and a phlegmy cough with which he often spoke more than with words. If he was unhappy about something, his cough would be short and terse, *khe, khe*. Two short coughs meant 'well, that's enough already'. When his cough was

185

longer and was not as intense, *khaa*, *khaa*, it signified that something was good and he was happy with it. If he was ever stumped without a ready answer, he would cough fast and sharp, *khi! khi! khi!*, meaning 'not so fast, not so fast, I have to consider this'.

Fishl Prochnik was not Mr Jacob Grossly's equal. He was a delicate young man with pale, slender hands like those of a ritual slaughterer and a pair of frightened but glistening eyes that seemed to ask, 'What should I do? It isn't my fault!'

It was God who was completely responsible for Prochnik's state. He was a newcomer, a wretched hawker who dragged himself from door to door with a suitcase full of goods that he always seemed to sell under cost price and on credit, and was so bashful that he avoided collecting his debts. He was therefore always in debt and no one wanted to sell him any goods on credit. So he wandered around the streets with a half-empty suitcase, looking around the houses and groaning about his misfortune. A solid student, Fishl was a genius in *Tanach* learning and had already received rabbinic ordination, but was now burdened by the shame of having to work as a hawker.

He had arrived in this distant land full of hope and great plans. He assumed that his learning would place him in an advantageous position that would see him swiftly snapped up, matched with a fine girl of a wealthy family and placed in a good position suitable for a man of his calibre. Fate chose events that turned out quite differently. No matter what he tried, he had no success in the new country. And what had he not yet attempted? What had he not tried? He had run a market stall, worked in the countryside for a Jewish farmer, tried teaching, even had a small factory manufacturing trousers, but in none of these had he had been endowed with good fortune and, after facing disaster in all these occupations, he had to confront the bitter prospect of tramping from door to door, hawking goods from a suitcase.

So how did a Fishl Prochnik get to a man like Mr Jacob Grossly? It was even a shock for Fishl. A little good fortune fell his way when the rich man himself noticed him. They met at the Anshay Israel synagogue, where Fishl prayed every Sabbath. Fishl prayed with enthusiasm, with fire, he did not omit one 'amen' or *Baruch Shemo*, he distinguished himself by his leisurely and drawn-out praying between the Morning and Additional Services. But Mr Grossly, the President, was somewhat perturbed by the greenhorn who prayed so deep and long in his synagogue. Once, when Mr Jacob Grossly said the blessing for *Maftir*, a very loud 'amen' escaped from Fishl; it emanated as an entrancing cantorial melody that resonated in the quiet half-filled synagogue. All those present, as well as Mr Grossly, turned around and stared at Fishl. Fishl stood bewildered, embarrassed and looking away with frightened eyes. Mr Grossly, however, let out one of his happy coughs, *khaaa, khaaa*. After prayers, he approached Fishl.

Mr Grossly was much warmer to Fishl from that time on. He always approached him after the service, asked him how he liked it and gave him a friendly pat on his back.

'You'll be all right, Mr Prochnik, never you mind!'

He invited him home every once in a while, and Fishl's hopes rose again. After all, Mr Grossly did not spend his time just with anyone. Fishl felt sure that this must mean something. He must have realised that he is not just a simple soul, that hawking was not a suitable profession for him and so must be considering him for something. Needless to say, Mr Grossly could do a lot for him, the most important thing was to know how to behave without downgrading himself; quite the contrary, it was important to appear in control and not to be in need of help.

This was the image Fishl wished to portray. He became a regular guest at Mr Grossly's. He often spent an hour there at a time discussing world affairs, with Mr Grossly, every so often, asking him how his business was faring, to which Fishl always answered, 'Thank God, I make a living.'

And if Fishl ever released a groan to indicate that things were not so good, Mr Grossly would himself respond with a terse cough and say, '*Khe, khe!* This is the best country in the world, there is no reason to complain!'

Whenever Fishl talked about *Tanach* or other religious matters, Mr Grossly would shake his head and cough his Khaaa, khaaa cough under his breath.

This gave Fishl encouragement and the strength to continue. He devoted more time to learning, marked with sayings from the holy books. When Fishl spoke thus, Mr Grossly, slowly and with great seriousness, pulled out a black silk skullcap from his breast pocket, placed it on the point of his big naked skull and casually sprawled himself out on his sofa. He then plaited his short, plump, stubby hands over his expansive stomach and, twiddling his thumbs, would call out into the next room, 'Mary! Mary! Tea for two please!'

Mary was Grossly's daughter, a girl about twenty years old, tall and slim like a real English girl with fine soft hair that rippled freely on her small proud head. With light rhythmic steps, she would bring in the tray of tea. Mr Grossly would then stroke her cheek in a fatherly manner with his meaty fingers and cough happily, saying, 'You good girl, *khaaa, khaaa*.'

He then glanced at Fishl, saw that all was in order and casually waved his hand, saying, 'Mary, meet Mr Prochnik, from Russia.'

Mary shook her light hair in a flirtatious manner without even look directly at Fishl. Instead, she looked upward towards the ceiling and said, 'How do you do?'

Fishl decided that Mr Grossly had some reason for repeatedly introducing his daughter. It must have been that he was looking for a buyer. Maybe he was thinking of him as a suitable match? And why not? There were many girls from rich homes that had been offered to him in the old country. After all, a young man who is already an ordained rabbi was nothing to be sneezed at.

This thought made Fishl very restless. Mary's image kept floating before his eyes as he was continuously drawn to Grossly's home. He looked for any excuse to visit Grossly more frequently and do all he could to find favour in his eyes. He continued his religious studies still more avidly so that every time he came to Grossly, he would repeat a whole page of *Gemarah* with its explanations to prove how well he could learn. His discussions with Grossly became more learned and profound. He brought with him new theories, turning and twisting his thumb while Mr Grossly coughed happily, himself continuously tapping his skullcap, which rested on the head, at times calling out into the next room in his authoritative manner, 'Mary! Mary! Tea for two, please!'

Mary brought the tea as before, her father patted her on the cheek and again introduced her to Fishl. This is Mr Prochnik, from Russia!'

'How do you do?' she said as always, with a shake of her head and an upward glance but with no acknowledgement of Fishl himself.

Fishl began to resent that Mary kept her distance from him. He tried to console himself: she's only a young girl, what would she know of the value of Jewish learning. She was surely more of a modern educated person, before whom he would need to appear not just learned in *Tanach*, but also educated in worldly matters. So it was not the end of the world. Worldly matters were not altogether so foreign to him and he did have some knowledge of sciences. Mr Grossly could rely on him in most matters.

Fishl decided that he had to impress Miss Grossly by proving that he was not a religious fanatic, no greenhorn, but also an educated person, a modern person.

And when she entered again carrying the tray of tea, Fishl would swing the conversation from *Tanach* to worldly matters and say loudly, 'Albert Einstein, you know? I have been studying his works. He was a clever, a very clever man!'

'Well, well, Albert Einstein, ha! *Khaaa, khaaa,*' Mr Grossly coughed happily. 'He is a scientist, no?' Taking the tray from Mary, he gave her a pat as always on the cheek.

'Good girl, Mary! Meet Mr Prochnik from Russia.'

Mary responded with her usual 'How do you do?' and danced out of the room as if nothing new had happened.

'She could not care less about Albert Einstein,' thought Fishl. 'She's just a silly kid, completely uneducated!' and returned to explaining a detail from the *Gemarah* to Mr Grossly.

One evening at the conclusion of a Holy Day, Fishl was sitting at Mr Grossly's talking about *Tanach*. Fishl was still in a festive mood. He got carried away with his talk, and began an involved excited explanation of the Sacrifices. He spoke with fervour, threw his hands around, and his eyes were aglow with deep religious devotion.

Mr Grossly was also in a particularly good mood. The reverend of their synagogue had spoken highly of Mr Grossly in his sermon, stressing his importance and devotion. He wore a deeply intense, devoted look as he listened to Fishl's talk while his vivid eyes swiftly followed each gesture of Fishl's hand. He happily responded with his cough, and his hand did not for a moment leave his skullcap lest it slip off in the midst of Fishl's holy talk.

Mary brought in the tea, this time accompanied by a cake in honour of the Holy Day.

Mr Grossly, who was feeling particularly religious,

called her by her Jewish name. 'Miriamle, you good girl!'

Fishl sat vulnerably silent. He assumed that Mr Grossly, as always, would introduce her to him and she too would reply with her customary 'How do you do' and disappear without a glance at him. But, this time, she remained beside him. She exuded the rich delicate aroma of expensive perfume that made Fishl feel drunk, dizzy. He deeply inhaled the scent that was mingled with the cool freshness of her slim body. His mouth suddenly became dry as if he had been chewing cotton wool, his hands began perspiring profusely and a wild idea raged in his head.

'If only she would look at me! Just once!' A feeling of deep resentment and anger spread through him. He gave a dry cough, wiped his hands on his knees and said in a tense and halting voice, 'Mr Grossly! I do not believe in God! There is no God in the world!'

Mr Grossly's eyes halted stock still. He began to tap his finger on his big flabby belly, his face stretched and the skullcap moved crookedly to one side of his head. '*Khe! Khe!*' he coughed, sharp and angry, '*khe, khe!*'

Mary, as if nothing had happened, lightly placed the refreshments on the table and danced out of the room with her rhythmic step. As always, she did not stop to look around at Fishl, who was sitting in his place, helpless, vulnerable, looking at Mr Grossly with his frightened eyes as if he were silently pleading with him, 'It was not my fault. Woe is me, what could I do?'

—*Australian Jewish News*, 11 June 1937,
*Dertzeilungen* (1939)

# OLD FRIENDS

*for Jacob Waislitz*

## Old relics, dead and alive

JOE BENJAMIN'S PAWN SHOP looked as if it had stood since the first six days of Creation. It was situated in a run-down, crumbling wooden cottage, which stood secretly, as if squeezed between the high concrete walls of the surrounding buildings. Over its narrow perpetually closed door and cracked windows that were covered with yellowed newspaper hung three copper plates in the shape of a seagull that had turned green with age – the secret and unholy sign of the Lombard shops.

The low display windows that had not been washed for years were full of all manner of objects: rusty hunting rifles, scratched porcelain, worn clothing, patched shoes, binoculars, ironware, books and hats, to name a few. Old-fashioned pocket watches and rings with large fake diamonds hung from a wire in the middle of the window. A holy picture in a broken frame peeped out like an orphan from between a pair of red pants and a bicycle wheel that stood in the corner of the window. The entire collection of old bits and pieces was attended by the pathos that often remains after long use by human hands. It emitted poverty and neglect as it looked out into the busy street with silent longing, awaiting some form of deliverance.

Joe Benjamin himself looked like an old relic that had climbed down from one of his dusty, musty shelves in his narrow dingy shop. He was an old, fat and bald man and was only ever half-dressed, whether it was summer or winter. He always wore a dirty shirt with rolled-up sleeves and a pair of old pants that kept sliding from his large prominent belly. He looked as if he had just woken up from sleep and his fat face had the appearance of never having been washed.

Joe, like all single men, had been quiet and reclusive. He was rarely seen outside. Occasionally, in the great summer heat, he would sit on a crooked chair outside his shop and look into the street with a pair of clear unconcerned eyes that seemed to have been made from glass.

Suddenly, as if he had just sprung out of the ground, his neighbour, Abe Rosen, would appear.

'Well, well, well, so how are you, Mr Benjamin?' he would say, rubbing his hands on initiating a conversation. 'The heat has completely ruined business, hasn't it, Mr Benjamin?'

Abe, a quick-witted blond Jew, had a haberdashery next to Joe's pawn shop and never failed to begin talking on the rare occasion that the other would appear outside. He was a pauper, forever bankrupt and subsisting on charitable loans. He had a persistent clandestine desire to hook Joe into giving him such a loan, but Joe would not, could not be hooked under any circumstance. Abe would chat to him at every opportunity and smile at him in brotherly fashion, but Joe held himself cold and aloof as if he did not know him.

Abe never got offended. He had great respect for Joe whom he believed to be secretly filthy rich. He always bragged about Joe's wealth to all his family and friends as if he were party to the fortune. Other neighbours in the street, especially the Jews, also estimated that Joe was worth many thousands. Fantastic stories were spread about Joe's chests filled to bursting with valuable gems. Joe's isolated and reserved manner further fired his neighbours' imaginations as they looked with awe, respect and latent jealousy upon the perpetually closed doors of Joe's shops.

Occasionally, clients would stealthily sneak out from there: mostly older women in black with sad teary eyes and moist face or, conversely, heavily made-up women in brazen brightly coloured wear. At other times, it might have been half-drunk hedonistic boys of the underworld whom the neighbours would follow with suspicion, shake their heads and wink at each other, saying, 'So, that is how you hoard your money.'

Rosa, the short fat widow from the tailor shop who was once interested in marrying Joe, would stand with her fat hands folded over her bosom and scream at the top of her voice in unsavoury language down the street, 'You old idiot! You are not worth the earth that you stand on! You are a swine, a piece of old junk, that's right, no more than just a piece of old junk!'

Original illustration for 'Old Friends' by Noel Counihan

## Isaac Green

Joe lived totally alone and isolated from the world outside. In his solitude, he was paralysed. His solitude seemed to have sucked from him all spark for living, all joy. He hated people. They lusted after the fortune that he had amassed over many years, this fortune, his money, being itself like a living entity to him. Whenever he would pick through his iron chest that was constantly growing, its contents breathed with life and sang quiet songs of debts and profits that only he could understand, doing so with his soul that had been encased in miserliness and old decrepit junk. The money that he paid for the items that people had pawned brought interest; those items passed through a trail of other people's hands, wandered through distant highways and byways, and eventually returned to his chest, from there to go out once more, as every transaction made his coffers grow, grow, transformed into money, money, money!

Joe dedicated his entire life's purpose to the pursuit of money. He adulated it with all the passion still left in his otherwise solitary, paralysed heart; the dark pawn shop was his whole world. He took on the life of a devout hermit bewitched by the unholy ministry of pledges and interest.

The only person to set foot into Joe's secret world of money and antiquated wares was Isaac Green, a tall, elongated man with a bulbous nose, prominent Adam's apple and high cheeks who was as stingy as Joe. He owned many houses and spent his days trudging across town on his long, shaky, black feet, requesting rental payments in lachrymose tones as if he were demanding a dowry. He maintained a uniformly dour expression, continually complaining about the weather whose heat was drying out his houses and eating up the bricks and mortar, while in wetter seasons the rains were seeping through their foundations and dampening the walls, causing him to bemoan the losses he had to sustain, the tenants themselves becoming enemies who were sorely abusing their homes and bleeding him dry.

Isaac had most trouble with the homes that he owned in the shady back streets where prostitutes lived. He always found the walls scraped, full of insect nests, peeling wallpaper hanging in strips, broken doors and windows smashed that repeatedly had to withstand the fights between the cheap and slovenly women and their clients and guests. Those houses were degenerating in filthy neglect and rotting in the dirt that had never been cleaned. Whenever he came to collect the rent, the women would flirt with him, tickle his Adam's apple, wink at him and make advances to him with lewd and suggestive gestures.

'No money, darling,' they would frequently say.

'What do you mean, no money?' Isaac would whine. 'I am an old sick man, I also have to make a living.'

Rita, a young Spanish woman with black curly hair and fiery black eyes, always laughed at him, hugged him, kissed him on his lips and offered him cigarettes. Resignedly, Isaac would take these offerings, smile foolishly and leave bitterly downhearted over not having received his rent.

He would pour out his bitterness to Joe every night, show him in black and white how they were making a pauper of him and, pulling wads of paper from a pocket, thrust them under Joe's nose and say, '*Nu*, see! More taxes to pay! For water, for rates, for everything you can think of. They are ripping bits off me from all sides. Who can understand this?'

Joe would hear out his friend in silence, empathise with pity and understanding, and, groaning, would raise a hand, point at all the junk around them stacked to the ceiling and sigh.

'Do you think that it is any better for me? I have thrown good money into this stock. There is a fortune lying here unsold. The place is becoming a cemetery and I can't squeeze even a penny out of it.'

Bitterly enveloped in self-pity, they would seat themselves at the table and, as if by magic, an old greasy deck of cards appeared in Joe's hands. Isaac pulled out the half-broken cigarette that Rita had given him and savoured the delicious taste of its smoke and the tender thoughts of that beautiful Spanish girl whose image rose like a dream-like visage before his eyes.

'Do you want to pay a game?' Joe interrupted him, shuffling the cards.

'Of course. Why not?'

## Cards

And so, their card-playing began and extended into the early hours of the morning.

They played for high stakes, but never paid. They borrowed to get themselves back on their feet and kept strict accounts of their debts that stretched far back over many years. Joe was usually the loser, never managing to win back his arrears that had long continued to mount and now stood at several thousand dollars. It became of utmost importance that he redeem his debt; so, every night he sat down to play again with a beating heart and the hope that this time, his luck would turn his way. He played impatiently, trying to keep his anxiety under check as, with his short fat working man's fingers, he dealt the cards.

Isaac Green, on the other hand, played coolly and controlled, even somewhat disinterestedly, so used to winning was he. He would leisurely light another of Rita's delectable cigarettes, lackadaisically pick up the greasy cards, spread them out in his hand, study them nonchalantly and proceed to withdraw a slip of paper from a pocket.

*The Card Players*, Yosl Bergner, c. 1940

'So, where are we up to in our accounts? Mm, over three thousand pounds already!' he said, avoiding excessive enthusiasm.

'No, two thousand pounds,' countered Joe.

'Two thousand and ninety-six pounds and four and a half shillings. Not a paltry sum,' corrected Isaac, beginning to hum briefly a dreamy tune. 'Over two thousand live pounds. Quite a fortune!'

'It's not all that bad,' Joe took heart. 'We will play some more. After all, I'm not a dead man yet.'

It took some time for the game to get moving. Isaac Green had not yet managed to shake from himself the outside world; his feet were still wandering between his houses and the streets were still before his eyes; and his ears, too, kept ringing with the cacophony of the city.

'Joe,' he said, remembering some news he had heard as he dealt the next hand. 'Did you hear about Rothman's bankruptcy? They say that he is half-a-million in debt.'

'What's it to me? I have enough of my own worries.'

'But nevertheless, half-a-million ...'

A little while later, Green was reminded of something else. 'I heard in town that there's been another pogrom on the Jews in Poland.'

'Another pogrom. I wish them health. What do I care?' said Joe, shrugging his shoulders as he took up his cards.

'And there is a lot of talk about a new war against Russia. People are saying that there might be another new world war,' said Green after a further spell of silence.

'Why are you thinking about all this foolishness? We

are playing cards and since we are playing, so let us play. You have birds flying around your head. Pogroms, wars, do think you can take care of ... the world?'

Tensely, bitterly, he swiftly dealt another hand of cards.

Green stopped talking altogether after that. He allowed himself to become more involved in the game, his bony fingers moving his cards more rapidly. His eyes burned, his cheeks took on a red shiny sheen.

Joe, however, was now becoming more excited and his breathing grew louder with an asthmatic wheeze. 'Father in heaven!' he exclaimed. 'Save me from the cards that I am getting, *kotsheres*, *lapates* and *shikses*! Boy, you really have dealt me some hand, Itsikl!' They had a nickname for every card. They called the small cards *kotsheres* and *lapates*, the knights and dames were *shikses*, the king was 'Reb Tsats', and so forth.

The cards were like living beings to them, each with their own wills and fickle desires. Both Isaac and Joe had well-established friends and enemies amongst the cards. Each time they threw down a card, they propelled it with all manner of greetings, pleas and wishes, as if they were sending it into the world on some important mission. Each card was also sent as if bravely to fight a difficult battle, to do extraordinary things and withstand arduous challenges. Hence, they would talk to the cards kindly and angrily and praise them and abuse them. They put their whole heart and soul into those fading greasy cards, all the hopes and desires, love and compassion that still flowed through their aging miserly hearts.

'Come here, you black dame, Reb Tsats is calling you!'
exclaimed Isaac with a laugh at one point when he took the
queen that Joe had dealt for his king. 'The dame is crawling
to me, hee, hee, hee! Take her away!' sang Joe as he threw
down his knight.

'A *shniek* is also worth something, and how do you like
my black strongman?' Isaac would hurl back as a brave jest,
a black ace.

'Hee, hee,' responded Joe with a laugh of his own as he
threw down another card. 'Where have you been hiding,
my baby? See how the ace of hearts showed up just like that,
so unexpected. Now show him what you an do!'

'Bad luck Joe, bad luck,' laughed Isaac as he took up
Joe's card. 'Sorry to say it, but you didn't hit the mark this
time. Your ace of hearts is dead, I'm afraid, the poor thing
fallen as a sacrifice. Hee, hee, hee.'

'It is not going, by Christ!' Joe threw down another
card, angry and bitter.

The ace of hearts was his beloved. He would play with
it, call it by endearing names, always flip it upon the table
with triumph and pride like a lord throwing down his
gauntlet. The ace of hearts had a special, secret and important meaning for him. It was a proud card; it was hard to
tie it down. It was always hiding somewhere, then either
suddenly swimming out from between the other cards or
suddenly disappearing from the pack with the self-will of a
high-ranking personage.

And if the ace of hearts ever fell into Isaac's hands, his
face would erupt into a broad smile and he would say again,

'Died, poor thing! Fell as a sacrifice! Its importance is wiped out!'

They had been playing like this for many years, night after night until the early hours of the morning. They dedicated their energy into the cards, invested in them their emotion, tested their fortunes through the games, tried to discover their secrets, and trembled and grieved through waiting and anticipation, until their final victory or defeat. The hours passed quickly in the quiet of the night until the two men were collapsing from exhaustion, until the blood that ran through their narrowed arteries beat wildly in their temples.

'Nu, that will be enough for tonight, Joe,' Isaac would say, barely able to rise from his chair to put on his overcoat.

Joe would not respond, himself riveted to his spot, looking about him as though he were in a trance.

Joe returned more immediately to the present.

'You owe me two thousand three hundred and sixty now, Joe,' Abe said, carefully noting Joe's latest debt on his tally sheet and replacing it in his pocket, uncertain and shakily making his way to the door, repeating, 'Two thousand three hundred and sixty pounds. Wow, it is so easy to say ...'

He then left, wrapped his worn-out overcoat more tightly around him and disappeared into the quiet darkness of the night.

## Dead

Suddenly, Mr Green stopped coming to see Joe. This did not unduly bother Joe. It did not even occur to him to inquire if anything untoward had happened to his friend. The long years of their association did not leave any impression on his heart, which had turned to stone amidst the dust of the old bric-a-brac around him and had become paralysed by the ongoing accounts of debits and credits, which had become the core of his life. Slowly, the fact that Isaac had ceased to come seeped into his consciousness. He took to wandering around the darkened rooms of his empty house after he locked the shop and sorting through the different wares that lay about wrapped in dirty yellowing paper, after which he took out his cards out of their packet, dealt them to himself and settled down to games of patience. This, he quickly came to find boring.

'There is no one with whom to play a real game,' he yawned. 'Where on earth has that old *shtinker* got to?'

Then, extending a hand over the cup of tea he had been drinking, he went on to groan and said, 'May as well go to bed, it is a shame to burn the light for nothing.'

But he could not fall asleep. He lay in his old, narrow and rickety bed pervaded by the acrid smell of sweat and dirt, and looked with sorry eyes into the darkness. The night was eerily quiet and still. The street noise could not penetrate the heavily covered doors and windows. From time to time, he heard the sound of an insect crawling around the junk. In his semi-conscious state, he set to imagining wondrous fantasies involving cards.

The characters of those cards grew to great proportions. They swam in the darkness, wove in and out, then appeared once more with strange distorted faces and threatening hands. The card that he pictured most was the ace of hearts, with its bulging belly that bobbed and rolled until it filled the entire space with its deep, dark and clouded redness. His own fat overgrown chest, in which his fat-saturated heart was barely moving, rose heavily with spasmodic laboured breath until he finally fell into a sleep filled with weird dreams, from which he woke exhausted, his body moist from head to toe with thick, clinging sweat.

One morning, after another sleepless night, he went out to the front door of his shop to get a breath of fresh air. As usual, his neighbour, Abe Rosen, appeared instantaneously.

'Have not seen you for ages, Mr Benjamin! What has been happening to you? I was getting worried that something was wrong. I have not seen you at all recently. You were not even at Green's funeral.'

'Whose funeral?'

'Nu, Isaac Green's funeral,' he said, looking directly into Joe's eyes. 'I don't believe it. You did not even know he had died. Yes, he died.'

'Everyone dies, Mr Benjamin, and no one can take anything with them to the grave.'

Joe glued his watery eyes on Abe. He appeared about to say something, but stopped himself, turned around and went back inside.

There, he was acutely attacked by a frightening silence. The shop appeared even darker then usual and he felt that someone was behind him, watching. But there was no one in the shop.

'He died, well, well,' he mumbled to himself, wanting

to shed that silence. 'Itzikl, Itzikl, you can now forget about the three thousand pounds that I still owe you from our games. I managed to get out of that one, well, well.'

He was unable to settle down. The empty quiet rooms were stifling. He wanted to go outside again and chat with Abe. He kept feeling that someone was hidden in the shop and watching his every move. The place harboured fragmented secret voices. He took to walking around the house with loud and heavy steps. He turned to opening his chests over and over again to count the bank notes there, examine the jewels wrapped in tissue paper and leaf through his ledgers inscribed with outstanding debts until he stilled the unsettling thoughts he had been nurturing about Isaac Green. He then proceeded to prepare his meagre meal, which he went on to eat with a hearty appetite, seated at his customary place behind the counter that stood opposite the door, having finally dispelled Isaac Green fully from his mind.

## The end

Customers began arriving at the shop. This brought Joe back to life. It was with joy that he counted the bank notes and groaned happily to himself – as he had become wont to do – while he valued the diamond rings and other valuables that his customers brought to pawn. He calculated their worth, filled out receipts, climbed his ladder to store them, and immersed himself joyously in the business like one diving into the pleasures offered by warm water.

But late in the day, when the deaf Jessie came, he

experienced a special secret joy, as if a long-awaited guest had finally arrived. Jessie would come once in a while to clean up his place a little and wash his laundry that would by then have substantially mounted. She was a spirited lady, a neighbour with a drawn face covered by hair, ruddy from the alcohol for which she had a man's predilection. Like most deaf folk, she rarely spoke, but tended to stare with glazed half-mad eyes. She was a little in love with Joe, drawn to the solitary lonesome bachelor who, himself, remained always silent. In her own moments of intense loneliness, not even the spirits that she drank could assuage in her destitute heart her affection for him.

So, she would come, even when Joe was not expecting her, and begin to clean his home or wash his clothes. And he would watch her quietly, his own face flushing brighter by the minute, his eyes becoming glassier and his breathing hotter and faster; until, finally, he would approach with his bear-like gait, embrace her from behind with his stirred excited breath, and Jessie would respond to his passion with a quiet laugh and allow him to do with her whatever he wanted.

This time he greeted her with a friendly smile and wrapped his arms around her even before she had the op-portunity to begin her cleaning. He was unusually gentle with her. He spoke to her, nestled into her flat bosom as if here seeking sustenance from her. But suddenly, memories of Isaac Green arose to overwhelm him. With a bashful laugh, he tried to catch her eye with uncertain timid glances of his own. She, in turn, embraced him, stroked his brow with a work-worn hand and let herself be carried away by his passion, by his need to dispel his own loneliness – by his recognition of his loneliness that returned to gnaw once more in his heart.

Jessie left late that night. Joe turned on his lamp. An acute wave of fear came upon him. He seated himself at his table, picked up his packet of cards and, before he knew what he was doing, he began shuffling them and dealing them as if he were about to play with someone. He looked at his cards and flung down a trump. His cards shone in his sight. Never before in his life had he held such a good hand.

'Oh, would I have shown him a game tonight!' he cried out cheerfully as he turned over the cards that he had dealt to his imaginary opponent, starting then to play both for himself and on behalf of his adversary. He won one trick after another, counted out aloud his winning score, boasted about the fortune that he was amassing. And so he continued, victoriously tossing down one card after another, constantly talking to himself.

'This is how you teach the idiot! This is what I call a game!'

Then, suddenly, he stopped, afraid. He had thrown down the ace of hearts and began searching madly among his opponent's cards.

Somewhere, he had let his mind wander. He had made a mistake. The ace of hearts had been lost.

'Dead, poor thing,' he heard Green's voice, 'it had to be sacrificed, hee, hee!'

His eyes sprang open widely and large beads of

perspiration gathered on his brow. His face twisted into a mask of terror as his heart took to pounding as if with hammer blows, rapidly, forcefully, painfully.

'Dead, hee, hee!' kept buzzing in his ears, 'Dead, hee, hee!'

The cards fell from his hand. He was too afraid to move, to take a breath. The silence hung over him, dense and threatening. He wanted to cry out, to scream, to move from the spot, to escape the silence. But his voice was caught as if in a vice and his body weighed down with cold lead.

'Dead!' he finally managed to utter under his breath as his head fell to his chest like a log.

—*Oystralier Leben*, 25 Dec. 1931,
*Dertzeilungen* (1939),
*Collected Writings* (1949)

# THE FUNERAL

THE DEATH OF REB ALTER created a big commotion in Drummond Street. Since early morning, a group of Jews had been gathering in front of the brown weatherboard house in which Reb Alter had lodged, distractedly looking up at the closed glass door that gave out on to the high balcony with its rusty iron railings.

Occasionally Mrs McCarthy, the landlady, a large unkempt woman, appeared at the door and surveyed the noisy group below. When the Jews noticed her they would move forward, waving their hands. Merkel, the Lithuanian, a lean agile little man with protruding eyes, confidently pushed himself to the front, for, among the Jews he was the one who could speak English.

In a drawn-out voice he appealed to her: 'Mrs McCarthy – please – excuse me!' Mrs McCarthy shook her head with the red cap angrily. She scanned Merkel up and down and, without a word, slammed the door in his face.

The Jews stared at one another and shrugged their shoulders then, with a sigh, muttered, 'You see? Much account we are.'

'We, we Jews in exile meet with the same treatment everywhere,' said Moyshe the hawker, an ascetic-looking man with his hat pushed back to the top of his head.

More Jews appeared. Silent, sleepy Drummond Street, with its long rows of dark neglected houses, narrow verandas and wild gardens, was filled with noise.

Moyshe circled around them and, rubbing his hands, he mused with a careworn expression, 'Yes, Australia, the Angel of Death will find us wherever we are.'

'A golden land,' sneered someone in the rear.

Feivel, a tall striding figure, arrived. He looked at the crowd with pinpoint eyes and, loudly for the benefit of the whole street, cried out, 'Well, *Yidn*! What do you say now, ha? What do you say now? It's just as I told you! A great country! Was it life we came here for or was it to die here?'

Then he spotted Merkel. An enmity existed between the two, for Merkel had wormed his way into a job, made good and thought the world of Australia. Feivel had contempt for jobs, and even if gold had been showered upon him he would still have maintained that Australia held nothing good. He habitually annoyed Merkel with questions such as, 'Like the place, eh, you Lithuanian? Getting on well?'

'Well, if you don't like it, why don't you go back?' Merkel would reply. 'Nobody's going to stop you.'

This time, catching Merkel by the lapel, Feivel screamed in his face, 'What have you got to say now, you Lithuanian? To hell with your job and your profits! How do you like the country now, you devil?'

'Leave me alone, you fool!' protested Merkel. 'It's a

calamity, of course. A man has died. All right! What can you do about it?'

'A lovely fate!' came from the crowd. 'A lovely fate to die in this God-forsaken land!'

Into the street rolled a luxurious dark-blue car that halted near the group. A thin man with a dapper little black moustache stepped out and approached them, mumbling something in English. The Jews blinked, shrugged their shoulders and called to Merkel, 'Come here, Lithuanian! We don't understand a word of this.'

Adjusting his glasses, Merkel came forward and shot an enquiring glance at the new arrival.

'*Chevra Kadisha*, Burial Society,' explained the man, the Hebrew words rolling clumsily off his tongue.

'From the *Chevra Kadisha*,' translated Merkel.

'Yes, yes, *Chevra Kadisha*,' a voice from the car, out of which stepped another man, a stiff thick-set individual with a large clean-shaven face and a pointed little beard over a shiny white collar turned back-to-front like a Christian clergyman's.

'Rabbi Stone,' murmured someone.

Merkel became altogether flabbergasted. His narrow shoulders sharpened, his eyes filled with awe. Approaching the rabbi, he indicated the brown house, saying, 'Here, Rabbi Stone, here!'

The rabbi nodded to the little man and the pair advanced towards the house. Glancing back obsequiously at the rabbi with every step, Merkel ran ahead. On reaching the front door, he struck it with the heavy knocker.

'Rabbi Stone himself!' said Frenkel, a large Jew with a round belly, smacking his lips appreciatively.

Of the newcomers to Australia, Frenkel was one who had done well. He owned a trouser factory with eighteen hands under him, and considered himself quite a big shot. Parting his yellow two-pronged little beard and drawing in his short neck, he said, 'After all, it's not such a bad place, this Australia. To think that Rabbi Stone himself has condescended to come! A human being is certainly of some importance here.'

This was waved aside by Moyshe the Hawker.

'A great privilege! A rabbi who's shaven and can't speak Yiddish!'

'Yes, and his collar back to front, just like a Gentile parson,' added someone. 'You'd think he was going to preach in a Christian church.'

Frenkel scanned the speaker up and down, muttering contemptuously. 'Church, shmerch – just tongue-wagging.'

'It's a topsy-turvy world all right,' commented another. 'Judaism is in a bad way here.'

'In a bad way?' angrily repeated Frenkel. 'And what about General Monash? Did Jews reach positions like that where we came from?'

The tall Feivel set his feet wide apart and, fingering his beard, snarled, 'Look at the prosperous businessman! Thinks he's important, doesn't he? Against Monash, he's just tendered swine!'

'A businessman lectures us?' added someone.

Suddenly, everyone became silent.

Rabbi Stone and the thin man with the dapper moustache who had earlier appeared first returned to the dark-blue car. Only when it began to move away did the man stick out his head and patronisingly announce, 'The funeral will take place this afternoon.'

A large crowd turned up for the funeral. Those Jews who were newcomers kept themselves apart. It was their first funeral in the new land. The hawkers, market-stall owners, tailors and others had put aside their businesses for the occasion. Drummond Street became black with people.

It was a sweltering afternoon. From the white-hot sky, such a blinding heat beat down that the softest word or murmur cut sharply through the thick flammable air.

With heavy, mournful steps the crowd paced about, looking into one another's eyes and muttering, 'Golden opportunities indeed! Much good it was coming here!'

A group of women appeared, suitably bedecked in black shawls and with vinegary, piously-mournful faces. They kept to themselves, conversing in hushed melancholy tones. Mrs Ackman, a tall bony woman from the kosher butcher's shop, repeatedly beat her chest as she wailed, 'Ai, Ai! Ai! He left a widow and two orphans at home.'

Representatives of the community had also come, arriving in shiny cars that stood scattered along the street. These folk looked highly dignified and self-important, reluctantly returning the greetings of the 'newcomers'. After them, a long-bodied black-lacquered car with a luxurious hearse at its rear turned into the street. At once, silence fell and a tremor passed through the crowd. The newcomers drew closer, casting timid glances at the car, driven by a non-Jewish driver in black cap and gloves. He sat behind the wheel upright, his face as emotionless as frozen dough.

Feivel, with his deep-set eyes rolling rapidly and craning his neck in all directions, muttered, 'Did you get it? A car with a Gentile driver!'

'What a country this is!' moaned Moyshe the hawker. 'A Gentile employed at a Jewish funeral!'

'They're just making a game of us. Why?' asked Feivel, a little louder.

'Yes, they're just making game of us!' echoed the crowd.

Some of them went up to Gutman, the wholesaler, from whom they usually obtained their goods on credit – a man who was on a somewhat friendly footing with the elders of the community.

'How does this come about – a Gentile taking part at a Jewish funeral?' asked Frenkel angrily, now in agreement with the crowd. He raised his two-pronged beard towards Gutman, thrusting his hands aggressively into his waistcoat pockets.

'A man of your position should know better than to ask that,' retorted Gutman. 'Things are done differently in this country.'

Feivel spat furiously while the community leaders in turn were themselves also annoyed.

'What insolence from these newcomers!' growled Gutman. 'If they don't like this country, let them go back to where they came from. They're only a worry to us.'

'Anti-Semites! Persecutors!' hit back the newcomers.

There might have been trouble if it had not been for the appearance of Merkel. He was with the little man from the *Chevra Kadisha* and two elderly Jews who wore felt hats high above their foreheads. With swift, quiet steps they went towards the brown house, looking at no one.

The crowd, pushing and clamouring, moved towards Merkel.

'Where have you been all this time, Merkel?'

'How are things?'

'What did Rabbi Stone say?'

'Say something, Merkel, please explain.'

'Just a minute, just a minute!' pleaded Merkel, fanning himself with his hands. His eyes fell upon the community leaders, who stood at a distance, observing the rowdy newcomers with disapproval. At once his expression changed. Craning his neck and nodding, he cast a skewed smile at them. He was about to approach them, but Feivel grabbed him by the arm, snarling through clenched teeth, 'Stay here, Lithuanian! Don't crawl where you're not wanted.'

Just then, a stir arose around the house. Its glass door was flung open and the men from the *Chevra Kadisha* appeared, bearing a black-covered body on a bier. Through the narrow door, they angled their way and hurriedly bore the load to the hearse.

The women let out a wail. With hands folded, Mrs Ackman rocked from side to side. 'The poor widow! The orphans!'

'What are the women wailing for?' asked Merkel in bewilderment. 'This isn't the old country! Women don't wail at funerals here!'

'Never you mind!' snapped Feivel. 'We don't care a damn about what is or isn't done in this country. Let the women wail. It's the newcomer's funeral!'

And he went towards the *Chevra Kadisha*, who were busy with the bier. As it was being placed inside the hearse, the crowd moved towards it with melancholy steps. Softly and slowly, the car began to move away, the hearse rocking behind it, gradually gathering pace. The mourners tried to keep up with it.

Frenkel, his belly heaving up and down, called out, 'Stop! Stop! The devil take you, Gentile!'

But the hearse gained momentum, leaving behind the mourners who halted in bewilderment. The cars of the Congregation's leaders swished past them in pursuit of the hearse.

With a warped smile on his lips, Feivel stood holding his hands on his chest. 'What have you to say now?' he mocked. 'We're properly ditched.'

'Unheard of,' growled Moyshe the hawker.

Frenkel stood open-mouthed, trying to get his breath. His double-tapering beard hung limp and dishevelled like a rag. 'Such an insult!' he gasped. Upon which, elbowing his way through the crowd, he began suddenly to run, protesting, 'This can't be allowed. Such levity isn't to be so easily overlooked.'

Before long he was back on a large ramshackle lorry with Big Bill.

A thick-set, ruddy-faced fellow with prominent eyes and a cigar between his lips, Bill was a familiar figure to the newcomers. He conveyed their goods to the market and did a bit of business there himself. With an assortment of wares such as shoelaces, cottons and rubber heels that he would lay out on the ground, he would call out, 'Ladies and gentlemen! Best quality bargains! *Mazl tov! Mazl tov!* Congratulations!'

The Jews, traders and customers alike, would delight in his smattering of Yiddish words and speculate whether he himself had some Jewish ancestry. When they asked him outright, he would respond with a stream of Yiddish expletives, gathered from no one knew where.

Having returned to the mourners, with his hat on his head and dispelling the sweat on his brow, Frenkel climbed down and motioned all to come on board.

'Get on! We're going to the cemetery – at my expense!'

'But what about the women?' asked Merkel, afraid on their behalf. 'Women aren't supposed to take part in funerals in this country.'

'Let the women come, too,' insisted Frenkel. 'I'm responsible! At my expense.'

Pushing and struggling, the women clambered aboard with the men. The lorry began to shake and roar, as if undecided whether to move. At the wheel, Bill worked busily with his hands and feet until finally the vehicle leapt forward and, with a cough and splutter, clattered off down the street.

The cemetery caused fresh consternation. As far as the eye could see, tombstones, crosses and holy figures, unmistakably Christian, reared themselves above the wall. Outside, women with baskets of flowers crouched like hens.

The mourners fretted helplessly at the gate.

'Frenkel, where have you brought us?' they exclaimed indignantly. 'This is a Gentile graveyard.'

'How am I to know?' Frenkel retorted. Turning to Bill he said desperately, 'Jewish cemetery, Jewish cemetery, you idiot!'

'Yes, yes, Jewish cemetery,' cried the others.

Pointing a finger in the direction of the crosses, Bill winked knowingly and boomed, '*Mazl tov! Mazl tov!*'

'Maybe it really is the Jewish cemetery,' said Feivel with his crooked smile, shifting from one foot to the other. You can expect anything in Australia.'

'Feivel's at his jokes again,' commented someone.

'Going a bit too far this time,' muttered another.

'Anything is possible,' demurred Shimon Loivitcher, indicating a number of cars parked down a side street. Gradually, his gaze became more intense and he screwed up his eyes. 'Those cars seem a bit familiar. I'll bet that's Gutman's Buick and that's Switman's new Dodge. Went bankrupt and bought himself a Dodge,' he added.

'I'm afraid Shimon's right,' unwillingly conceded Frenkel. 'It looks as if the Jewish cemetery is somewhere near.'

He told Merkel to make inquiries and, adjusting his glasses to appear important, Merkel capered across the road, stopping a passer-by to question him in English, much to the envy and admiration of the crowd.

He returned with a long face. 'God knows. They say it really is the Jewish cemetery.'

'We'll take a walk through and see,' decided Frenkel. 'Maybe the way to the Jewish cemetery leads through here.'

But Shimon hung back. 'Nonsense! I won't set foot in a Christian cemetery.'

'Well, what else can we do? We've no choice,' argued Frenkel. 'We're here now – we might as well have a look.'

Treading cautiously and without a word, the Jews stole into the cemetery, while among the trees stood a host of stone figures and crosses as the late afternoon sun, which was descending towards the horizon, tinted the sky with a reddish hue.

Along the broad sandy paths, the crowd moved silently. Merkel, in front, removed his hat; the others also bared their heads one by one.

'Fancy looking for a Jewish cemetery here,' Moyshe the hawker complained. 'Heaven knows where we are being led to. This place is endless.'

Suddenly, in the deep evening silence they heard footsteps. A procession of human figures moved against in the dark background.

'A Christian burial!' gasped voices among the mourners. Then their ears caught the strains of a Hebrew ritual. Hurrying forward, they saw Rabbi Stone in a long black cloak with broad dependent sleeves and a tall peaked cap on his head. He was pacing with slow measured steps, his hands folded high on his chest, chanting Hebrew words in a deep solemn voice. Behind him followed the men of the *Chevra Kadisha* with the bier on their shoulders, in turn succeeded by the community leaders piously bowing their heads in keeping with the rabbi's chant.

The newcomers stood horrified, the men forgetting to cover their heads. Rabbi Stone paused, knitting his brow disapprovingly. Without interrupting the liturgy, he pointed to his head, motioning them to put on their hats. Then, with a shrug of his shoulders, he raised his folded hands higher on his chest and continued piously to lead his retinue ahead. Still keeping their distance, the others followed timidly until they reached a freshly-dug grave.

Alongside it, the mound of dug-out earth was replete with greasy clumps of whitish clay that looked as if they had been mixed with oil. With downcast faces, the mourners stood in silence around the grave.

Moyshe the hawker picked up a handful of earth and rubbed it between his fingers, pensive as he looked at it. 'Strange earth, this,' he sighed. 'Altogether different from home.'

'No difference,' countered Frenkel gloomily. 'The worms will devour you just the same.'

As the body was lowered into the grave, Rabbi Stone rapidly recited the prayers from his prayer book. Then, with a light cough, he took up the shovel that stood upright in the mound and, digging up a small quantity of earth, he sprinkled it over the body in the grave. Having done this, he looked about him, sighted the tall figure of Feivel and handed him the shovel.

Feivel sank it into the mound and then stopped, his

eyes wandering about the fellow-mourners. The newcomers stood tense, the women looking at the men as if seeking some sign.

'Go on!' urged the rabbi. 'Go on! It's the right thing to do!'

'I can't, *Yidn mayne*! I can't!' I can't!' Feivel burst out and let the shovel fall.

His compatriots looked away. Frenkel sighed deeply and his chin with its forked beard quivered.

As if that had been their awaited signal, the women splintered the heavy evening silence with a long protracted wail.

The newcomer kindred tentatively drew nearer to the grave, each tossing in a handful of earth.

Upon which, Moyshe the hawker began to intone the Kaddish, the traditional prayer of mourning for the departed.

—Translated by Naomi Kelly

*Dertzeilungen* (1939),
*Collected Writings* (1949)

# THE FIGHT

W., A SMALL TOWN in Western Australia, was covered with huge glaring signs announcing:

Sensation! Sensation!

First time in Australia,

the phenomenal Hungarian muscle man

**Arnold Kirka**

fighting against

**Fred White**

Champion of Western Australia.

Be sure to get your tickets in time!!!! Do not miss this opportunity! All of W. must see this sensational fight! A major attraction comes to W.

The advertisement caused the town of W. to sizzle, a rare experience indeed for this far-flung provincial town that lay some twenty miles from the nearest train line.

When the night of the fight eventually arrived, the temporarily erected circus tent was packed to capacity. People were pressed one on top of another. Any place where a foot could find a spot or a hand something to grasp, there you found humanity: broad-shouldered farmers with thickly-veined necks and tanned rounded faces; unhappy gold-diggers wearing hungry looks; happy, free and easy sheep-shearers; dirty and tattered rabbit-shooters; swaying women and children squeezed into a mass of humanity, which filled the hall with buzzing. The air was permeated with the sharp and bitter smell of beer, tobacco and human bodies compacted into a thick damp fog of evaporating perspiration, hot breath and tobacco smoke. The strong electric reflectors shining through that fog cast a smudgy dull light that resembled a sauna.

All the faces in the audience were screaming with the heat and the excitement of the imminent fight. There was lively rambling conversation and laughter, the sound of nuts being cracked, and smoking. There was constant betting over the expected winner and every so often a fight would break out in a corner over an empty inch of space. One could hardly hear the jazz band above the noise, no matter how loudly it played with its drums and saxophone.

On the arena, as if through a cloud, one could see the entwined bodies of the second-rate athletes that filled in the time before the championship bout. Nobody even looked at them. The whistle of the referee, the flat voice, like a duck's, of the announcer, and the ringing of the bell sounded almost lost in the hall. The audience was becoming more restlessly impatient, stamping feet echoed more frequently, as did threatening cries:

'Kirka!'

'White!'

An aging, rotund ex-sailor who was standing on his

crooked rheumatic legs, smoking a clay pipe between his huge brown teeth, looked at his pocket watch every few minutes, then, looking around at his neighbours, said in deep bass tone, 'When are those damned champions finally coming out? It is already after ten o'clock. They will not even have any time to warm themselves.'

'Don't worry, old sea-wolf,' replied a tall farmer with a long moustache. 'Our champion will quickly wipe out the Hungarian. You can't play around with White.'

'Never mind, boss. Kirka is not just anybody. I saw him arriving by bus this morning. He's a real elephant; it's frightening just to look at him,' butted in a farm hand with a seeping eye.

'Hi! Hi! Kirka!' cried out a fancy Italian with a black waxed moustache. 'I will give him ten to one! Who will take my bet?'

'Nick off, you bloody dago! This Kirka is one of your dago brothers,' a squeaky half-drunken voice was heard.

'Who is a bloody dago, Sacramenta?' retorted the Italian, threateningly putting his hand in his pocket.

A pockmarked man arrived instantly and raised a fist under the Italian's nose. 'Are you after a knife, you dirty dog?'

The argument was brought to an abrupt halt by an outburst of applause and cries of wonder and surprise. 'There they are. Hooray!'

Two huge athletes appeared in the arena, draped in light-coloured dressing-gowns. The announcer, a pale tall elongated man with the face of an over-ripe apple, dressed in a greasy waiter's tuxedo, raised his right arm with great bravado and called out in his duck-like voice, 'The fight between the champion of Western Australia, Fred White, and the famous Hungarian, Arnold Kirka, will be fought over eight rounds.'

The air filled once more with cries of 'Ho, hey, hooray!'

Both athletes threw off their dressing-gowns. In no hurry to approach one another, nonetheless, after having surveyed each other with intense concentration, they did so and shook hands. It was clear from their slow reserved movements that they had never met before.

A loud shrill whistle sounded – the sign for the fight to begin. The athletes grabbed each other with strong muscular hands. The fight promised to be lively and gripping. Fred White was tall and blond; he had a mighty and grandiose body that appeared to have been sculpted from stone. His movements were agile and light, his steps elastic and sure. Kirka, however, was heavily-built with a mean, dour, square face. Muscles as tight as knots rippled over his massive frame, performing dramatic acrobatics whenever he made the slightest move.

At the beginning, they fought slowly and carefully as if merely testing their opponent's strength. White, with his agile steps, easily manoeuvred around his opponent without strain, thwarting Kirka's attacks without moving from the spot. It appeared as if they were playing a game but the audience watched their every move with enthralled breathless attention.

Second round. Third round.

The fight was becoming more heated and fascinating. Their movements quickened, became more powerful. White began to attack his opponent. He leapt about Kirka with the agility of a cat, moving upon him with lightning speed with his long agile arms, or drawing away to avoid a solid thrust. The other, meanwhile, stood immobile, weighed down in the middle of the arena, keeping White at a distance with his own sharp, powerful and solid punches. Slowly, Kirka, too, became more aroused and launched into a strong attack on White, pummelling him with the full momentum of his body. Both turned red and were covered with sweat. White, in turn, also mounted his attack, seeking to overwhelm Kirka with his agility, confounding him at times with some new manoeuvre. It was now Kirka who was barely able to defend himself and resist White's accelerated tempo.

The audience was becoming even more engrossed in the fight. Their eyes were aflame, their loud bellowing screams, hooting and whistling carried more vociferously throughout the tent.

Fourth round. Fifth round. Sixth round.

Now, the real fight truly began as, incited by the crowd's constant yelling, both giants fell upon each other with murderously menacing ferocity. Streams of perspiration poured from them, their deep-throated breathing reached every side of the tent. The Hungarian gathered his utmost strength and threw himself upon White who skilfully sidestepped him. His movements had lost their earlier agility and momentum as he changed his tactics towards avoiding the attacks, much to the dismay of the audience. Kirka, meanwhile, was becoming increasingly wilder. His body turned fiery red, his small angry eyes lit up with a hostile glow, he bent his head and, like a charging bull, he threw himself upon White who, again, slipped away like a snake from the Hungarian's arms. Suddenly, to everyone's surprise, White leapt upon Kirka's shoulders in a swift move, twined his legs about Kirka's torso and clasped his neck with both hands. Kirka turned about on his elephantine legs to shake off the hold. It seemed that he was about to topple as an astonished excited tumult, applause and joyous cries spread throughout the tent.

'Bravo!'

'Hooray!'

'Bravo!'

Resorting to all his might, the shaken and startled Kirka managed to free himself from his burden and, before anyone fully saw how he had done it, he picked up White, lifted him above his head and threw him to the ground. But White was quickly on his feet again, ready for further battle.

Once again, the audience went wild with more excited applause and tumult.

'Bravo, Fred!'

'Good on you!'

'Well done!'

Then, seventh round. Eighth round.

Both athletes were now verging on total exhaustion. Each was trembling from the strain, barely able to stand on his feet. They grasped each other tightly with their last reserves more out of madness. The audience watched with bated breath. Their entwined bodies were so red and sweaty that steam exuded from them, as if their bodies resembled creatures skinned alive. Time moved slowly and tensely. A dense silence pervaded the tent, with only the heavy panting of the combatants being heard. Not releasing their hold upon each other, they fell to the ground and rolled like moving mounds of flesh to the edge of the arena. Their muscles twisted and twitched in seeming pain and it appeared that one was about to be defeated. The silence deepened.

Suddenly, the Hungarian rose swiftly to his feet, tightly clasped and dragged White by the neck between his arms. White tried desperately to free himself from Kirka's hold, his body turning ashen and his brow perspiring with beads of sweat as thick as oil. But his efforts were futile. He began to tremble and a stream of thick dark blood began to stream from his nose. His legs were about to crumble beneath him as with a deep desperate sigh, he groaned, '*Oy, Mame!*'

Kirka was nonplussed. His opponent had spoken Yiddish, *Mameloshn*. It could not be! Kirka must have heard wrongly. Or had it just been his imagination? But the quiet Yiddish groan continued to resound in his ears. And melted his heart.

For his part, White felt the clasp about his neck loosen. He broke altogether out of its hold and quickly spun around to attack his opponent. But he came to a standstill, when he saw two sad gentle Jewish eyes looking at him.

The audience broke out into another wild tumult,

stomping their feet, whistling and threatening the fighters angrily with waving fists.

'Come on!'

Fight!'

'Get him!'

'Come on!'

The entire tent shook with the uproar. Flaming eyes and raised brandishing fists urged, insisted, demanded that the fight be resumed.

But the two men did not move. They stood facing one another, each of them quietly smiling.

—*Oystralier Leben*, 17 April 1931,
*Collected Writings* (1949)

# IN THEIR OLD AGE

'SHLOYME-ZALMEN, will you put on your Sabbath tie, the silk one!'

'Really Shloyme-Zalmen, you could trim your beard a little!'

'Shloyme-Zalmen, you are not really going to wear those shoes to the children, those dirty, old shoes.'

'Shloyme-Zalmen!'

'Oy, Shloyme-Zalmen!'

Shloyme-Zalmen slowly turned his face away from the mirror where he stood engaged in a battle with his stiff, starched collar. He stared at his wife with his clear eyes that sat cushioned within his flabby, wrinkled flesh and spoke with a calm, forced voice that so belied its tenseness that threatened cracking at any moment.

'Bashe, it is enough already!'

'Oh, I have already insulted his honour, my lord and master, have I?' said Bashe, angrily crossing her arms across her bosom and bouncing her head as if it was suspended on a spring. 'As far as I am concerned, you can go out in your undies, why should do I care? At the same time, shame our children, why not? Are they so nasty to you?'

Shloyme-Zalmen pulled in his lips so tightly that the hair on his moustache stood up angrily. He was controlling his rising anger with all his might. His words passed through the tightly pulled lips, with a whistle.

'Maybe I should also stand on my head for them? Big deal … the children.'

'May my enemies stand on their heads.' She rested her head upon her shoulders and said, 'What have you got against the children? Other people would pray to have such children. What do they take from you?'

'The children, the children,' said Shloyme-Zalmen, turning to face his wife, boiling in rage, the skin cushions around his eyes red and burning. 'Who needs their favours? I can look after myself! I will go out and earn my own living! I will look for a job! I can live without their favours.'

'My God, Shloyme-Zalmen, what are you saying?' Bashe said, frightened, her eyes narrowing.

'It is all your fault, only your fault!' Shloyme-Zalmen remonstrated. 'You wanted to come here to the children! You forced me to go begging for bread, you turned me into a scrounger. Now, I have to sponge off my own children!'

'Shloyme-Zalmen, please stop, I beg of you!'

'This has to end!' he screamed wildly. 'I refuse to go to the children again! I have finished! I will earn my own money! I will go back home! You can stay here with your darling children and beg your living from them. Not I!'

Bashe pursued him around the house with out-stretched

arms and a weeping, moaning tone. 'Shloyme-Zalmen! Shloyme-Zalmen!'

This happened every Thursday morning. Thursday was the day on which Shloyme-Zalmen went to his children to collect his 'wages'. This he found regularly degrading, even though they were his own children and he had to admit that they were good children. They did not forget aging parents in the old country as did many other children. They sent ship passages and they set them up in a decent home and offered them a generous allowance. What more could one ask from children? But if only they had continued to treat them as they had when they had first arrived. The children had been overjoyed to see them, they came often to visit their parents, they placed their allowances on a shelf and often added a little extra and showed a great deal of respect for them.

Unfortunately, the early joy the children had felt upon first seeing their mother and father cooled off in time. Such was the 'way of the world'. The visits became less frequent and more careless with the allowances. Helen, their daughter, was the first to falter, even though she was the richest. Hers was a happy married life with her husband Phillip. He was a spendthrift, a philanderer, he spent his nights in cabarets and made his wife's life miserable. Meanwhile, Helen had so many troubles of her own that she tended to forget her parents' needs. The sons too had problems. They ran big businesses, they were always busy and they had little time for their own wives and children, let alone for their parents. Slowly the situation changed so that Shloyme-Zalmen had to go to his own children to collect his stipends.

From that time on, estrangement evolved in the parents' and children's relationship. Shloyme-Zalmen could not look them in the eyes. He felt as if he were coming to them for charity. He came to believe that they had done this on purpose to shame and degrade him.

Bashe was just a woman, he thought, what did she understand of such matters? She treated his weekly trip to collect the money as a holiday. After all, he was going to visit the children. Every Thursday, she woke up before dawn and began to put out his clothing. Everything had been washed, dry cleaned and pressed as if he were going to a wedding. She did not leave him for a moment while he dressed and fluffed around him, noticing every minute detail. God forbid that there should be a speck or spot on his clothing.

She would repeat continuously, 'You will be embarrassed when you see the children, Shloyme-Zalmen.'

This truly riled him. Not enough that he had to degrade himself before his children and rely on their favours, but now he also needed to spruce himself up for them, to put on a show! Rarely would a Thursday pass without a fight with his Bashe. He would pour all his embitterment upon her. But in the end, it no made no difference. Invariably, she won out with her pleading and her crying, and got her way. He wore the silk tie, his new suede shoes and the stiff high collar and trimmed his beard as she demanded.

Angry and dressed to the hilt, he would then set out with beaming Bashe seeing him to the door, her cheeks glowing and smiling as she said, 'Shloyme-Zalmen, did you take your glasses?'

He gave her a sideways glance. All he needed were the glasses. His wife flattered him, telling him that he looked aristocratic in them, almost like a rabbi – an image that Bashe liked to see him portray. What she did not realise, however, was that every visit to the children was cutting years from his life.

'Why not take the glasses, Shloyme-Zalmen? Let the children have some pleasure.'

'Maybe I should also hang some liver and lung on my nose?' he fumed under his breath set out on his way with heavy, laden steps.

Nonetheless, after a few steps he felt his breast pocket to see if he had his glasses and with a sigh, said, 'Woe is to those who have to depend on their children in their old age.'

He spent a while standing in the street. It was not so easy to go to the children for those few shillings he brought back. He could not decide whom to see first. Should he go to Helen or maybe Dave or Henry? Helen would not run away, she always stayed at home until lunchtime. With the sons it was not so easy. They were busy people whom he had to catch at the right time. Dave, the elder, not only operated a big business but was also deeply involved with communal affairs. His office was always full of people where, as soon as one left, another entered. Sometimes Shloyme-Zalmen had to wait for hours before his son could spare a few minutes for him. He was also forever forgetting the amount that he gave his father.

'How much do I have to give you, *Tate?*'

'Thirty shillings, as always.'

'Thirty shillings, you don't say,' and he would begin to speak in English, taking a handful of small change out of his wallet.

He paid his father the money, but no longer had time for him; his business called for his attention and he quickly farewelled his father.

'Regards to Mum,' he would say. 'Goodbye.'

Things were even more difficult with Henry, his younger son. Henry actually did spend more time talking to his father but he was not all that generous and it was not so easy to get those few shillings out of him. Poor man suffered enough stress before he finally left with his stipend.

Yet he decided to make Henry his first stop. He lived quite a distance away and the journey would allow him the time necessary to prepare mentally for the demeaning task of asking for his allowance.

Henry welcomed his father with a great deal of fuss. He invited him into his office, bade him sit on a luxurious divan and asked him about his mother, whether he had received mail from their family back home, what news he had heard but avoided any mention of money. Shloyme-Zalmen did not feel right about raising the subject in the midst of their conversation but, increasingly, time was running out. Henry was slowly becoming more impatient. He looked at his watch and nervously began to kick the legs of his chair. Shloyme-Zalmen was becoming more distressed. He could see that Henry was in a hurry, he was itching to leave and he would soon rise and dash away. But Shloyme-Zalmen was not prepared to leave without his dues as he had had to do on numerous occasions. He summoned up all his will and with a flushed embarrassed face stammered out, 'Henry, today is Thursday.'

'So it is! Thursday already. How the week flies, fancy that, it's Thursday already.'

'Yes, Thursday, you know, Henry, that we have to prepare for the Sabbath.'

'Hm, Hm,' Henry suddenly became lost in thought, spending time staring into space. He slowly dragged a wallet out of his breast pocket, heaved a deep sigh and brought out spanking new crisp bright ten-shilling notes.

'Just got them out of the bank, yes. Money, may it serve you well!' Sadly shaking his head, he handed the money to his father.

Shloyme-Zalmen breathed a sigh of relief. That was at least one out of the way. With light steps, he set out to see Dave. He took his glasses from his waistcoat pocket, placed them on his nose and immediately felt like a person of some importance. He imagined his forthcoming meeting with Dave. Just let him try to forget how much to give him.

'Do you think I am a fool, Dave?' he rehearsed. 'That's what I will say to him. Do you think I am not up to your tricks? You are a man of the world, you should honour your father, not aggrieve him.'

These thoughts endowed him with courage. He felt stronger, more determined as he bravely boarded the bus to Dave's office. On reaching it, he wanted to meet with Dave as usual, but was approached at the entrance by one of the workers who handed him a closed envelope.

'The boss is very busy, he asked me to give this to you. It is money.'

Shloyme-Zalmen was disturbed as he stepped outside. He had not been expecting this. He was so upset that his glasses slipped from his nose and bounced on their string. He twirled the envelope as he tried to recover from the slight he had encountered. Dave, it appeared, would do anything to avoid seeing his father.

'May it turn out for the best. What do I care anyway?' he tried to comfort himself. 'He just wants avoid seeing me.'

With that, he set out for Helen's, even though, hurt and rejected as never before by Dave, he lost the will to visit Helen. Who knew how she would be feeling today? She was always depressed, forever wore a tragic face, it was impossible to talk to her. Her Phillip was destroying her life. He, her father, understood her and never had the heart to discuss money with her. If she herself remembered, then everything was good and if not, then … it was lost. More than once had he left her empty-handed.

On contemplating the matter further, he reasoned that he really could get by that week with the amount that Henry and Dave had given him, hence considered that Helen might not feel like dealing with his own troubles today.

Alas, he has a sister back home, Chanele, who showered him with letters repeatedly reminding him that he should not forget her own great need. She was a widow with a brood of children. Whom should she ask for help if not her brother in the golden land? If only she knew how much heartache and resentment he spent in getting every penny out of his children! But what choice did have? He could not allow her children to simply expire from hunger.

Yes, what choice did he have?

He had to get money from Helen today to send to his sister. He could not be too proud and wait until Helen herself remembered the money. He had cause for shame. After all, she was well aware of his reasons for his weekly Thursday visits. Why should he be hindered by false pride in his old age? Chanele was more important to him than pride.

As soon as he stepped into Helen's, however, his resolve all but disappeared. She was particularly distressed, with her face distorted from pain and her eyes shimmering from withheld tears.

'I will not get anything today,' passed immediately through his mind.

Father and daughter did not utter a word for some time. Helen kept avoiding looking directly at her father. Her appearance spoke for itself. For his part, Shloyme-Zalmen let his gaze wonder over the opulent and luxurious surrounds. Several times he was about to speak until finally he did so. He moved his lips a few times, as if he wanted to say something, then finally he spoke out with a heavy, worried tone. 'You have regards from you Aunt Chana I received a letter from her.'

'From Aunt Chana,' she replied absentmindedly. 'How is she?'

'Surely you can imagine. How can it be for a widow with such tiny children.' Shloyme-Zalmen sighed forlornly, bolstered by some hope and expectation. Maybe she will give something? he dared to think. He sat on his chair, stroked his beard and placed his glasses on his nose.

'You should read her letters, Helen, they could move a stone to tears.'

'Everyone has his own package of troubles, believe me, *Tate*!' Helen interrupted with a show of impatience as her face of became more inflamed.

'Woe is me, she won't give a cent!' Shloyme-Zalmen now thought, becoming more distraught, upon which he drew Chanele's last letter from his pocket. 'Still, it will not hurt you to hear what your aunt wrote. She and her children are in such desperate need.'

'I know, I know!' She fell silent and lost in thoughts as, slowly, she approached her desk and pulled out her handbag from a drawer.

'She is giving money, she is going to give!' Shloyme-Zalmen recovered heart, his glasses beginning to shine. He held his breath as he followed Helen's every movement. She seated herself at the table, took out a letter from a scented pink envelope and handed it to Shloyme-Zalmen.

'*Tate*, better you should take this letter to read. My Phillip now receives love letters at home.' She bit her lip and her whole face contorted. Her eyes were enraged, her breath thick and fast, her chin quivering once, then again and again, suddenly throwing her face upon the table in heart-wrenching sobbing.

'Helen, what is the matter?'

Shloyme-Zalmen became distressed, raising his fingers into the air.

'*Tate*, my life is such a tragedy. I can't stand Phillip any longer. I have nothing to live for!' Helen continued to sob violently.

'Quiet, my daughter, there, there, my child!'

Shloyme-Zalmen put his hand on her head and stroked her with fatherly tenderness and pity. With the other hand, he stroked his beard with worry as his mind replayed its other thoughts.

*All is lost, she will give nothing! Not a penny! All is lost!*

—*Australian Jewish News*, *Literary Supplement*
no. 2, March 1938,
*Dertzeilungen* (1939)

# THE LAST MINYAN

## 1

REVEREND FELDMAN, the *shammes* of the Netzah Israel Synagogue, had bad news for Rabbi Cohen: the minyan, the ten men whom they had hired to pray at the synagogue, were demanding a pay increase; they were insisting on it with gross audacity and arrogance. They had asked him to inform the rabbi that they would no longer attend services until they were awarded so much and so much and not a penny less. They also wanted morning prayers to be held one hour later since they were elderly men who had difficulty being on time so early every morning at the services.

The rabbi listened to the *shammes*, but said nothing in reply. He sat silently at the writing desk in his cold, high-domed office, wrapped in a thick bulky black coat, his rabbinic top hat pushed down on his forehead. The day was cold and wet. The stained glass on the tall curved windows appeared wrinkled as the raindrops fell in their angular zigzag pattern. The smeared, smudged light was reflected on the rabbi's face that contorted into a crooked smile as he

243

became lost in thought while his fingers twirled one end of his thick grey moustache.

The *shammes* who had brought the news was a much-wrinkled old man, with a matted beard that looked as if formed from tufts of wool. He wore an old beaten-up hat with a dusty grey brim, perched above his two bulging ears. He stood a respectable distance from the rabbi's desk, nervously blinking. He could tell from the rabbi's smile and his unresponsiveness that they would not reach any early agreement. He wanted to relieve the tension before departing so, apologetically he said, 'It's no use, Rabbi, the minyan will not come.'

The rabbi's face hardened.

'Well then, Feldman, there is nothing to be done.'

Whenever he spoke to Feldman or any of the other 'foreigners', he employed a hybrid mixture of German and English. As an Oxford graduate, he zealously guarded his highly educated Oxford English and only honoured the wealthiest and most respected of his congregants with his more refined linguistic skills.

The *shammes* spread out this arms and tilted his head pleasantly to a side. 'All right, Rabbi,' was all he said, disconsolately shaking his head.

Silence fell once more. The raindrops sounded on the stained-glass windows as the rabbi seemed to withdraw deeper into his coat. He contracted and relaxed his eyebrows as he shook his head.

'There is nothing to be done, Feldman,' he repeated.

The *shammes* nervously scratched his beard, his floppy lips fallen open like those of a fish.

'How will this end?' he ventured to ask. 'They are poor old men. They do not want the minyan to end.'

'Oh, God!' said the rabbi impatiently. 'I will not put up with this, this strike. And it is a strike, a strike in a *shul*, which is intolerable!'

'What can we do then? We need them! After all, the *shul* must have a minyan!'

'I will not tolerate a strike! We will just have to close the *shul*, that's all!'

The *shammes*' face grimaced with alarm and fear.

'Close the *shul*?'

The rabbi banged a fist on his desk, turning his face to avoid looking at the *shammes*.

'Yes! We will have to close the *shul*!'

The *shammes* stood for a moment more, scrutinising the rabbi, then with a shrug of his shoulders, he dug his hands into his pockets and edged towards the door.

The rabbi absent-mindedly began rubbing his thick protruding wrinkled chin and threw an agitated look at the departing *shammes*. The *shammes* caught sight of the glance and responded to it as though he had been expecting it.

'Feldman,' the rabbi called him back. Uncertainly, he rose from his chair and began pacing back and forth, then approached Feldman and grasped him by the lapels.

'Maybe we can still find a way of saving the minyan. After all, we are all Jews, so we should try to work something out together. Try to persuade them. Inform them that the *shul* is poor, there is no money in our coffers. Feldman, you do understand, don't you?' He spoke out in his Oxford English to show Feldman how he was relying on him, entrusting him with serious responsibility.

'Certainly, Rabbi, certainly!' replied the *shammes* cheerfully, relieved that the tension had broken.

'But I have not changed my position. Punctuality is of prime importance!'

Sternness and anger returned to the rabbi's mien and he returned to his native German as he proceeded to pace about restlessly, no more acknowledging the presence of the *shammes*, who was still smiling with relief.

But, with several coughs, he tried to draw back the rabbi's attention, there being something else that he wished to say. However, the rabbi now ignored him whereupon, sighing and saying to himself, 'I just told him how things stood, but he is too obstinate to tolerate their demands,' he left the rabbi's office.

Rabbi Cohen was now alone. He was a tall, bony old man with a hard square face covered by a thin layer of fine skin verging on a pale shade of yellow, wholly different from his thick white eyebrows and moustache. His moist blue eyes possessed a sharp birdlike look. Even after the *shammes* had left, he continued his pacing with long steps. His shoulders were hunched and rounded. Taking out his old-fashioned monogrammed watch from his bag, he looked at the time and stopped moving. He was already late. It was a quarter past eleven, while the now-rusted sign outside his office stated clearly that his consulting hours were from ten to twelve every day.

Quickly throwing off his overcoat, he removed his top hat and replaced it with a silk skullcap towards the back of his head. He stepped towards his bookcase, searched through its diverse volumes and removed a large linen-bound *Gemarah*. He sat down at his desk and opened the book, placing his watch by his side that sounded a prominent tick-tock throughout his office.

This had been rabbi Cohen's established routine from his first day as rabbi of the Netzah Israel Synagogue for more than forty years. He was always punctilious about his consulting hours, sitting out the established two hours at his desk with his watch beside him, knowing well that no one would come, except for the *shammes* Feldman when he needed to speak with him.

## 2

Once, things had been different. Rabbi Cohen was not the sort of man who dwelt on the past. However, on occasions when he sat alone in his quiet office, he allowed his mind to wander back in time. To the time, for instance, when he had completed his rabbinical studies at the rabbinic seminary after having acquired his newly completed Oxford degree; or his long journey to Australia to fill the position of rabbi in the gold town of Wattle Hill at a time when there was still no train to the town and he had to travel with difficulty by post-wagon through wild bushland between spiky grasses, bent and wizened eucalyptus with leaves the colour of rusted iron. It had been a hot and dusty day. The sky had extended incredibly high, its blueness so fine and tinged with red as if it, too, suffered from the dryness and the heat. Four sleepy horses had slowly pulled the old battered wagon that squeaked loudly and churned up dust storms around it.

The wagon had been packed. There had been a cluster of gold-diggers travelling with him. They had been sitting there, hot, sweaty and weatherworn. Their shirts were open, their sleeves rolled up. The wagon was loudly filled with their talk, their laughter, their shouting to make themselves heard. They smoked and drank beer from their only cup, themselves smelling of sweat and spilled beer. The driver, his face weather-beaten by the ravages of sun, wind and storm, carried a gun and took happy part in all of the gold-diggers' revelries, sharing his own jokes with them, although he did at times request some order, pleading, 'Hey, more quiet, you guys! Getting to Wattle Hill is no child's play. This area is teeming with bandits, you can take my word for it.'

'Haa, haa,' laughed a broad-shouldered, pockmarked man with an extinguished pockmarked cigarette dangling from a corner of his mouth. 'What can they take from us? Our bags are empty. We will only get to stuff them with gold once we're in Wattle Hill.'

Another, a small man with a tapering, widely freckled face, looked about him with authoritativeness and said, 'It's told that bandits actually bring luck. If you confront a bandit, afterwards you go on to make your fortune. I heard of one gold-digger called Jim Lorry who was attacked by them. They stripped him down to his singlet. A few days later, he found a nugget that weighed eight pounds!'

'I still think we should move on with the beer,' intervened a rotund man in a duck-like tone. He spoke in earnest but, with a wink, added, 'Any bandit would be happy to get his hands on a beer on a day like today.'

The sticky glass was passed around several times more. The driver, too, had his share. With froth clinging to his lips, he declared, 'May you all make a fortune at Wattle Hill!'

'I know only too well what you will find at Wattle Hill,' piped up an old-timer with a yellow moustache extending over his mouth. He banged on his chest and said, 'I have seen it all. I was in Ballarat during its heyday of gold. Now that was really something! You could sweep the gold from the streets. They brought some actress down from one of the big theatres and, boy, was she a dish! When she started singing and dancing, the audiences went wild. They took off her shoes and filled them with gold. And they then said that if she also took off her clothes, the gold would be hers, haa haa! And you know what? She did, the trollop, but she also held a gun in each hand, threatening to shoot anyone who dared to touch her.'

'Shame on you!' protested the freckled man, 'an old man like you telling such stories before one of God's people.'

He pointed at him, at Rabbi Cohen, the rabbi recalled.

The team broke into united laughter. The old man winked, looked at him and went on to jest, 'It's a good sign if God's people are already also on their way to Wattle Hill.

I can't say I ever saw one in Ballarat before. No, I'm sure!'

Rabbi Cohen retreated even further into his already tight corner. He raised his book higher before his face, using it as a *mekhitse* to separate himself from them.

The wagon finally arrived at Wattle Hill at dawn. Lights were sill shining in some of the pubs and gambling houses. Already, the din of morning activity could be heard in the streets. A Syrian with a shiny curly moustache stood proudly next to a camel laden with water bags, crying out, 'River water! Just arrived! Fresh and clear! Real river water!' Groups of gold-diggers with wild gleams in their eyes wandered around the dusty streets. Upon a sudden billowing of wind gusts, cloth tents were blown down. The houses that the rabbi saw, haphazardly knocked together from wood and iron, were arrayed at random. People were already crowding the few stores while street traders with leather pouches wound about their bellies strode around loudly peddling their assorted wares.

'Digging irons! Boots! Gold-pans! Spades!'

A cluster of Jews surrounded Rabbi Cohen the moment he stepped down from the wagon. Hands reached out to greet him from all sides.

'*Sholem aleykhem*! *Sholem aleykhem*!' they greeted him.

A short, rotund man with a nose that resembled a cucumber, and a patch over one eye, took Rabbi Cohen's arm and took control over the people.

'Hey! What's the matter? Move over a little! Make way for the rabbi!'

A lean man with a plush beard but mild eyes approached

the rabbi cordially with an extended hand.

'Welcome, Rabbi! My name is Feldman, Reverend Feldman.'

Reverend Feldman, accompanied by others, led the rabbi to a large dark weatherboard house. A long unpolished table occupied the centre of the room with shelves around the walls filled with assorted goods. Between two dusty windows on the eastern wall stood the *Aron Kodesh*, the Ark that housed the *Sifrei Torah*, a simple cupboard covered by a curtain of tartan fabric.

'This is our synagogue,' said Feldman proudly, swinging an arm about the room.

He then pointed towards a short tubby man in the retinue.

'Mr Smith, our President, donated his house to our *shul*.

The highlighted man who basked with pride, his fingers intertwined over his belly, modestly but clearly joyous at the mention of his name, said, 'It's all right, all right. Each man does what he can.'

In his stern way, Rabbi Cohen looked about the ill-lit synagogue that was steeped in the odours of raw wood and leather. He alighted too upon the other men who had joined him and Feldman, huddled together out of his way, but not removing their eyes from him for a moment. Dressed in gold-diggers' clothes, heavy high-heeled boots and with scarves about their necks, they were deeply tanned; they worried and whispered secretively amongst themselves.

'So,' Rabbi Cohen said, nodding, 'So, this is the *shul*. Ah, well, it's not important.'

Mr Smith, with a grand gesture, placed a tray with beer and glasses on the table. The people suddenly came alive, keenly approaching the table and reaching out to the beer.

'One minute, fellows, no grabbing! Show some respect for the rabbi!' called out their host. He took up a glass and filled it until the foam had begun to pour over its edge. Reverend Feldman, in turn, took the glass and transferred it to a small tray customarily reserved for the Kiddush cup and, beginning to rock back and forward as if in prayer, intoned 'In the name all the Jews of this town ...'

'Hear, hear!' interrupted Mr Smith immediately, raising his own glass high, upon which, waving it around, he broke into a chorus: 'For he's a jolly good fellow ...!'

'It's unnecessary! Unnecessary!' The rabbi impatiently waved a hand. 'The first thing we will do is pray together. Serving God always comes first.'

The men looked at one another in surprise as they began to slowly edge away from the table.

'It's all right, boys! We will pray!' called out Mr Smith in his most welcoming voice as Reverend Feldman struck the table with the flat of a hand to draw them together.

'Now, quiet! Quiet! We are all going to pray!'

The gathering reluctantly moved back, mumbling to themselves as they kept their eyes on the rabbi, draped in the *talith* that Reverend Feldman had provided.

Thus was normal procedure established from the outset. Rabbi Cohen knew what he was up against. He asked that all goods be removed from the *shul* shelves; they took out the unpolished table; he brought in a decent *Aron Kodesh*

Original illustration for 'The Last Minyan' by Noel Counihan

and a dais. Every morning, he and Reverend Feldman would go out to gather a minyan. They forcefully dragged the men from the streets and the pub into the *shul* where Rabbi Cohen held long and important sermons every *Shabbes* in his immaculate Oxford English. After prayers, he would stand at the door and personally shake the hand of every congregant, wishing them a good *Shabbes* and sending them off with God's blessing. He began keeping a book in which he detailed the name of every Jew in town. He made a large sign in both English and Hebrew that he hung on the outside wall, identifying the Synagogue Netzah Israel of Wattle Hill.

Reverend Feldman was overjoyed by the way Rabbi Cohen conducted himself. He followed him like a shadow, picked up every word, every look, every gesture. He would then run with the details to the half-blind Mr Smith.

'Well, then, what do you think of our rabbi? He wants to make a Jewish society of us all,' he said with wonder. 'He will be calling a meeting of the congregation to set up an appeal.'

'A Jewish society? A congregation? Wattle Hill is really turning into something, isn't it, Reverend Feldman?' said Smith, keenly rubbing his cucumber nose and contentedly shaking his head.

Soon after, Rabbi Cohen indeed summoned a meeting of the congregation. He called on all Jews to register in his book. The proud Mr Smith, dressed in his holiday best, wearing a new hat in a most outlandish light brown colour, sat on the platform holding a bell. He looked around the room, calling all the people in his irritating grating voice. 'Order, please! You are now at a meeting, friends. The rabbi wishes to address you, please maintain silence!'

The rabbi made a long and heated speech. He called them 'children of lsrael' and 'my respected brothers'. He made his words ring with festive joy. He itemised his plans for the 'Jewish Society' from a long sheet of notes. The first item was to provide the community with a proper synagogue.

'Hear! Hear!' cried out the audience, delighting in the fact that the rabbi referred to them as 'my highly respected brothers'.

'Order, order! We must have silence!' called out Smith, vigorously ringing his bell while constantly adjusting the patch over his blind eye. 'Out with that pound, mates! Give it here, if you want a synagogue! This is my donation, pure gold!' he said, throwing a leather pouch on the table, which landed with a loud thud.

'Lord above, a contribution of pure gold from the President, Mr Smith!' exclaimed Reverend Feldman in a cantorial tone. The rabbi carefully raised the bag with his fingertips, weighed it in the palm of his hand, a smile spreading over his lips.

Mr Smith became obsessed with the notion of a synagogue. Dressed in his new hat, he and Reverend Feldman spent the ensuing days and nights marching through the pubs pursuing the Jews. They collected money, for which he wrote the receipts with the stub of a pencil in his chubby fingers. Every evening, he would then bring it to Rabbi Cohen.

The rabbi himself never accepted it into his hand, gesturing instead that it should be left on the table while saying, 'Yes, the money, we must call another meeting.'

Before the community was wholly aware, a new synagogue stood on Wattle Hill's main street, its most favoured street that boasted of the finest residences with immaculate porches and high balconies. The rabbi had instructed that the synagogue be built along the lines of the wealthy English temples with their towering domes and high cornices over their circular stain-glassed windows. He ordered *Sifrei Torah* to be brought from the holy city of Tsfat; he furnished the synagogue with fine furniture carved from imported wood, elaborate exquisite chandeliers and menorahs, and decorated velvet drapes and curtains.

The Jews were proud of their new synagogue, leading them to take enhanced pride in themselves. Abandoning their former thick woollen shirts and heavy boots, they came to *shul* looking very respectable in high hats, high collars and ties. Mr Smith took the patch off his blind eye and took to wearing glasses with a darkened lens. He ceased his tendency to shout and began to speak in a quieter, more refined tone and clearer enunciation, similar to that of the rabbi.

'Well, we now have one fine *shul* indeed, thank God,' he said.

Reverend Feldman was no longer compelled to run in pursuit of a minyan. The *shul* was filled for every service, even on weekdays. But even this was not sufficient for the rabbi. He brought in a number of poor old men from

Melbourne, hiring them so that the synagogue would have a salaried reliable minyan as was customary in the larger British synagogues.

This was the way that the rabbi established the community that he ruled over with a firm hand. Apart from the Jewish Society, he founded other organisations: a charity fund, a sick-visiting society and a burial society. The *shul* buzzed with constant activity. Reverend Feldman's days were filled with meeting communal needs; he was forever running errands and his sheepish eyes shone with happiness. He now also dressed in a manner befitting a reverend with an elegant black jacket and a white shirt with a stiff collar closed at the back. He shaved off his plush beard, leaving only a little goatee on his chin that he kept twirling between his fingers.

However, he did not feel altogether comfortable, despite all that activity, which only increased when Harry Goldstone arrived.

Harry Goldstone, a young man from Liverpool, organised *shul* dances and parties. He was short and undistinguished in appearance with a red face that looked as if he had rubbed too hard with a soapy brush. He had watery eyes with thinning eyebrows that gave him a bare, startled appearance like a fish. As if to compensate, he had the gift of the gab that immediately made him a man of importance in the *shul*'s affairs. He became involved in every aspect of community work and had something to say on everything. The rabbi esteemed him highly, would walk with him arm in arm and greatly appreciated Goldstone's social functions because not only had they stopped their Jews from frequenting the pubs and gambling houses but also created profits for the *shul*.

Reverend Feldman did not much like the young man from Liverpool. He could not stand his large eyes and light brisk step that made him look as if he were dancing. The matter that disturbed him most, however, was the rabbi's exaggerated regard for him, which made the man seem an important personage.

'What's the big deal about him, anyway?' Feldman would at times confide in Mr Smith. 'We managed to build the *shul* without his wonderful dance. If you ask me, he is just a bluffer, full of hot air!'

Smith would rub his nose, reduced to pensive thought while peering over his tinted glasses, then would bellow hoarsely, 'It's all right, Reverend Feldman!' Smith appeased him. 'Such is the way of the world.'

Reverend Feldman's intuition had been right. Goldstone was involved with the synagogue only as long as it remained a hive of activity. As long as there was plenty of gold to be mined, the Jews who did substantial business with the gold-diggers were content to donate some of their profits to the *shul*. Goldstone was always hanging around, involved in communal activities, rubbing shoulders with the rabbi.

But then a new era dawned. In time, less gold was to be found, monetary returns tightened and the people found it harder to eke out a livelihood. The Jews, too, had reason to complain about the more difficult times and stopped donating as generously as they had been accustomed. It was then that Goldstone disappeared from the *shul*, and Reverend Feldman patted his belly with no mean satisfaction.

'I can always recognise such types!' he prided himself. 'We won't be seeing hide or hair of that Liverpudlian bluffer now that the coffers are empty!'

Not only Goldstone, but many other Jews also began to turn away from the *shul*. Their financial situation deteriorated as the gold fever became extinguished and Wattle Hill died. Those folk who had arrived in wagons, venturing through dangerous terrains, began leaving to seek fortunes in more-promising greener pastures, while the streets that had but a short time before been filled with hubbub and excitement were now reduced to silence as desolation descended upon them. On the rare occasion when one did see a remaining gold-digger, he would walk with short cautious steps, peering into every shop, bargaining for the best price he could still get for the few small fragments of gold that he had kept rolled up in dirty old rags stuck deep in his breast pocket.

'Wattle Hill has seen its day,' the Jews told each other, shrugging their shoulders. 'The pot of gold that lay at the end of the rainbow has emptied!'

Quietly, they packed their belongings, told no one where they were going and vanished as if they had fled from the plague, not even bothering to tell each other where they were going.

Dim-sighted Mr Smith spent most of his days walking around the town, watching it die. Ever more shops were closing, their windows boarded up and heavy locks hanging from the doors. It made him feel his age more acutely. His rotund belly drooped further like a stuffed bag. His face had its own loose bags of flesh while his glasses sat askew on his bulbous sagging nose.

Facing Reverend Feldman with his one good eye, bloodshot from weariness and with a dark patch of red from a burst blood vessel spreading over its whiteness, he said disconsolately, 'What has gotten into everyone? Where are they running? But what's it to me? Let them go. I'm not moving. I've had enough wandering in my life, believe me!'

But in the end, he, too, left. One morning after prayers, he knocked gingerly on Rabbi Cohen's office door and entered. The rabbi greeted him with a tight-lipped smile, he shut the book he had been studying, straightened the skullcap on his head and sighed.

Smith sat down tentatively on the edge of a chair, spent an inordinately long time wiping his hands on his knees and finally revealed his reason for coming in a thick, strained voice: 'Rabbi,' he said, 'I have come to say goodbye! My children say there is nothing here for them. They want to leave, they insist that I join them …'

'Certainly, Mr Smith, a family should remain together. So, it is right that you go with them,' replied the rabbi genially.

'I trust that you will understand how hard it is for me to leave this place. I have spent half my life here in Wattle

Hill. I know its every tree, every stone ... But what I find hardest is leaving the *shul*. Rabbi! Everyone is leaving. There is hardly a Jew left in the town. How will it end?' His voice quivered, threatening to break into sobs.

The rabbi knitted his brows and looked at Smith as if from a distance. He cleared his throat with a dry cough, his neck swelling. 'You need not worry about the *shul*. It will be well looked after, set your mind at rest, Mr Smith.'

The rabbi sat back stiffly in his chair and reopened his book.

The *shul* was becoming progressively emptier and quieter. There was scarcely anyone left who needed communal attention and only infrequently did anyone wander in, even for a *Shabbes* service or to recite *Kaddish* for a deceased relative. More commonly, the rabbi prayed with his hired minyan.

He was alone day after day in his office, gloomily tearing off each page from the day calendar and glancing at times towards Reverend Feldman who roamed around the *shul* with dragging tired feet and short-sightedness, his shiny sweat-stained cloak drooping loosely from his hunched and rounded shoulders, himself of late given to vague mumbling into his beard, which had become particularly more wool-like over his sunken cheeks. The rabbi would be stirred to anger just by looking at him, pulling at his moustache and murmuring irately in German, '*So was! Gott in Himmel!*'

Soon, there was almost no one left from the old community. The street on which the *shul* stood had become quiet, lined by the one-time splendid houses with their old-fashioned towers and balconies between the wild palms, but now abandoned. The sounds that had once emanated from them had ceased, their doors and windows were boarded up and the street itself was dusty, dirty and gloomy like a cemetery, the *shul* itself with its tower and domes in their midst. The *shul*'s interior seemed to peer out through its high stained-glass windows like a man with dark glasses scanning the high crooked noses that lay outside.

The Jews who had been hired to pray, meanwhile, straggled slowly and weakly into the *shul* every morning and evening as if they had come from some distant place. Rabbi Cohen marched stiffly in the street in his long, black rabbinic coat buttoned to the top, with his rabbinic top hat pushed down severely to the rims of his eyes.

His steps were measured and determined, his gaze, hard and glazed, firmly fixed ahead.

### 3

Twelve o'clock had come and gone but the rabbi remained seated at the desk, his head drooped over his chest. The clock sounded out each second with its regular tick-tock. The rain had stopped and the wintry afternoon sun's damp-laden rays fell upon his office walls in muted yellow sloping lines.

The rabbi rarely remained after his ten-to-twelve consulting hours. During all his years of administering the *shul*, he was most exacting in the schedule he observed. On this day, he felt compelled to stay, holding back from leaving at his accustomed time. The *Gemarah* lay open before him, but his thoughts were not with his learning. He was thinking about the *shul*, about the years gone by and about the men who had made up the minyan but who were now prepared to desert it on account of such a small inconsequential issue as an increase in their wages. He took out a thin ledger engraved with a golden Star of David from a desk drawer. It was a ledger of the *shul*'s accounts whose stiff white pages he turned slowly as he examined the figures with a despondent shaking of his head.

The *shul* truly did not possess the means to pay the increase demanded by the minyan. He would need to put aside some of his own earnings and live more frugally. Maybe God would help, maybe Feldman would succeed in persuading them to keep accepting their present wages. He would try to talk to them himself after the following day's prayer service. If either he or Feldman proved successful, well and good; if not, he was personally prepared to carry the extra cost. He could not allow his *shul* to be shamed on account of money.

He sighed deeply. He was relieved that he had overcome the anger he had felt against the minyan. He remembered the holy words, 'Who is mighty? He who has overcome his inclination.'

He rose from his seat and put on his coat and top hat, yet he could not bring himself to leave. Aimlessly, he roamed about his office, tidying his bookshelves, making order of his books, straightening the writing materials on his desk and clearing a cobweb from the wall. He then walked through a narrow doorway screened by a dark velvet curtain that led directly into the *shul*. He opened the door slowly and was accosted by a profound silence. The stained-glass windows dispersed a multitude of colours across the solid dark wood benches that delicately melded with the glow of the brass edging around the dais. A wide passage led to the *Aron Kodesh* covered by red velvet, the scrolls within steeped in a dim incandescence of twilight. The high ceilings, on the other hand, were so dark that the *Ner Tamid*, the Eternal Light, had no effect in according them brightness.

The rabbi stood there, his shoulders hunched as he inhaled the air in that darkness, his mind weighed down by the heaviness oft experienced after a prolonged exhausted sleep.

The minyan arrived at the *shul* the next morning to hear the rabbi's response to their demands. They stood huddled together by the door, mumbling under their breaths in their tired aged voices and blowing their noses, their tense faces both winking and gesturing to each other. They usually sat right in the front row, but on this day they stood stubbornly near the exit, refusing to move a jot nearer despite Reverend Feldman's appeals to come close.

'Come in, dear friends! Why are you clinging so far back like strangers?'

He wore a broad black rabbinic robe that reached to his knees. In addition, he wore a shabby worn-out eight-cornered *spodik*, commonly a tall fur hat but, in his case, made of velvet. He was disturbed by their resistance and kept moving restlessly here and there, disconsolately tugging at his beard as he looked at the minyan. He had already spent the entire morning arguing with them, ranging from gentleness to anger. And now, they refused both to budge from their stand by the door and their stand on their original monetary demand.

'So, what is your response to our raise?' they challenged Rabbi Cohen.

Rabbi Cohen's was no less forceful. 'You will become a laughing-stock over the matter! Jews of your age making such demands! It does not become you. How dare you get angry and make such demands on the *shul*? What has gotten into you?'

'Say what you like, but no raise for us, no prayers from us!' called out one man whose vehemence may have stemmed from an associated toothache.

An older man with a tiny head retracted between his shoulders glanced sideways at Reverend Feldman and fell to laughing in a thin voice, his prominent turned-out lips making Feldman in turn think of the spout of a kettle.

'I think, hee, hee, you wasted your time getting dressed up in your *spodik*, Mr Feldman! There will not be a minyan today, oh, no!'

'Will you have a good a reason then to celebrate if there is no minyan, Reb Boruch?' the reverend said severely as he turned to him. 'You should be ashamed of yourself, your behaviour is outrageous!'

'Now, now, Mr Reverend, don't be rude or we will leave right away and this entire business will be finished!' said a small, shrivelled man with a squeaky voice, a Sam Sunshine who, because of his feminine voice, was nicknamed Sonche.

He was the minyan's spokesman and smoked imported cigarettes from a shiny tin that had a naked woman engraved on its lid. He continuously chewed strong mint sweets. even during prayers. He wore light-coloured tight-fitting clothes of a past fashion that did little to hide the sharp angularity of his skinny body. His green eyes had a curious look about them that seemed poised, about to leap out and seize others by the hand and call them thieves. The other men feared him, listened to all that he said, enjoyed his cigarettes and mint sweets and wanted to stay on his good side. They exchanged tales about him behind his back, believing that he had been a criminal and had escaped from Siberia.

'You have to be careful of that Sonche! You would not want to cross him! Your life would not be worth living!'

The reverend was infuriated by Sonche's words. He ran up to the men with his arms outstretched, the sleeves of his robe billowing out like sails.

He appealed to the others. 'It is easy for Sonche to talk, what does it matter to him, he could not care less whether we do or don't have a *shul*! You will look like fools if you let yourselves be led around the nose by the likes of him.'

'Hee, hee,' Sonche burst out laughing with a squeal. 'Should we instead be led by the rabbi who would want us to pray for free?'

Zelig Hirsh butted in, saying, 'Mr Sunshine is right! What do we get for our praying anyway? We don't get enough to live on and not enough to die.'

This Zelig Hirsh was seen as a strange man. His eyes were close to his nose like an owl's; the rabbi had found him in an old age home in Sydney to replace a former member of the minyan who had passed away. Even though he had already served the minyan for several years, the others had never fully accepted him, regarding him always as a stranger. They disliked and made fun of him for he prayed sincerely, never omitted any of the prayers and extended his Amens and *Boruch Shemos*.

He was often the target of their grumbling, as shown again on this occasion. 'Who are you to talk? You are afraid to cheat the rabbi of one word!' they grumbled when he took his time praying and swaying to the *Shmoneh Esrei*.

'You too, Mr Zelig?' Reverend Feldman gazed at him disappointedly. 'Is this why we brought you from Sydney? My friends, what do you hope to achieve from this? Will you deem it a victory if we close the *shul*? Will you then leave, expecting to earn some great fortune elsewhere? Go into business? Somehow I doubt it! Listen to me, my friends, leave things well alone! The *shul* has no money, the rabbi is denying himself needs of his own, even food, to keep you. Do you want to be responsible for shaming this holy place, God forbid!'

'So, we should be the shamed? Be the rabbi's puppets? Let him realise that we also have a say in what happens!' protested Meyer Segal, a solid man with a square chiselled face and drooping eyelids, who was dressed in cheap, ragged clothes.

'If he wants us, he can come to us! Talk to us like equals and not hold himself so high and mighty, isn't that right, men?'

'Yes! Absolutely!' cried out the hard gravelly voice of a certain Jimmy, a strongly-built man with a wooden hand who depended upon the Salvation Army for his meals and was by some his colleagues almost considered to be Christian.

'Yes!' he repeated. 'What is the matter with him? Why does he not come to us?'

The reverend shook his head in disbelief. 'Even Jimmy seems to think that the *shul* owes him a living! I should like to know if he is as bossy at the Salvation Army as he is here! I bet he kisses their cross, just to get some of their *treyf* food. One is led to wonder whether we should include someone like him in a minyan. We really pay him for nothing.'

'For the money paid here, who knows?' said Reb Boruch.

'Money, money, all you think about is money,' said Feldman heatedly. 'The time has come that you should be worrying more about what you will be taking with you into the next world, Reb Boruch!'

'For the present, I am still here.' The old man laughed mockingly, his face displaying all his crinkles. 'When I reach the age of a hundred-and-twenty and am no longer among the living, then will I come to the *shul* again and pray for all the dead and, I promise, will not charge a penny!'

'Not for me!' responded Segal, raising his droopy eyelids. 'When I will pray after my death, I will do so back home in my old *shul* in Stashev!'

'For sure! Of course!' The members of the minyan became suddenly animated as one. 'Yes! After our deaths, pray at home amongst our own people! Where else? And from there, we will laugh at Rabbi Cohen and his *shul* and at this place.'

A frightened shiver rocked Reverend Feldman. In an instant glance, he took in the entire *shul*. 'Enough of this kind of talk! So now we are talking about the dead, even though it might be easier to deal with the dead than it is with you.'

'And how are we different from the dead?' sighed Zelig Hirsh with a tragic air as he turned his owlish eyes towards the reverend. 'Do you believe that we are truly amongst the living?'

The assemblage suddenly fell silent.

The rabbi had entered from his office into the *shul*. He was dressed like the *shammes*, except for a broader, wider robe and a higher *spodik* of silk with an insignia at its summit. In addition, he wore a small *talles* over his shoulders.

Upon entering, he scanned the front rows where the minyan usually sat and stopped still. Looking around the *shul*, his gaze paused briefly upon the cluster of people who stood by the door. His cheeks and jaws stiffened.

With his customary measured steps, he ascended the dais, drew his *talles* more firmly about him and began to leaf through his large cantorial prayer book lettered in gold. A deep lull hung over the *shul* and the rabbi began to pray, his voice echoing in the stillness. The minyan eased closer to the door. The rabbi's words froze on his lips; his entire body tensed in its entirety; his fingers, white, stiff and splayed reached out from his robe.

Meanwhile, Reverend Feldman was quietly pleading

with the minyan, his face so contorted by distress and pain that he seemed about to collapse into an outburst of tears.

The minyan men remained stubbornly quiet. Sonche stepped forward, his arms outstretched, and looked angrily about him. The others kept crawling back until they were almost standing in the doorway. Zelig became confused and agitated; he seemed to double over and began to slowly inch forward.

'I am going to pray! They will get me into trouble with the old age home! Oh dear, what will become of me?' he mumbled in a distraught voice.

Sonche restrained him, gave him a murderous glance and held him painfully back. He almost stopped breathing from the pain, and nervously retreated.

The rabbi resumed his prayers. His voice rose, fell and fluttered. Only the reverend joined him. In an agitated tone, he alone recited the amens to each prayer that made the others' silence all the more profound. The rabbi placed his hands heavily on the dais and dropped his head. He sang in distress with his fullest strength that was nonetheless so weak that his voice was lost in both the loftiest and deepest corners of the *shul*.

He had reached the *Shmoneh Esrei*. He quivered, took a step back and stopped still and stiff with his head thrown back. The folds of his robe hung down straight as if it were chiselled from black stone. The minyan began to fidget uncomfortably and agitatedly whispered to each other.

The rabbi suddenly turned to face them. His eyebrows and moustache were disordered, his eyes bloodshot. 'Out of here!' he shouted. 'Everybody get out!' He shook, raised his arm and fell to the floor.

'*Gevalt, Yidn!*' cried out Reverend Feldman, hurrying towards the rabbi. 'What have you done? You have killed him!'

## 4

A few days passed. Services were no longer held at the *shul*, although Rabbi Cohen still arrived each day at his usual time. They were wet and wintry days. Winds swept through the streets, blowing sheets of rain into people's faces and tearing at the boarded-up doors and windows of the empty houses. The rabbi walked with slow, halting steps, his head trembling and his shoulders hunched. He had aged markedly over the preceding days. He seemed shorter, shrunken, with his limbs loose. He was unable to harness his thoughts, so scattered had they become, as scrambled and sifted as sand through fingers. Only his eyes remained unchanged in their sharp, bird-like look. Whenever he walked along the main street, he kept staring at the *shul* that continued to stand like a fortress with its lofty towers and domes.

He removed its old eroded sign and replaced it with two others, one outside and one on its office doors. He always paused, with head quivering, before the one at the entrance.

But still, every day, he was at his desk for his customary two hours, sitting stiffly with raised shoulders and a drawn face, not permitting himself so much as to study his books lest this diminish the time he reserved for *shul* duties.

Through the wall, he could hear Reverend Feldman

as he swept the old and worn carpets, frequently gagging in the dust and clearing his throat with a hard dry cough. He listened attentively to every movement, to the way he dragged his feet, to his every sigh and to his roaming on the other side of his office door. Ever since he had collapsed, the reverend had been watchful over him and kept close, should the need arise for urgent aid.

But Rabbi Cohen kept asking himself: What did Feldman want? Why was he always hanging around? He, Rabbi Cohen, could well manage by himself, he did not need the reverend to look after him! Since there was to be no more minyan, he preferred to be alone, totally alone.

Reverend Feldman, however, was wholly devoted to the *shul*. He could not understand why the rabbi, who had never seemed so bitter, had become so stubbornly inflexible. He kept sitting in his office, moved not a muscle and said not a word. It disturbed him; he was beside himself. Since the rabbi had driven out the minyan, a fearful stillness had fallen upon the *shul*. It appeared larger and emptier. And he began to notice details to which he had previously been oblivious: cobwebs on the ceilings, cracks along the walls, rents in the carpet, loose planks of wood in the benches, the Eternal Light flickered tenuously while, one morning, a rat scuttled past him and disappeared amongst the benches.

'So, we have come to this, have we?' he thought with an inner ache.

That day, upon leaving, he made for Sonche's home. Sonche lived in a poor, narrow, dilapidated street where the houses stood in tight huddles. Sonche had a dingy little shop there with shelves laden with glass jars filled with sweets and half-melted chocolates. A girl sat there. She was ugly, had humped shoulders, a pinched face and broad forehead and wore make-up and lipstick. In her silk red dress with its profuse ribbons and bows, she resembled a new doll just bought from a shop. She was curling her hair by the glow of a flimsy light when Reverend Feldman entered.

Inspecting him with her piercing green eyes, she asked him in a grating voice what he wanted.

The reverend did not immediately reply. He was somewhat confused and unable to gather himself in the sweet-smelling air permeated with the scent of the girl's perfume. She, in turn, hastily rose from her seat and cried out with a frightened, 'Daddy! Daddy!' that brought Sonche instantly running into the shop.

He was dressed in a wet woman's apron and dirty rolled-up shirtsleeves while his hands bubbled with soapsuds. When he saw Reverend Feldman, he quickly pulled off his apron and wiped his hands.

'Why! Reverend Feldman, such an honoured guest!' he exclaimed, overwhelmed, approaching the girl whom he embraced and kissed on her head.

'This is the reverend of our *shul*, dear daughter, Reverend Feldman!' he reassured her.

She angrily threw back her head with its small, thin curls.

'You have to be polite to the reverend, my dear child!' he

said, taking her chin. 'He will find a boy for you to marry, handsome and rich, eh?' He bent towards her, smiling right into her eyes.

'No, no, no!' she shrieked, releasing herself from him and running away.

Sonche followed her with a proud look and shake of his head. 'She is embarrassed, my only child! She really is a refined girl, though, may she be always be well!'

'A fine girl,' the reverend replied with a mild smile.

'Oh, Reverend Feldman, forgive me, such a distinguished guest and here I am receiving you in the shop! Please come into the house!' Sonche quickly pulled down his folded dirty shirtsleeves.

'It's all right, Mr Sunshine, I will not keep you long. I just came to speak to you about the minyan. I want to know how you feel about …'

'Do you really need to ask? But, since you have troubled to come to me, then I will tell you the truth. We regret the whole business.'

'Do you truly mean this?' the reverend ventured with a tremor in his voice.

'Well, yes. If we had any idea that it would end like this, then we would have started nothing.'

'Does that mean you are prepared to settle for what you had before? So that the minyan will be a minyan once more?' Reverend Feldman could not believe the good news.

'Sure. We will return to *shul* tomorrow!'

'Let me tell you, Mr Sunshine, you have just lifted a heavy weight from my heart! The rabbi will be so happy.'

They stood silently for a time, neither of them knowing what else to say.

The reverend was overwhelmed. He tugged at his beard and smiled absent-mindedly. Sonche, in his turn, kept wiping his balding head, rolled his eyes and finally said with a worried tone. 'What shall we do about Jimmy, Reverend Feldman? He has gone over fully to the Salvation Army. They hung a drum on his stomach and he walks around playing their music.'

'What can we do? First, he is still a Jew and as long as he hasn't converted he can remain in the minyan,' the reverend replied, waving his hand. 'Second, we have no one to replace him. Do you think that the *shul* should lose the minyan because of one fool?'

The reverend left Sonche in an elated state. He did not expect such an easy result and it made him a little resentful. He had expected to do a great deal of persuading before he could proceed far.

In the end, however, he had to do nothing. Sonche himself asked to have the minyan reinstated! The reverend had expected he would have to argue with a stubborn man. But it turned out he had nothing to worry about.

Well, it seems that little girl really does lead that big tough man, Sonche, by the nose! he thought.

He returned home exhilarated, sat down comfortably to eat a late dinner that was served by his wife. She was a tall heavy-set woman, stiffly bound in a corset that pushed out her bosom. She wore her hair combed in a stiff high style full of combs.

Theirs was not a peaceful existence. She was from a well-respected, long settled family that was related to the Adelaide Montefiores. She had come to Wattle Hill looking for a match with Rabbi Cohen. The *shul*'s congregants would complain that the rabbi was still a bachelor and seemed to have little interest in becoming married. He was offered many different prospects but turned up his nose at them, saying they were not suitable for him. When Miss Montefiore was suggested, he was caught in a dilemma. One could not simply ignore the Montefiore name. He wrestled with the idea, could not make up his mind, did not have the courage to say 'No'. So the community made a great show of paying for her passage to Wattle Hill. They met on several occasions over an extended time. The rabbi kept deferring any decision until he declared that she was not the match for him! No arguments persuaded him. Rabbi Cohen had made up his mind, 'No' meant 'No', hence nothing came of the match.

The congregation felt that it would be too demeaning to return Miss Montefiore empty-handed, so it decided that she should marry Reverend Feldman. Securing this match proved not as easy as it seemed. But, in the end, he conceded. Like the rabbi, he, too, had preferred to remain a bachelor, but Miss Montefiore was too great a test for his convictions: stemming as she did from a distinguished family and coming with a fine dowry, he relented. The more difficult task lay in persuading the would-be bride. Marriage to an ordinary reverend and a 'foreigner', what's more, had not been particularly alluring. She was a woman with high ambitions and pride. However, wanting to show the rabbi that he was no better than his reverend, she also finally agreed.

Miss Montefiore, as she insisted on being called even after the wedding, felt herself to be superior to her husband. She led an independent life of her own, slept in a separate room and ran her own business – a small shop filled with flower pots and porcelain knick-knacks with cut-glass shelves that held reading books. It was an honourable and refined business and she earned more than her husband did at the *shul*. She declined all money from him to manage the household. Instead, he paid her a regular amount for his food and accommodation, as if he were a boarder.

She had no children from him. Silently and angrily, she would roam about the house that smelled of camphor and washing starch. She rarely spoke to her husband and, when she did, she would place her golden pince-nez, pinned to her bosom by a string, on her upturned fleshy nose.

As for Reverend Feldman, he was in terror of the way she stared at him through her glasses. Her grey watery eyes appeared strangely huge and flat behind her glasses, like two silver buttons; she looked at him with such bitterness that his words gagged in his throat.

For him, however, that day had been different. He felt victorious after his meeting with Sonche. And he ate heart-ily, rolling bits of bread between his fingertips, smacking his lips and wiping his moustache with satisfaction. He knew that his wife could not tolerate this and felt her criti-cal gaze upon him. He had not recounted the day's events, so he said in an ordinary, indifferent, uninspired tone, 'I really achieved something today! The rabbi sits around with folded arms! Everything falls on my shoulders!'

She looked at him in surprise, placed her glasses on her nose, then removed them and nodded, eagerly, opening her eyes wide. 'What is the matter? I heard that you had some trouble at the *shul*. There are rumours in town …'

'Everything is all right, there is no trouble,' he interrupted. He wetted his fingers in the *Mayim Achronim* water, closed his eyes and belched loudly.

His Miss Montefiore rose grandly from her seat, turned away her shoulders, gave him a measured glance and said angrily, 'It is already the second week that you haven't paid me for your living expenses, Reverend Feldman! What are you going to do about it?'

'*Nu, nu, nu*,' he replied, closing his eyes, continuing to belch and pulling at his beard.

The next morning, Reverend Feldman reached the *shul* at the first break of day. He energetically swept the carpets and dusted the seats to glowing point. The *shul* recaptured its previous honourable appearance. It held nothing more to fear in its silence and from its high ceiling emanated a joyful, welcoming, religious solemnity. He quickly donned his ministerial robe and *spodek* that he had not worn since the minyan had ceased.

On hearing the rabbi now come to work, he went towards his office and knocked on the door. On entering, he gave a slight cough, stroked his beard and looked straight into the rabbi's face. 'Everything is all right with the minyan, Rabbi. I spoke to the men. They are ready to forego their demands.'

The rabbi sat silently, his head bent low. His breathing was deep and long, his eyebrows twitched as if he were lost in thought. He waved his hand almost dismissively and said in an unresponsive voice, 'Never mind, Feldman, we will make do without a minyan.'

The reverend was speechless. His face turned askew, his chin and his beard began to tremble. This was not the response he had expected. He knew that the rabbi did not like him to mix too much in *shul* affairs. From the outset, the rabbi had not permitted him to take responsibilities. He had been a reverend but the rabbi had turned him into a mere *shammes*, never letting him lead the congregation in services, even on a weekday, treating him as he did all the other men of the paid minyan, speaking to him as he spoke to them, using solely his German dialect. He made a point of avoiding his reverend as if he were a stranger. They had spent so many years together, experienced many different eras, both good and bad, and he had always been loyal, had done everything the rabbi had asked of him – surely, he had earned more than this from the rabbi. Why, then, didn't the rabbi now want a minyan? Did his pride stand in the way? Could he not tolerate that Feldman had acted without his permission?

For the first time the reverend faced the rabbi with resentment. The rabbi sat hunched in exhaustion with his head shaking as if he were napping, the flesh of his face and chin hanging loosely. How the rabbi had aged, thought

Feldman. Even the former white of his eyebrows and moustache had adopted a straw-coloured yellow hue.

Whereupon, the reverend's resentment dissipated. A heaviness weighed down upon him as he said resignedly with a sigh, 'Yes, we will manage without a minyan. We don't need a minyan.'

The rabbi's shoulders turned further inward. He did not reply. He only shook his head a little harder.

Feeling increasing dryness in his throat and mouth, Reverend Feldman wanted to approach the rabbi, take his hand and sit beside him, but he was too embarrassed to make such a move. Yet, he felt unable simply to remain standing there in silence with words struggling for release, each word hurting him, each word was eating him up.

'After all,' he did manage to say, bending over the rabbi, 'to tell the truth, which *shul* does have a minyan every day? Even in Melbourne, and in the large synagogues there, they only pray on *Shabbes* and on the *Yontoyvim*. It is certainly better to have no minyan than one like ours! Jews like these do not even deserve to enter a *shul*. They said we should pray with the dead, with the dead, hee, hee.'

'What? With the dead?'

The rabbi suddenly sat upright, having taken notice of what the reverend had said.

'Yes, yes! With the dead, haa, haa! The clever Reb Boruch invented the idea. He thought he would scare me!'

The reverend began chatting freely, telling the rabbi how Meir Segal intended to return home to Stashev after his death and pray with the dead in his own *shul* there. 'And

I told them that it was easier dealing with the dead than it was with them.'

The reverend was becoming more and more talkative. 'They thought they had the *shul* in the palms of their hands and that they would receive everything they demanded. I warned them that they would regret this. They refused to heed my words and now they regret what they did. They would now be happy to return for their old pay, even for less ...'

The reverend fell silent. He realised that the rabbi was barely listening to a word he was saying. His eyes were eclipsed by a deep concentration, aimlessly looking around. His head had fallen tiredly to one side. A faint smile manifested under his moustache. Then, raising his eyebrows, he scrutinised the reverend and laughed softly. 'The dead, hee, hee, hee! The dead ...'

An icy chill coursed down the reverend's back as if a harsh wet brush were being dragged down the length of it. He lapsed into a state of agitation. His last previous talk with the rabbi had distressed him. His laughter now ringing in his ears terrified him and stirred dark and fearsome premonitions.

He set to attending the rabbi even more vigilantly. He waited for him every morning outside the *shul*, followed him constantly with his eyes as he shuffled along with his short steps, his head shaking as he talked to himself in a thin vulnerable voice with a smile brooding across his lips. He tried on a number of occasions to engage him in chat, but the rabbi did not reply, shaking his head instead and regarding him with a puzzled look as if he were unknown to him.

## 5

From then on, the reverend was perturbed. He was just as concerned about the *shul* as he was about the rabbi. What should he do? Just stand by with folded arms while someone was expiring right before his eyes? After all, were we not all responsible for others in this world?

He would approach the few congregants who had remained in the town and forewarn them; tell them to attend the *shul* at least once a week. Mr Mendelson was still there, the old Mr Gudman and his son, Mr Teper, Mr Goldstone, the Liverpool bluffer and Mr Levy. He would visit them all and ask Sonche and some others to come so that they could have a full minyan. The *shul* would have a proper minyan at least once a week. It would not remain perpetually abandoned.

He knocked confidently on the door. With a slight cough, he stroked his beard and with sheepish eyes looked directly at the rabbi.

'Everything is all right with the minyan, Rabbi! I spoke to the men. They are ready to forego all their demands!'

The rabbi sat silently, his head bent low. His breath was this way, it would help the rabbi, it would restore his will, bring him back to life.

He decided to see Goldstone first, who was now an eminent man, a tycoon, one of Wattle Hill's richest men. Unlike so many others, he had not deserted the town during its initial lull. Instead he had turned to business during those bad times. Where everyone was caught in the panic of finding a means to escape, he had remained and taken advantage of the situation. He had bought up abandoned shops and houses, in which he proved successful. Every day, he became wealthier and more powerful as half of the town fell into his soft pudgy hands. He had bought the entire front bench of the *shul*, the one nearest the Mizrach that he had upholstered with the softest velvet and to which he had attached two silver plaques, one in English and one in Hebrew bearing his name. He attended the *shul* only during the High Holidays and sometimes on another *Yontev*, demanding from the reverend that no other be permitted to sit there, even if it did remain unoccupied throughout the year.

Reverend Feldman still disliked the man as much as he had when Goldstone had been a favourite of the rabbi and arranged the dances and parties that had financially aided the *shul*. Indeed, his dislike had mounted over the years for, since he had become so rich, the rest of the world ceased to exist. He would not speak straight to anyone. His protruding eyes had become even milkier and more glazed as he walked with short light steps as if he wished to deny the earth the pleasure of his gait.

When he did come to *shul*, he dressed in a frock coat with silk lapels and a high top hat that shone like steel. He always felt the velvet padding of his seat before sitting down, then looked about him, his face glowing with pride. The rabbi always made a big fuss over his coming, cleared his throat and, in praying, would strain to reach the higher octaves as he had done in times past, employing a tuning fork to attain perfect pitch. What particularly infuriated Reverend Feldman was Goldstone's attitude to the *shul* about which he seemed, with a thin smile, to say, 'Oh well, what do I really care about it?'

It took the reverend some time to summon his readiness to face Goldstone. But his purpose offered him no choice. Goldstone was the only person who could restore the *shul* to its feet. He, above all, had the strongest influence on the congregation. He had only to say the word and not only would the people attend every *Shabbes*, but even every day. Nothing would change Goldstone's character, but once he heard about the most recent events and the rabbi's condition, he would surely use his influence and bring together a minyan for every *Shabbes*.

Goldstone welcomed the reverend into his small study like a long-lost friend. Two wide iron chests stood in the study, its walls lined halfway in dark cedar wood. A lit kerosene lamp covered by a green shade hung from the ceiling even though it was still day outside. It threw warm shadows over the study.

Seated in a deep armchair that seemed to swallow his small lithe body, leaving visible only his red scoured face with his milky glazed eyes, Goldstone rubbed his hands with glee as if he were about to be the recipient of good news. Upon which it was he who, merrily, began to ask about the latest events at the *shul* and the wellbeing of the rabbi.

The reverend had not expected such a cordial reception.

Original illustration for 'The Last Minyan' by Noel Counihan

Goldstone proved so warm and his tone full of anticipation of good news that the reverend did not have the heart to relay all that had been taking place as he had intended.

He sighed, stroked his beard and replied circumspectly, 'Well, you know it all, what news can I tell you?'

'It's all right then, I see,' Goldstone beamed with joy. 'You can rely on our rabbi to take care of the *shul*, believe me!'

'Yes, yes …' the reverend mumbled under his breath. Then, as they continued speaking, he mentioned that the *shul* was now without a minyan and referred to the rabbi's condition.

'The rabbi has become a walking shadow!' he said with emphasis. 'He can't tolerate what is happening much more. Things might improve, though, if there were a minyan every *Shabbes*.'

A stern look arose in Goldstone's expression. He rose from his seat and began to pace unsettlingly around the room, striking his hands against his chest.

'Terrible! Terrible! That such a thing should occur! Nothing like it has happened anywhere else in the world! What a scandal! And now you come to me about a minyan! Everyone comes to me with all their troubles!'

He began to shout with rage rising in his face.

The reverend moved back guiltily and embarrassed, pleading in a shaky apologetic tone.

'What shall we do? This is a disaster! Is this to be our fate?'

'Hmm, a tragedy, a disaster indeed!' Goldstone

mumbled irately to himself, with a sad shaking of his head. He returned to his seat, lapsing into thought, drumming with his fingers against his chair.

'Well, we must do something, yes, Reverend Feldman!' he said, taking a cheque-book from his breast pocket and repeating, 'Yes, we must! Nothing should or can be too much!' He wrote out a cheque.

Reverend Feldman left Goldstone with a heavy heart. He walked through the streets with slow tired steps. The cheque lay in his wallet like a piece of dead metal. He drew out that strip of coloured paper and considered its broad rounded script that appeared to melt right away as did his milky eyes. He contemplated tearing it up or burning it so that no memory would remain of it. But then, no! He would not destroy it. Why should he so misuse the rabbi's money? Instead, he would go to the rabbi's office the following morning and give him the cheque and at the same time return his own keys of the *shul* and say, 'Here are my keys, Rabbi! I have no further reason for coming, while you have no more need of me.'

Or, maybe, he should explain nothing at all but simply place the keys and the cheque on the desk, say a brief 'Goodbye' and leave?

He began to feel sorry for himself as he roamed along the dark empty streets with his head drawn into his shoulders. The wind blew a yellowed fragment of newspaper through the air, whipping about wildly. He raised his robe collar and thrust his hands deep into his pockets, his eyes stinging as if they were about to weep.

He arrived home late in the evening. The house was empty. His wife, it appeared, had not yet returned from her business, even though she usually returned much earlier. This gladdened the reverend greatly. The way he felt, the last thing he needed was to have a confrontation with her! He would fix himself something to eat while she was still out, thereby being able to avoid the repeated angry and recriminatory plaints she had been giving him since he had ceased paying his board.

He went to the pantry, but found it locked. He pulled at its door, once, twice. It did not yield. He then tried to open a drawer but it, too, was locked. She was denying him food, he saw. And it was on purpose that she had not yet returned. She was deliberately punishing him on account of his arrears. What a nasty piece of work she was! Rage welled within him as, in his fury, he pulled the pantry door from its hinges and reached for bread and cheese and gulped them down in haste, omitting his ritual washing of hands. The food stuck in his throat. A tense threatening silence permeated the house. He stood before the broken pantry, disoriented and with his heart palpitating. He kept imagining that he was hearing his wife's footsteps. Quickly, he threw on his coat and ran from the house.

He was on the streets again, oblivious to where he was heading. His mind was in chaos with wild imaginings. What would his wife do when she discovered the broken pantry? How would he summon the courage to face her? If he had any option in the matter, he would never again set foot in their house. But, in the meantime, what should he do with himself? Where could he go?

Night fell. The sky was stark black, almost devoid of stars. A wrathful silence – so it seemed to him – surrounded him, enclosed him. The houses, cottages, streets, street-lamps and gardens were at that moment remote and alien to him; he was walking through an altogether strange and unknown terrain, wearily dragging his feet as a voice in his head kept repeating, It's over, it's over!

Then, suddenly, the evening silence fell apart; it shattered before the singing, spirited and joyous, accompanied by tambourines and drums. A procession of the Salvation Army passed by, bearing torches whose bright red, orange and yellow flames danced in the darkness, throwing shadows upon the pavements while lighting up the drab walls, doors and windows on their passing.

Reverend Feldman paused to watch and remembered Jimmy who had been a member of the minyan – Jimmy who had never had it so good. For, now that, on abandoning the *shul*, he had found the Salvation Army, where everyone, even the lowest of the low, could belong, he, too, had found his place. Just as Sonche and his daughter had theirs in their sweets shop, and Zelig Hersh in his elderly people's home in Sydney and Meir Segal in his homely *shul* back home in his native Stachev.

Only he, Feldman, had nothing – no home, no children. He was desolate, alone, a nothing.

He recalled the morning when Rabbi Cohen had collapsed, with every detail so engraved that it replayed itself before his eyes. Likewise, there returned to him his discussions with the minyan, still lucid, word for word, the insistent demands made by Sonche on the one hand and the old man Segal's blessings on the other.

Yet, he, Feldman, remembered almost nothing from his native home. So many years had passed. He did recall that he had been Yashe then, but, now, Reverend Feldman to all – even his own Montefiore wife.

'Yashe, Yashe,' he repeated to himself aloud, the sound itself resounding strangely in his ears, his very voice as he uttered it overwhelming him with a sense of dread.

Whereupon, unsettling premonitory fantasies flooded his thoughts. He felt that he was being followed. Worn out as he was, he accelerated his own steps with no clear inkling where he was heading until, to his own surprise, he found himself nearing his *shul*, seeing which, he reached once again into his pocket for its keys, their familiarity emitting warmth, which spread through his fingertips to envelop him entirely.

The street on which the *shul* stood was darker and quieter than any of the others that he had walked along, no longer the street that it had been in more prosperous times. But above, across its vault, between the clouds, clusters of glinting stars appeared, while alongside the footpaths, the palm trees with their drooping branches and fronds rose high. Reverend Feldman made out the silhouette of the *shul*'s lofty rounded dome between them.

But, as he neared the *shul*, he caught his breath and froze stock-still. He saw it lit up while a shadow was moving slowly across its window.

'The dead' was the first thought that came to him with alarm, making him want to escape. But his feet became at once wooden stumps. He could not turn his eyes from the window where the shadow moved back and forth in prayer, so devotedly, so serenely, that the reverend's anguished thoughts steadily dissipated, transforming into a warmth and peace that enveloped him like a loving friend.

He entered the *shul*. It was open. Having removed his shoes, Feldman entered softly. All the lamps had been lit as if it was a *Yontev*. Rabbi Cohen stood on his dais, dressed in white with a high *spodic*, also white, embroidered with gold.

Reverend Feldman watched him pensively, a gentle smile forming across his lips. He went to his locker, took from it his own reverential garments, dressed himself in them and placed his *yarmulke* upon his head, not for an instant taking his eyes off the rabbi.

—*Dertzeilungen* (1939),
*Collected Writings* (1949)

# A WORD FROM
# PINCHAS GOLDHAR'S SON

WHEN MY FATHER DIED in the summer of 1947 we received a letter of sympathy from Nettie Palmer. She enclosed the text of her recent ABC announcement in which she paid tribute to Pinchas Goldhar as a writer, and regretted that his passing had deprived Australian literature of a unique talent.

Vance and Nettie Palmer were the doyens of the Australian literary scene. That she would recognise a Yiddish writer showed what an impact Goldhar had made. Here was a Yiddish author of Jewish subjects welcomed as an equal – the first 'ethnic writer' to be taken seriously and accepted into the Australian mainstream. And he set in motion a mode of writing that changed the perspective for all minorities and enriched the Australian scene.

Seven decades after his death, the time has come to look back on his career.

Born in Lodz in 1901, Pinchas was the eldest of four children. He attended yeshiva as well as a Polish gymnasium and a school of journalism. As a journalist, he first wrote for the *Lodzer Tageblatt*, then for its counterpart, the *Warshever Tageblatt*.

His father Jacob was a widower with four children when they left Poland in 1928, for Australia. An ardent Poale Zionist with a good command of Hebrew, Pinchas was to confide many years later to the Yiddish critic Shia Rapaport that it had been a mistake to choose Australia over Palestine, and it was too late to go there now that Australia had left him 'a broken man'.

In Australia, Pinchas worked in the dyeing factory his father established in Richmond. He spent his days standing over large and steamy vats stirring hundreds of pairs of socks with a wooden pole. Then he moved across the blotchy floor rutted with greenish puddles to the vat. The air was humid with the acrid smells of chlorine and ammonia. He did this for sixteen years.

While at the factory he ordered a printer's set of Hebrew letters, and arranged with veteran printer Dov Altshul to produce the small sheet that evolved into the first Yiddish newspaper in Australia. It was called *Di Oystralier Leben*.

The readers were eastern Europeans living in Carlton, just like himself. To them, the Jewish establishment seemed cold and lacked the vigorous cultural diversity they knew. Life in Melbourne in 1930 left them with an overwhelming feeling of remoteness. They were losing their sense of Jewish belonging and were unable to integrate into Australian society. They lacked a focal point. What were they all doing here in this place, Carlton?

Goldhar's modest news page took time to make its

impression. At first, it looked more like a pamphlet or brochure as it was a single sheet about 10 by 12 inches, printed on one side only. In spots where English letters appeared it was clear that there was a shortage of Hebrew letters. Pinchas wrote, edited and proofread it, paid Altshul for his expenses, then took copies out to the street where it was either given to passers-by, left on shop counters or placed into letter boxes.

The sheet came out regularly; more Hebrew type was sent for from America and the paper grew as more contributors greeted it with enthusiasm. It was essentially a one-man show, but Pinchas was happy. It was a labour of love. In 1932, he decided to go back to Europe. It was to be only for a year or so, among other things to look into new developments in dyeing techniques and machinery in England, Poland and Germany. There was also the matter of proposing to the girl he had left four years earlier, Ida Shlesinger of Lodz, who duly arrived in June 1934. She was to help him set up a creative environment for his literary work, help him revise and polish it, and enjoy a happily married life in Melbourne.

While in Europe, Pinchas was passing through the German city of Worms when he heard that Hitler was scheduled to address a rally there. He attended it; we still have the orange-coloured ticket. He left Europe in great fear for his people. The first story he wrote about his trip – titled 'Cain' – described graphically what he feared Nazism would inflict.

While Goldhar was in Europe, Dov Altshul sold *Di*

*Oystralier Leben*, now of respectable size with a growing list of contributors from its increased readership. The new editor-publisher, Chaim Rubenstein, continued to work with Goldhar and include all his articles and stories, which led to a warm friendship between them. The last editorial that Rubenstein would write would be for the first *yahrzeit* (anniversary of death) of his colleague Pinchas in 1948.

The new set-up gave Goldhar time to be selective in what he wrote and pursue his interest in Australian literature. Soon he had translated into Yiddish stories by Frank Dalby Davidson, Gavin Casey, Katherine Susannah Pritchard, Dowell O'Reilly, Vance Palmer, Louis Esson and his favourite, Henry Lawson. When he received a two guinea honorarium in 1945 for the translation of 'The Funeral', he bought a coloured print of Lawson as a housepainter. It still hangs on our walls.

The Yiddish writer Melekh Ravitch's arrival in Melbourne in 1933 led to the publication of two books about Jewish life. These so-called Almanac volumes with their essays on Australian literature and translations came to the attention of the leading group of writers and intellectuals who met at Vance and Nettie Palmer's home. The first one, published in 1937, contained Goldhar's first story, 'Der Pioneer' ('The Pioneer'). Artist Noel Counihan, who was also present, agreed to provide woodcuts to illustrate the stories. Many people who did not understand Yiddish came to ask for copies as late as the 1970s, when Counihan became famous enough for collectors.

*Dertzeilungen Fun Oystralie* by Pinchas Goldhar was

published in 1939. Among those who reviewed it favourably were Israel Joshua Singer in New York and his brother, Isaac Bashevis. The book brought wider ramifications with it. Counihan went on to illustrate other Jewish books, notably by Herz Bergner. Another painter from the Palmers' group, Vic O'Connor, also felt drawn to Goldhar's work. As late as 1996, he illustrated 'Old Friends', which he heard in 1939 for the first time.

When Melech Ravitch's wife and two children, Ruth and Yosl Bergner, arrived in Melbourne, they visited their father's friend daily. Yosl was introduced to Goldhar's circle of artists that included Counihan, O'Connor, Jim Wigley and Sidney Nolan. They all attest to the remarkable effects that meeting these Jewish creative people had in infusing their work with passion and a breadth of understanding that was rare in Australia.

Ravitchi's brother Herz Bergner also found his way into Australian literary circles through Goldhar. The two close friends encouraged each other. Goldhar found a publisher for Bergner's *Between Sky and Sea* among Palmers' group, the violin-maker Bill Dolphin. In 1944 the same publisher brought out a soft-covered collection of poems, pictures and fiction called *Southern Stories*. It contained Goldhar's best-known story 'Café in Carlton' and Yosl Bergner's famous Aborigine pictures.

Goldhar's novella 'The Last Minyan' had its origins in a trip to Ballarat to meet fellow author Nathan Spielvogel, who told of his memories of the community and the synagogue that had seen greater days. Aaronson of Ballarat had told his friends about the once-thriving *kehilla* (congregation), but Spielvogel's account captured Pinchas' imagination. 'The Last Minyan', his longest and some say finest work, is a finely-crafted account of the Ballarat rabbi's struggles to maintain his *kehilla* in the declining goldfields. Some of Counihan's most touching woodcuts accompany the story, which is appearing for the first time in book form in English.

Writing seemed like a sacred mission to my father. Certainly it was no money-spinner. Clive Turnbull, a leading critic, said Goldhar wrote the best war story published in Australia, which greatly pleased him. So did the two guineas sent for that, his first and only payment for his writings in nineteen years in Australia.

Although anti-Semitism used to be rare in Australia, my father once encountered it. For a sensitive person like him, it came as a trauma. In 1945 we caught a tram to East St Kilda one Sunday afternoon to visit Moyshele Hirsh, my father's cousin. As we got off the tram a drunk started hurling loud anti-Semitic abuse at my father. He reddened and silently put his head down, slumped between his shoulders. Shocked and depressed, Father looked fixedly at the ground with appallingly sad eyes, making no attempt to rebuff or reply.

Later the same year my parents said we children must stay home while they went to a special showing at the Liberty Cinema in Lygon Street. We found out that it was the so-called Nazi horror films which revealed the aftermath of the concentration camps. Again my father reacted with the same shocked silence, only this time it lasted for weeks. Though he did not talk about it, his pain was clear.

He was soon stricken with diabetes, then a heart attack. He survived for another year, but then his father Jacob died. That sent him into a deep depression and the next heart attack at the age of forty-five proved too much. It is ironic that just when the world was entering a happier phase, an author who had worked so hard to build bridges into the future should die.

Four years later, the Kadimah issued his collected works in Yiddish. It seemed too risky a venture to bring out a book in English. Since then occasional stories, essays and articles by and about Pinchas Goldhar have kept his name alive. But surely it is his due that the curiosity that piqued the writers of the 1930s and impressed the Yiddish-reading public should lead to the publication of an English collection of his works. Aside from its literary quality, such a collection would also have great historic interest. Pinchas Goldhar is a pivotal figure, whose extraordinary pioneering efforts gave expression to early Jewish experiences and dreams in the new society of Australia.

My Kaddish, though sad at his early death, is a grateful one for all that he worked so hard to achieve, and for the love he showed his family and all the Jewish community of his new homeland.

—Joshua Goldhar